CROWN OF SHATTERED THRONES

AN EMPIRE OF CURSES AND DREAMS NOVEL

THE NIGHT AND RAINS SERIES
BOOK TWO

SUSAN PERSON

For all those who refuse to waste a second chance,
especially in a waterfall or by a lagoon

AUTHOR'S NOTE

Dear Reader - Please be advised that this book series contains content that may be upsetting for some readers. Should you wish to learn more information for your best reading experience, please scan the QR code below for additional details and content notes.

THE NIGHT AND RAIN SERIES
SUGGESTED READING ORDER

The Night and Rain Series

Crown of Night and Rain, Book 1

Crown of Broken Promises, Prequel

Crown of Ruined Oaths, Book 1.5

Crown of Shattered Thrones, Book 2

Crown of Storms and Starlight, Book 3 (Coming in 2026)

CROWN OF SHATTERED THRONES

PART ONE

NYX'S BLOOD

Held in secret by the curator of the War Museum at General Daphina's request resides an ancient document written in a language only a few can read. Daphina, in her many hours of examination, believed it to be a thoughtful poem. Whit had many more years with it and considered it a forewarning of what was to come.

When Nyx's blood returns to the realm, all the magic shall be replenished to the glory of old. Those who bear the burden must prove their worthiness not only to Nyx but to the realm. From darkest night and raging storms to the brightest stars and dancing moonlight, life will be reborn.

CHAPTER 1
TAPESTRY
ARI

I vanyshened inside the palace wall to the courtyard where a poison-tipped arrow had nearly taken my life not that long ago—my traitorous father's seat among the vampire. No guards met me. Strange, but it was hours before the sun would set. I noted the spot I'd landed. My knowledge of the area or maybe a memory brought me to this exact place—the place where Griselda had died to save me. All the air left my lungs. I knelt and ran a hand through the pebbles. She'd given her life for me though she barely knew me, and I knew little of her other than she'd become vampire after the death of her brother. But she'd been a follower of Nyx before that. I hoped she'd been granted passage to reside in the next realm with the Goddess, and if she were blessed, her lost family would be there too. She'd sacrificed herself so that I would live because she trusted in Nyx.

I raised my head to look at the palace where my father...I no longer wanted to call him that even though my brain hadn't quite caught up to my heart...Albert held my sister and her mate as his prisoners.

The gray stone walls seemed even darker than the last time I was here, but I hadn't had much time to study the structure, either, while my father had me beaten. I dropped my head to the side as if the simple action would erase the memory and stop the bile from rising in my throat. He wouldn't be allowed to scar anyone else, especially my sister, the same way. I scanned the windows. Most of the curtains were drawn except for those in the area where I'd been kept. I recognized them from the view below I'd memorized while a prisoner. Griselda had been the only kind one, and she was gone. I shook the thoughts away because I had one task—save my sister and her mate. There was very little movement in the daytime, even though I knew the vampire here drank concoctions of unicorn and fae blood to be able to travel in daylight. They preferred the night and only entered daylight at my fath... Albert's behest.

Thunder rumbled as if it rolled across the sky in my direction. A whoosh of air tousled the hair around my face. My mate's minty scent drifted on the breeze. His boots pushed softly into the pebbles. I took him in. Worry wrinkled Rain's fine face, hiding the scar at his jawline. No one existed in this world as handsome as the fae I loved, despite how pale his skin was and how weak he looked.

He hadn't recovered from the overuse of power where he rained hell down from the skies on Father's vampire army.

I suspected he would follow me, but I'd hoped I could make it to Albert first. My heart belonged to my mate in every way. My bloodline caused the attack on his city, though, and I had to fix it. The last thing I wanted was for the incredible man beside me to see me become just like my father. Because that was what it would take to defeat the man who raised me.

"Rain, this is my battle."

"Laurel is my brother, and you are my mate. Gemma is my family. I unleashed destructive lightning on my own city to try to save them. This is my battle too." He was out of breath, each inhale more labored than the last.

My mate needed to recover.

"Whatever you want to do, Ari, I'm by your side, but know Marius has called for forces to join us here. You do not have to do this alone." The corners of his eyes turned down, and I didn't need to be his true mate to see he believed we would lose if we went forward.

Gods dammit. I'd been rash. Remorse tangled with my anger and strangled it, even if momentarily. My decision to come here put Rain in danger. I wouldn't sacrifice my mate, my friends, or my family for emotions. I wouldn't let Griselda's sacrifice be in vain. And I wouldn't let Albert win. "Where is Marius assembling them?"

"In the forest right over the border. The same one—"

"We came through when you rescued me."

"I think Nyx did the rescuing, but yes."

It was foolish to go in without a plan. I knew this, and yet, I'd still come. My childhood belief that I could do anything on my own had taken over in a moment of desperation, but I hadn't been a naive girl in many years. Stupid at times, yes. Reckless, yes. Naive, no. I slid my arm around his waist and looked in his eyes. "I love you, Rain, but you'd better hold on."

A wicked grin spread over his face. He slid his arms around my waist, pressing his hard body against me. "With pleasure."

I vanyshened us to the edge of the forest. A black deer, dark as midnight, crossed in front of the spot. I'd never seen a deer that color. The majestic creature seemed the opposite of nonplussed by our presence. I sensed Marius a short distance from us, and the familiar comfort of my unicorn guardian settled over me. Our bond seemed even stronger now after he refused to break it when I attempted to release him to save him and my family from Albert's wrath. "Can you walk from here?"

"Yes, I'm fine," Rain said, sounding stronger, though he was still leaning heavily on my shoulder.

Marius emerged from the trees in his natural form— glossy black coat, white mane and tail, and that glorious golden horn. Concern etched his eyes, but he looked healthy otherwise. Relief he wasn't injured washed over me. He took me in. A twinge of annoyance and worry slid down the bond. I resisted the urge to squirm under his scrutiny like I would have a few years ago.

I must have passed approval because he turned to Rain. "We have a healer on the way for you."

"I need food and rest...if we have time." He slumped against me.

Panic gripped me like a vise around my heart. "Rain?"

"It's exhaustion, Ari. Listen to his breathing...the rhythm of his heart." Marius shifted to his faelike form and lifted Rain off me. Torn between being thankful for the help and not wanting to be separated from Rain, I acquiesced to Marius's assistance.

Marius hefted Rain's dead weight into his arms. "We don't have supplies or tents yet, so you have two options. We can take him back to the city to rest. Or we can wait here for the healer, who should be with the next group who vanyshen in."

Moving Rain back to the city in that method of travel didn't seem wise to me in his state. Although we had vanyshened from the Forgotten Forest when he'd been stabbed in the leg by my fath...by Albert. "I want to wait for the healer."

"Let's take him to where the others are gathering," he said, his tone pragmatic. He led the way through the trees.

About a dozen fae, some in the blue and silver uniforms of Rain's kingdom...our kingdom...and some in regular clothes with tunics or sweaters and those heavy blue pants I'd seen in Rain's wardrobe, were already at work. The fae made a perimeter around the clearing. Magic swirled and hummed around them. A dome took shape above us, and the sides cascaded down. It was like the protective wall Gemma used with her wind magic, but what I witnessed with these fae was different elemental magic woven together like a tapestry to create a shield. "It's incredible."

"We used those protections during the Great War many times," Marius said. "It's the first time I've seen one built in two hundred years."

"I'm assuming they weren't needed after the war ended?"

"That, and they take considerable magic to construct and maintain. Those fae will be in a similar state to your mate after they finish. Others will rotate in, though not as many, to keep it intact."

"And they came for my sister and Laurel? Without hesitation?" Tears pricked my eyes.

"They came for you, Ari. They came for the one touched by the Goddess herself."

My confusion as to why they would so freely help morphed into concern for what would happen if word got out. "How do they know? We didn't tell anyone."

"After the war, the fae learned of your power and direct line to Nyx, and those gifts are passed down the maternal line—one per generation. When your mother passed, you might not have realized it then, but your power, already stronger than hers on its own, grew. They might not know the extent of your magic abilities, but they do know you are your mother's daughter."

It was common knowledge that power passed down the maternal line, but what was uncommon was to receive a parent's power upon their death. Her last actions made more sense. A tear escaped and slid down my cheek. My grief threatened to leak out along with it. "Was that why she sent Gemma away and called for me when she passed?"

"Yes," he said, setting Rain down on a blanket another fae had spread out. My mate hadn't regained consciousness, and as much as I wanted him awake, I wanted him to recover safely more. I dropped to the pallet, pushing the hair off Rain's face.

Marius squeezed my shoulder. "Even though it's not Nyx-given, your sister has her own power from your mother, but her greatest gift is the one element that can only be passed through paternal lines."

"Wind," I whispered.

He nodded, letting his glamour go and turning back into the large black unicorn with a gold horn. His white mane and tail lifted with the subtle breeze as if the elements were confirming what he'd just told me.

"Wind is my weakest..."

"It will match the others in time, but your greatest defense will always be your power from Nyx. It's as if all the elements were forged from a fraction of the goddess's power."

A few fae gathered nearby and worked on construction of a tent for us.

Marius knocked on my mental door, but I wasn't ready to let him back in yet. I needed a break. He lowered his head in acknowledgement and slipped away.

I glanced back at where the fae worked on the shield around the camp. A seed of hope grew in my chest like when I planted the young moonflowers in the garden with Mother. The fae behind me tended a different kind of garden. "Like a finely woven tapestry of power."

CHAPTER 2
NICKNAME
ARI

The magic shifted, and I went on alert. Someone powerful vanyshened nearby. I wasn't able to sense the ripple of power before my time with Nyx.

Now, it feels like a feast prepared just for me, and I don't know what the fuck that means.

Marius mentally knocked on the door to our bond. I'd shut the pathway when I vanyshened to the vampire palace. A less powerful unicorn could have broken through. Although I could sense he was near, he didn't force his way into my mind. Hist showed me respect with his request, and I was thankful for it.

I dropped my shield, and he eased into my mind like a gentle breeze.

I'm not glass, Marius.

No, you are one of the toughest fae I've seen in my three hundred years.

Thanks. He was being too nice. What was he about to hit me with...

The person who came through is not your father.

I inhaled and let the breath drift out slowly through my nose. *His power is different. I can tell it was someone powerful, but not as powerful as him.*

Good. You're learning to read the essence of the magic.

I am. Thanks to Nyx. Is this fae more powerful than me?

No, there is no one more powerful than you. The question you should be asking is if she is more practiced.

His word choice put me on edge. *Is she?*

Yes. Trained for almost two hundred years to be the best.

I scanned the area for a new arrival, hoping to see one of the healer coats some of them wore in the kingdom. Rain shifted and made a soft grunting noise. I laced my fingers with his. *So, is she here to help, and where the fuck is this healer?*

She is the healer. Not by birth, but she has channeled her energy into it the past four years.

A stunningly beautiful fae stepped out of the grove of trees. Her blonde hair dropped past her shoulders in waves. She wore tight black pants and a light blue top that accentuated all her curves. Her lips were painted the brightest red I'd ever seen.

That's the healer?

She is.

I shook my head. There sure weren't any healers like that in the prison I grew up in. I rose to meet her.

She approached me and held out her hand. "We haven't met yet, Arianna. I'm Merrick."

Not using any titles or bowing was a refreshing change. I placed my hand in hers, and her nervousness radiated between us like a wave. My palm started to sweat, and I hastily pulled my hand away. "Thank you for coming, Merrick. Rain is this way."

She stayed in step beside me. I assessed her as she trained her gaze ahead. Her posture was straight—perfect, really. She was highborn, but the strength of her power had already confirmed it.

The group before her had finished erecting a temporary tent around Rain's cot. I drew the flap back. "He's here."

Merrick's throat bobbed like she was afraid to enter. Was I going to have to push her inside?

"Do you need some assistance or some supplies?"

"No." She paused, swallowing hard again. She glanced at me with a small smile. "I should probably—"

"Ari..." Rain called to me. His eyes were still closed, but it was the first sound he made other than incoherent grunts. Hearing him say my name was the sweetest song.

I motioned for Merrick to follow. "He won't hurt you. I promise."

She moved to the opposite side of the cot from me and pulled a couple of instruments out of the small bag at her hip.

He looked peaceful but pale, and it was because of me.

His recovery was the most important thing on my list of priorities. I knelt beside Rain and whispered next to his ear. "I'm here, my mate."

His eyes darted under his lids, but he didn't open them.

"Normally, I'd ask someone to tell me what happened, but I believe the whole city saw it," Merrick said. "At least the ones who survived."

Her nerves seemed to have given way to another emotion—one I was quite familiar with—anger. But it told me she wasn't afraid of him or me, so another matter had caused her to hesitate.

"Marius, my bonded, said you only came to healing about four years ago, Merrick. What did you do before?"

Her eyes widened, and she turned her gaze to the instruments. When she looked back up, she met me with a distant and cool stare. "Mostly drank and fucked and spent my father's fortune."

Her candor caught me off guard, but I appreciated her honesty. "I've done my share of drinking and fucking, so I can relate."

Merrick smiled. "Thank you. I expected you to be prudish, but you are quite refreshing."

I slipped my hand into Rain's. His skin was warm and melded to mine, but he didn't squeeze back. "Now that we've established we have fucked to our fill, can you help my mate or not?"

Her smile widened. "I'll have him better by half the hour."

"Good," I said, comforted by her confidence in her abilities.

She held her hand over Rain's forehead and her other one over his chest. Merrick's eyes pinched closed tight with concentration. "He's not responding to me," she said, her tone frustrated. Sweat beaded along her perfectly sculpted brows. "This has never happened before."

Fuck. Rain, if you are being stubborn, you can stop now. "Is he fighting you?"

"No," she said, her face turning bright red. "It's like there's a barrier around him I can't get through."

I fought back a smile, because as soon as she said barrier, there were only two things it could be—his mate connection with me or Nyx. If it was me, I would need Nyx's help to bridge it. If it was Nyx, there was a reason. I closed my eyes.

Nyx, I know he'd heal in time, but I need him by my side. Just as your blood and love run in my veins to give me power, he is the source of my fortitude and where I draw my strength. I can't face his people without him. I can't rescue my sister without him. I can't stop my father without him. Please, Nyx.

When I opened my eyes, a sheer layer of darkness, like smoke, enveloped Rain's body. It turned nearly opaque like the darkest night, but light shimmered in the shroud like stunning twinkling stars. "Beautiful."

Though I'd only whispered, Merrick's eyes shot open. "Is this you?"

"No. Have you not witnessed this before either?"

"Never," she said, sounding a little breathless.

Thank you, Nyx.

Darkness and starlight could only be her. I smiled. "We have the Goddess herself to thank then."

"That's not something I thought I'd see in my lifetime."

I didn't tell her another of the blessings from Nyx sat across from her. The way Marius described the situation earlier, she might know anyway. I was hoping I was close to making my first real friend on this side of the forest. Telling her I'd basically died and Nyx had saved me seemed like a weird thing to tell someone I'd just met anyway.

"Especially not with Rain." She used his nickname. His friends and family were the only ones who did that. She was familiar with my mate.

My curiosity lowered the wall I normally kept up when I first met someone. "You know him?"

If she was caught off guard by my question, she didn't flinch, and that earned some respect from me.

"I do." She nodded.

Rain hadn't woken up yet, but he wasn't so pale. Nyx's magic became translucent like smoke again. "Are you friends?"

"We've known each other our entire lives." She looked down at him. "His pulse is stronger and his breathing deeper. He should wake up soon."

"Thank you," I said, sincere with my gratitude for Merrick's honesty and Nyx's help.

Merrick stood. "I did nothing. This was all because of you and your relationship to Nyx."

"You came and you did what you could," I said. "That's more than many would do."

'Maybe in your former home, but here it is different. The people here—"

"Merrick? What the fuck are you doing here?' Rain sat up, looking between me and Merrick with a confused expression on his face. He took my hand and pressed his lips to my fingertips in a brief touch. "What's going on, Ari?"

"Merrick is the healer who came to restore you." I glimpsed an alarmed expression on Merrick's face. She looked ready to bolt from the tent. I studied Rain, and he appeared to be the epitome of good health. "How are you feeling?"

"Like I never used my power."

He looked healed, but he pushed himself in the same way I did, so I worried that he might be persevering for me. If he sensed my guilt, he'd want to shield me from it. Looking at him, I only saw strength. Rain didn't show any lingering signs of overused power. He smiled at me with his full radiance.

"I'll leave you two alone." Merrick ducked out of the tent before either of us could respond.

"Why did she leave like a fire had been lit under her?"

"I don't know." He studied his hand, flipping it back and forth as if it didn't belong to him. "She was the one who healed me?"

"No, she tried, but she couldn't," I said.

"So, you did? That's why I feel like I do when you boost my magic," he said, sounding relieved.

"Actually, it wasn't me. It was Nyx."

CHAPTER 3
HAZE
RAIN

My mate believed Nyx had healed me, but I was convinced it was Ari. The ghost of magic coating my skin was all hers. Beyond the relief on her face, I noticed the concern behind it. Her hair was a little more disheveled than what I remembered, and damn the goddesses and gods if it didn't make her more beautiful. I cupped her face in my hands and pulled her toward me, brushing my lips across hers. "I love you."

"I love you," she said, draping her arms over my shoulders. "So, you don't have any lingering effects?"

I liked where she was going and winked at her. "None."

"That's wonderful." She leaned back slightly. "Then you can tell me how you know Merrick."

Not what I expected her to say, and I ran my hand over my face. Merrick wasn't my past to share, and an awkward pit formed in my gut. "She's been around my family since I can remember."

"Hmm," she said, studying me. I could almost see her brain dissecting that answer like a scientist. "You never courted her?"

I glanced toward the flap of the tent, half expecting Merrick to emerge and tell her side. "Look, Ari, I don't know what Merrick told you—"

"She said nearly the same thing you did, but it's the hesitation you both had in how to phrase it that I'm curious about." She didn't sound pissed, but she was annoyed for sure.

I had to give it to her straight, but some of this would be better coming from her sister. My one night with Merrick was to keep her away from Laurel, because I'd known even then he'd fallen for Gemma. Merrick was a different person then too. Ari and I needed to get past this and refocus on rescuing my brother and her sister. I expected her to go stab Merrick and maybe me, but she'd asked the question. I wouldn't withhold my part of the truth from her. "There was a circumstance years ago that led to Merrick and me sharing a bed. It wasn't anything for either of us."

"You slept with her?" That single eyebrow quirked up like it did every time she was about to unleash her fury.

"I did, but it was a long time ago and one time. I never had feelings for her."

"So, she was one of your conquests. No wonder she ran out of here so fast."

I had no argument for her point. After the war, many fae had shared my bed until I'd tired of the constant rotation. I'd lost the only person I'd loved outside of my family, and I never wanted to feel that pain again. It made sense why I never found anyone I wanted more with when I met Ari. There was no one else, and I wouldn't lose her over my brother's ex. "Merrick would be offended to hear you say that. She has won more fights than most men, so I doubt that was the reason she ran out of here."

She shifted, relaxing her shoulders slightly. "I trust you, Rain, and I know you had a life before we met. I wasn't expecting your ex-lover to be the healer sent to heal you, though."

Goddesses and gods, she had it wrong. My brother would understand that I needed to divulge more of his story to untwist the past for Ari. "She's not my ex-lover. She's Laurel's."

Ari's eyes narrowed at me. Her face scrunched up in a disgusted look. "You slept with your brother's lover? That's revolting."

"There's a reason, but it's not my story to tell. When the three of them were—"

Ari's eyes widened. "I'm sorry...my sister slept with her?"

"No, with Cyrus."

She looked at me like she expected me to further acknowledge what I'd said was true. "I'd known Gemma had feelings for Cyrus beyond the bond, but I didn't know they had...That's why she looked so sad when I asked her where he was."

"You and Marius haven't..." I paused, trying to think of a more sensitive way to ask if she'd been intimate with her bonded. If she had, she wasn't now, but there wasn't one ounce of my body that intended to share her. I studied her for any signs that there could be truth in what I asked. "You haven't been with him, have you?"

"Goddesses and gods, no." She covered her mouth. "That will never happen. I've called him Daddy Marius. We don't, nor have we ever had that kind of relationship."

"Could you call me Daddy Rain?" I wagged my eyebrows at her.

Ari slapped my bicep. "No." She crossed her arms. "So, Cyrus just fucked her and left. That had to have been painful for them both with the bond. Unless... He didn't break the bond, did he?"

"I don't know, my love. Can we table this for now? We have more important things to discuss than who is fucking who...unless you are straddling me."

She tilted her head and glared at me. "We do. We have a small force here, and Marius is coordinating the setup of the camp for us, but we should go see if they are ready to strategize."

I stood, expecting dizziness or weakness to affect me when I got to my feet, but there was none. Ari's careful gaze took in every move I made, so I pulled her up with me, kissing her cheek. Thankful the conversation about Laurel's ex was over, I needed to get caught up on where we were tactically...right after I gave her some reassur-ance. "You are my mate, my love, and my entire existence."

She smiled. "I know."

A laugh rumbled in my chest. I took her hand in mine, relishing the warmth of the skin-to-skin contact, and led her out of the tent. My gaze snagged on the expansive shield cast over the camp. Though not as intricate as what General Daphina had been capable of doing, the work rivaled much of what we'd used two hundred years ago while battling Albert and the vampire. I ignored the pit in my stomach from the flashes of the bloody battle-field that was now the Forgotten Forest. "How long was I out?"

"Not long. They did incredible work putting that cover together. Have you seen one before?"

"The last time I saw one must have been during the war." They'd been used frequently to keep vampire from locating us. While they were great for shielding us from sight, only the most skilled, like Ari's mother, could create one that prevented our scent from escaping into the air beyond the cover. Still, some protection was better than none.

"That's what Marius said too. I guess there hasn't been much need for them since then."

"No, there hasn't. We were able to live relatively without fear. I'd kept the vampire at bay on the border." And going to the edge of the vampire lands was the perfect place to release any pent-up power I had, so the trips served a dual purpose.

"Until my father was freed," she said, and the guilt in her voice broke me.

"None of this is your fault, my goddess. It is all Albert's doing. I know you don't want to be a victim, but you, like many of our kind, are when it comes to this."

Her shoulders straightened a little more. "I'll never consider myself a victim, but I will end my father's rampage that threatens to destroy our realm."

Godsdam. I respected the hell out of my mate. No one could ever come close to the strength she had in a single bone. I wanted to take her to bed right here and show her how much I loved her, but we had to figure out our next steps to get Laurel and Gemma out of the vampire palace.

Marius walked up in his unicorn form. "You look better."

I ignored the comment. Acknowledging weakness wasn't something I'd been allowed to do most of my life. "What do we know so far about where they are being held?"

"We don't know for sure, but we believe they are in one of the underground chambers in the palace."

Ari shivered next to me, and I slid my arm around her waist. She sank against my side.

"Thank the Goddess they aren't in that awful gallery," she said, shaking again.

I tightened my grip on her hip. "We'll burn that down to the ground."

"The guards are not heavy on the outside, but we suspect the closer we get to Gemma and Laurel, the more guards there will be. The consensus is they are trying to lure us in, making it look like there's not much protection." Marius shook his neck.

His assessment was valid, and I would have given the same based on the intelligence.

"So, Albert thinks we're stupid...or at least me. Let's make that work for us."

"Why don't I like the sound of that?" I asked, picturing Ari running straight into the middle of Albert's forces with her dual blades drawn. "I don't want you to be bait."

Marius moved closer to Ari. "Your father is expecting you to do something impetuous. We need another way to infiltrate and get detailed information about the layout and guard schedules."

"I've been inside there, Marius." My mate turned her fierce gaze on her bonded. He didn't flinch...never did when it came to Ari. Both of them were impressive forces, and I loved the strength my mate carried in every fiber of her being.

"I know you have." Marius's voice softened in acquiescence that wasn't a real surrender, but like he'd failed her.

"That's not what I need right now," she said. "I need my bonded to channel strength. There is nothing soft about this situation." A dusting of gray haze surrounded us.

"Your emotions are running your decisions. That never ends well," he said matter-of-factly.

She met his gaze like she was ready to unleash all of Nyx's power on him, but the fog disappeared. Whether she'd admit it or not, she understood what he meant. As did I. Albert knew Ari's emotions ruled her power, and if she gave in to it, she'd walk right into his trap. What I didn't add was that I'd walk in right behind her, even if it meant surrendering my existence to save her.

CHAPTER 4
CHALLENGE
ARI

The next day, a full camp had been erected, including a much larger tent for me and Rain. I'd insisted Rain sleep last night despite his assurance he was fine. While I welcomed the niceties brought in for us, I couldn't get comfortable. I itched to get away and rescue my sister. I'd gotten up to take care of personal needs at an area designated by the edge of the camp. It seemed like a lot of setup when I hoped we'd go in and get my sister right away. We needed a plan. I'd learned that lesson from my first time in this horrid land. Hanging a robe, one that had been brought for me, over a chair by the table, I slipped back into the bed that had been assembled for us. Rain rolled over, draping an arm over me. If I snuck away, would he know? He'd sensed things since we'd learned we were mates, but how much I wasn't sure.

His eyes fluttered open as if he'd heard my unspoken question. A lazy smile turned the corners of his mouth up.

He pulled me to him, and his hardness pressed against my belly.

"Were you dreaming about me?" I asked.

"Mmm." His grip on my hip tightened. "Always. Since the first time we met." He pressed his lips against my cheek.

"I need a bath." I wanted him, but the quick rinse I'd had yesterday wasn't enough to wash away the events of the day.

"If you've forgotten, I like it when you're dirty." A growl hummed in his chest.

"You are—"

"Fucking crazy about you."

"Fucking crazy is right."

He laughed and claimed my mouth. When he pulled back, he kissed the tip of my nose. "You taste like toothpaste. Minty and fresh. Who needs a bath?"

Marius had already told me the others were gathering. As much as I wanted to stay in bed with Rain, reality was waiting. "We have a meeting with Marius and your strategic leaders."

His forehead creased. "Our strategic advisors. They are yours more than mine."

"They know you and listen to you. I'm just the daughter of an incredible general and the worst traitor the realm has ever known." My stomach roiled. As proud as I was of my mother's accomplishments, I was equally outraged at the atrocities committed by the man responsible for one-half of my existence.

Rain rolled so he was on top of me, trapping me between him in the one place I always felt safe—his arms. He brushed the hair from my face. "You are a powerful, intelligent leader. You are the most beautiful woman I've ever seen, and you are my mate. You are so much more than your parents. I see the woman I will spend the rest of my life in this realm and the next with, but I also see the fae who will restore our kingdom."

My chest warmed, and my breath caught on a knot forming in my throat. I believed him when he whispered reassurances to me, but I wasn't sure I believed that was who other fae saw when they looked at me. I loved him more for having that kind of confidence in me. Hooking my leg around his, I flipped us and positioned myself over him. His hardness pressed against my core, and I ground myself against him. A moan tumbled from his lips.

Leaning forward, I nibbled on his earlobe. "Tonight, after our family is safe, I want you to make me scream your name."

"Challenge accepted." He grasped my hips and moved them back and forth. I remembered him doing that before and the lust in his eyes as he watched me unravel. A gasp escaped my mouth as my desire ratcheted up. "We need to get dressed."

Rain sighed and gave me a hasty kiss as he stood up with me wrapped around his waist. "As you wish, my mate."

A twinge of disappointment skimmed over me, but I

tucked it away. He guided me as I slid down his body. My mate was my perfect match.

The others are ready when you are. Marius's voice drifted down the bond. Although it was a mood killer, I was anxious to get to the meeting because each step was one closer to getting my sister and Laurel out.

On our way.

"Daddy Marius?" Rain asked.

"It's weird when you say it. Remember what I said earlier about screaming your name?"

"Of course." Rain smiled.

"Not going to happen now, and yes, that was my bonded unicorn, Marius." I winked triumphantly and turned away to find my clothes. Thankfully, one of the fae who vanyshened in had brought clothes and personal care items for both me and Rain, including the nightgown I had on earlier. I cringed a little, wondering who had gone through my things to find it, but at least they had packed the fluffy robe too. Otherwise, the walk this morning would have been chilly. I opened the bag for myself and looked for something appropriate for the strategic meeting.

Rain grabbed my hand and jerked me hard against him. He gripped my ass with one hand and slid the other around the nape of my neck.

I gasped, and my core throbbed. "What are—"

He claimed my mouth, and I sank into his touch. He licked from the hollow of my neck to the tender spot near my ear. "My name will be on your lips later."

"Later." I climbed off him, missing his touch as soon as there was space between us. I winked at him. "You'll be saying my name."

He rolled onto his side and studied me with so much love in his eyes. "Whatever my goddess wants, she gets."

Goddess...He could call me anything he wanted, but I wasn't sure I could live up to that one word.

MEETING

ARI

Rain's advisors had secured a map of the vampire palace and grounds. There were five fae gathered around the table. A woman, who looked a lot like Merrick and wore similar clothes, stood to my right. Marius took the position behind me as if he was ready to be a buffer between us. She waved a hand to the man next to her, and he unrolled the map.

Zabrina, Merrick's mother, is the fae beside you. Marius's words whispered into my head. *The fae unfurling the parchment is Whit. He's a historian and was a personal friend of your mother's. Gemma has become close to him as well.*

My gaze fell on the gray-haired man. He positioned paperweights to keep the map flat. He met my gaze with a warm smile. I inclined my head toward him.

"May I, Princess Arianna?" he asked, his eyes twinkling.

"Ari is fine and yes, please."

Whit pointed to the map. "There are a lot of hidden hallways and rooms in the palace." He paused. "It's important to note this map is fifty years old. We stopped monitoring the vampire activities as closely since then."

Fifty-year-old information wasn't very strategic. "Is there anyone inside like..." Griselda. I couldn't say her name out loud to people I didn't know. I cleared my throat. "An ally?"

Rain wrapped his pinky around mine and grounded me with the minor touch.

"None," Whit said, his tone grim. "That's why the map is out of date. Our last collaborator was hung on the wall until all the tonic cleared his system, and he burned in the sunlight."

A gruesome display, but based on the timing, it wasn't from Albert's doing. He'd probably laid the groundwork for such treatment. My anger seethed inward. "Was the tonic to prolong the suffering?"

"No," the fae female with the deepest skin tone the other side of Rain answered. "It was the same one that allows the vampire to walk in the daylight."

What's her name? I asked Marius.

Orla.

"Thank you, Orla." I met her golden gaze.

She inclined her head. "Our contact was lost when my team oversaw the border. It was a personal failure for me that I intend to rectify." Her skin shimmered with magic and a promise that said she wanted revenge.

Whit shook his head. "It wasn't your error. No one could have known."

"I should have, and I accept that responsibility." She met his gaze with the fierceness of a warrior. I respected her strength and understood how guilt often intertwined with responsibility.

"No one needs to carry that blame alone. We were all complacent. We will not make those mistakes again."

Haisley. Marius's voice named the striking brown-headed fae with skin covered in a golden sheen. Her hair, cut short, drew my focus to her beautiful features. Her tone was gentle, but pain floated just underneath the surface, visible only in her kind, olive-green eyes.

"It's time to let the dead vampire go." The pale-skinned man with black hair turned his gaze on Whit. "Show us what you know, old man."

And that is Dariel.

The way Dariel condescended to Whit angered me. I didn't know either of them, but I could tell he wasn't playing when he called Whit "old man." *I don't like him. He needs a punch to the throat.*

Rain gripped my hand in his as if he could hear the exchange between me and Marius.

Temper your anger. These fae, including Dariel, are our best chance of getting your sister and Laurel back. Marius stepped back behind me.

Are you afraid I'm going to use some of Nyx's power?

A chuckle rumbled down our bond. *Not at all. Cyrus has secured your brother and your niece. He's on his way here.*

Drew and Phina were safe, and that was the best news I'd heard in the camp. Seeing Cyrus face-to-face made me want to stab something. *You should be afraid for him.*

Rain tugged on my hand in an easy gesture for my attention.

"As I was saying"— Whit leaned over the map and pointed—"given the power we detected, this room is the most likely to be where they are keeping Gemma and Laurel."

An exact location was the answer I needed to have hope. We could vanyshen in and get them out quickly.

"Why put them that far underground?" Dariel asked.

"We can't vanyshen to that depth under the earth," Rain answered.

Fuck. I hadn't known that. I'd assumed we could use that power anywhere. I studied the path. No easy entry from what I could see. "If we can't vanyshen in, then what are our options?"

"We fight our way in," Haisley answered with all the confidence of a seasoned fighter.

Her I like. I sent the thought to Marius.

She has earned the respect of your kind many times over.

"We could vanyshen to here and then proceed to remove the obstacles," Dariel said, rubbing his hands together. He wanted to end some vampire, and I would have enjoyed that if he hadn't been an asshole to Whit.

Zabrina remained quiet, but her gaze looked over every inch of the map.

Orla drew a circle over a spot with her finger. "We would likely be surrounded by them here, Dariel."

He grunted. "If enough of us are there, it won't matter."

Orla lifted her shoulder in a half-shrug. "True."

Normally, I would be in full support of jumping into the middle of a battle, but I wouldn't make another reckless move. Dariel wasn't earning my trust with his brashness either. What we needed were more unicorn. *How long before Cyrus arrives?*

He should be here in a few hours. I know you are angry with him, but there are circumstances you need to understand.

I already know your brother and my sister... I let the thought drift away, and Marius didn't add to it. Cyrus was still bonded to my Gemma. He would want to protect her, and an additional unicorn would add significant power on our side. *We are going to get to them in time, aren't we?*

I believe so. Your father needs them alive.

You know what he's doing with them and haven't told me?

No, I suspect he is resuming his pre-war activities.

Which were?

Building an untouchable army.

I let that sink in and contemplated what it meant. *You mean he wants to use Gemma and Laurel's blood to create an army of vampire who can walk in the sun?*

The blood is only ever temporary. His journals from before suggested he thought he had a way to achieve the goal if he could combine some of the power of the fae with their blood.

My stomach bottomed out. Our power was as much a

part of us as our physical extremities. *That's basically an amputation.*

Rain shuddered next to me.

Can he hear us? I asked Marius. Not that I didn't trust my mate, but my bond with Marius had been private my entire life. The connection was like a private diary, and I wasn't sure I wanted anyone, even Rain, to have access to those parts of me.

I don't believe so, but he is your mate and will feel your emotions.

"The most vulnerable point is here." Zabrina looked directly at Rain. "If we concentrate your lightning there, it should give us enough time to get inside."

"To cover that much area will take a lot of my power." Rain smiled at me. "Unless someone can give me a boost."

His infectious grin was meant as a distraction, but my worry shivered through me. I didn't want him to repeat what happened last time he used his magic. If I boosted him, then someone else would be saving Gemma.

"Who is getting my sister and Laurel out if Rain and I are the distraction?" I took in the others, and their eyes focused on me. It wasn't scrutiny I saw. No, they looked at me with what appeared to be reverence I hadn't earned.

"I will." Haisley dropped to a knee. "In honor of General Daphina's sacrifice."

"As will I," Orla and Dariel said, taking the same position.

"My skills on the battlefield are rusty, but they are yours," Whit said, following the others.

"Someone has to keep the history, Whit, and that is you," Zabrina said, but she didn't lower herself in reverence. "I'll go as will my daughter, Merrick."

Goddess, I don't deserve this. I just want help saving my sister. They are willing to meet danger face-to-face for my family. The loneliness I'd experienced since the collapse of my home, the prison kingdom, lifted a fraction. A knot hardened in my throat, and I had to swallow several times to clear it. "Thank you."

Rain leaned in close to my ear. "They are kneeling for you. You need to release them."

Oh. Shit. Nyx, I'm never going to get used to that. After my family is safe, I'm going to request a no-bowing decree or whatever they call it in this kingdom. "Please rise. I thank you for the way you honor my mother."

She was the one who should be here leading these fae. I could never live up to Mother's greatness, but I would strive to make her proud every day. Hopefully, that was enough to restore the kingdom to a state of normalcy.

When they all rose, Orla stretched her neck to look at me. "We honor her, but it is you we look to for the future."

They didn't seem concerned that it was my father who had us in the situation. Everyone knew who he was, yet they focused on my maternal side. *How can they be sure I'm not like Albert?*

Because you are blessed by Nyx, and you are much more like your mother than you give yourself credit for being.

I blinked back the tears threatening to spill, because

I'd be damned if I'd cry in front of these battle-seasoned high-borns.

"When the rest of the teams are back from their reconnaissance, we'll compare and confirm plans. I want to move as quickly as possible," Rain said, squeezing my hand gently.

CHAPTER 6
DRAINED
RAIN

Marius scanned the edge of the woods as he walked me and Ari to the tent erected for meal preparation. "My brother should have been here by now."

"I'm not used to your outward concern. Do you think something happened?" Ari cocked her head in his direction.

He looked toward the trees once more. "He should be able to hear me through our twin bond, but he's not responding."

I wasn't an expert on unicorn anatomy, especially twins, but I knew there were limits to how far a unicorn connection could reach for the fae they guarded. I'd assumed it was similar for unicorn to unicorn as well. The bond between Marius and Cyrus was different than the average of their kind, even unicorn siblings. If what Casimir had told me was accurate, they were rarely out of touch with each other unless one blocked the other. My understanding from my conversations with Casimir was that Marius, as the leader, did the blocking. Was Cyrus ignoring his brother?

Ari reached over and patted Marius's shoulder. "Cyrus has been on his own for years. He can handle himself." She studied him with more concern. "Unless you think something happened? Are you sensing something?"

Her bonded grumbled something I couldn't understand.

I shook my head.

Sophus approached in hasty strides. With his dark golden skin, curly hair, and good looks, he still looked like what many fae called a god when we'd worked our way through the bars in the city. He walked with a slight limp. I doubted anyone else but me would even notice the subtle change in his gait. He had the leg mended during the battle where I nearly died. Years had passed since I'd last seen him, but I was thankful to know he was here. Given his role as a skilled magic weaver during the war, I suspected the fine net cast over us was largely his doing. I held my hand out to him.

He knocked his fingers against mine, pushing them out of the way. "Is that how you greet your best friend?"

"Sophus, it's good to see you." I embraced him.

"I missed you, my friend," Sophus said, stepping back. "This wasn't how I imagined us draggin' your brother out of the lab."

"No, and I fear it's my negligence that has put him in

this situation." A tingle smoothed over my skin, and I didn't have to look at Ari to know she attempted to soothe my fractured confidence. There would be no forgiveness for this mistake—only retribution. "Let me introduce you to my..." Did I call her mate in front of everyone? No one else knew outside of our family, but I trusted Sophus. He'd taken a blade to protect me when I lay bleeding on the battlefield. I looked at Ari, and she winked at me. That was the only confirmation needed. "Ari is my mate and General Daphina's daughter."

Sophus's brows lifted, and he dropped to a knee. "Nyx-blessed daughter of our friend, General Daphina, I am honored to be in your presence."

"Please rise. There's no need for dramatics. It's a joy to meet Rain's best friend. Were the circumstances different, I'd be asking you for all of Rain's secrets." She held her hand out to him.

He took her offered hand in his and placed a kiss on it. "I will gladly divulge anything about this horrible fae you want to know...for a dance."

This motherfucker. He was doing it to get a rise out of me. A chuckle rumbled low in my chest. While I'd told Ari about my affairs, mostly one-night stands, there were some stories best left between brothers. I trusted Sophus wouldn't share those.

Ari laughed and pulled her hand back.

As he stood, Sophus flashed his most impressive smile like he used in many a bar during our younger years.

A growl rumbled in my chest.

Sophus clapped his hand on my shoulder. "You are mated, brother. You have nothing to worry about."

I narrowed my eyes at him. "Touch her again and you will find out just how unbothered I am by you."

Ari cleared her throat. I moved to her, tucking her to my side. She sank against me. *Thank the goddesses and gods.*

Marius's head jerked to the side.

"Is Cyrus here?" Ari asked, her tone filled with concern.

"No, there are two fae missing. Their horses were found drained," Marius said.

A creature, particularly a horse, who was bled dry could only mean one thing—vampire, and they were too fucking close. They needed to be ended, and I hope to the goddesses and gods that the fae were still alive.

Ari shifted beside me. "We should join the search. Where were the horses found?"

My grip tightened on her hip. I'd follow her to the bottom of the ocean or, covered in blood, to a vampire horde. If the fae hadn't survived, I worried she'd feel that guilt deeply even though it wouldn't be hers to bear. "Are you sure you need to go? We do have things to do here."

Ari sighed. "It's because of us...our family. We should be the ones out there."

"I don't think it's wise." Marius sounded unusually distracted.

"According to you, I never do anything wise," she shot back.

Marius snorted. "Occasionally but not very often."

I bit back my amusement. We had more important things to do than listen to their exchange, but damned if I didn't enjoy it. My mate could hold her own with the unicorn leader, but then again, she'd had over a quarter of a century to figure him out.

Merrick emerged beside us. Worry lines creased her face. "Have any of you seen my mother? I know she arrived this morning, but I can't find her."

The fear in Merrick's voice quashed any awkwardness about seeing her. Zabrina wouldn't have been part of the patrol, but that didn't mean she wouldn't have gone with them either. It would take more than one vampire to bring her down. Zabrina wielded fire with some of the deadliest techniques I'd seen. In the Great War, she'd incinerated several thousand vampire before collapsing on the battlefield. It took three days for her to wake up afterward. Merrick was strong like her.

"Yes, we met with her a short time ago," Ari said. "She didn't mention what her plans were after the meeting."

Merrick's distress didn't ease. "She'd planned to stay until we got Gemma and Laurel back, but I can't find her."

"Maybe she had to return for something urgent." Sophus touched Merrick's upper arm. "She does have many responsibilities."

Merrick rolled her arm away. "I'm well aware of my mother's obligations."

"I'm sure she's here, but it is unusual, " I said, glancing at Marius.

Ari reached for Merrick's wrist. "I think we should look for Zabrina. I'll help you."

"Thank you." Merrick's face relaxed slightly. I didn't recall ever hearing her thank anyone before. I suspected the friendship between my mate and Laurel's ex-lover would be temporary once Gemma returned. Ari had dealt with so much loss in her short life, but she was loyal to her family to the point of her own detriment. She needed to make friends here, but I wasn't sure Merrick was that person either. I'd tracked down Valentina, her friend from the prison kingdom. She was on the coast, adjusting to life with her husband.

Ari glanced at me. "Given two other fae are missing—"

"What?" Merrick's anxiety was palpable.

I suspected Albert aimed to cause disruption and create uncertainty by sending vampire out to find us. Zabrina and the two other fae had to be found right away, or retrieving my brother and Ari's sister would be at risk.

Marius sighed. "Their horses were found but not them."

"The horses were drained," Sophus added.

Merrick's face twisted. "We have to find my mother."

"Maybe if we split up and start by searching the camp first," Marius said.

CHAPTER 7

GRIEF

ARI

Marius, Merrick, and I searched together. Rain went with Sophus. When Sophus wanted to pair with him, I encouraged him to go. I wanted to spend every minute with him, no matter what we were doing, but I knew that wasn't healthy. If we were lucky, there would be a thousand years together, and we needed our own friends and interests.

I can hear your thoughts. Marius popped into my head through our shared bond.

Well, get out if you don't want to hear them.

A chuckle reverberated down the bond. *So, you don't want to know that I liked how you were forward-looking and establishing boundaries.*

Why are you being nice to me?

I'm always nice to you.

Mmmhmm.

A piece of blue fabric hung on a low limb of a tree

ahead. Dread slid up my neck, causing the hairs to prickle. I pointed to the material blowing in the breeze. "Merrick, I think your mother was wearing that this morning."

She gasped and ran toward the scarf.

I scanned the area looking for other signs of Zabrina. "Would she need anything from the woods for any reason? Like medicinal?"

Merrick's hands shook as she studied the sheer fabric. "No, she's not a healer. Fire is the element of her affinity." She turned in a circle, surveying the area. "Mother? Are you here?"

A pair of boots came into view beside some underbrush a few feet from Merrick. I froze and reached out for Marius's shoulder. He stopped beside me.

"Mother!" Merrick called as she ran to Zabrina. Blonde hair covered her face as she knelt beside her mother. Tears rolled down Merrick's face. "She's alive. Help me."

I snapped forward and dropped down to the ground on the opposite side of Zabrina. Her lips were blue and her skin an ashen color. I recognized the pallor from when my mother was near death. Scanning her for injuries, I found no blood visible on Zabrina...except for the bite marks on her neck. "What do you need me to do?"

"Do what you did when you healed Rain."

Apprehension crept in on me. I wasn't even sure what I'd done for Rain. Nyx had helped me. I didn't know how to call on that power without her, and I wasn't sure I had the right to ask for assistance again so soon. Merrick did what she could to save my love, though. Didn't her actions deserve for me to try? *Nyx, you have given me a second chance. You helped me restore my mate, so he could stand by my side when I needed him. May I ask that you help my new friend save her mother?* Closing my eyes, visions of my mother passing in front of me flooded my mind, and I stifled a sob. All the crushing grief from that time smothered me. I wanted to stop, so I didn't have to relieve that pain. Merrick and her mother came to help me, each in their own way, and that made me more determined to press forward.

"Please," Merrick whispered.

Marius dropped his chin to the top of my head. His support gave me the additional strength to open my eyes.

Starlight glowed around my hand. Relieved the brilliance responded, I focused it. Merrick had hers out flat, hovering just above her mother's chest. I set my hands upon Merrick's. The sheen enveloped hers, and the luminosity radiated from Merrick's palms to her mother's chest. The soft, sweet scent of jasmine and vanilla filled the air, and I inhaled. Moonflowers. The aroma rejuvenated me, and I was able to send more power to Merrick.

"You can let go, Ari," Marius whispered next to my ear. "I can sense Zabrina's essence renewed."

Thank you, Nyx.

Happy Merrick wouldn't have to say goodbye to her mother today, I collapsed backward, into Marius. He'd shifted to his fae form at some point because he wrapped his arms around me.

"Ssh," he said, his voice low and soft.

My grief for my mother poured out. I'd thought I was done and moving forward, but the suffering never left my heart. Hot tears cascaded over my cheeks. Seeing Merrick so close to losing her mother reminded me of how helpless I'd felt when Mother wasted away.

"You're okay," Marius said.

I wiped my tears and pushed away from him. "I am," I said and added down our bond. *Daddy Marius.*

He stood and helped me to my feet. *Do you need anything?*

I expected to be weakened using the power, but I wasn't. Zabrina must not have been in as bad a condition as I'd thought. *Thank you, my friend. I'm fine.*

I turned to Merrick. Her cheeks were flushed, and her hand shook as she tucked a strand of hair behind her ear. "Can we vanyshen her back to the camp?"

"Yes, she is stable."

Zabrina opened her eyes. Her color wasn't quite normal, but she looked much better. "What happened?"

"Mother." Merrick helped Zabrina sit up. "You scared me."

Zabrina's hand skimmed over her neck. The bite healed, and her fingers found the blood left behind. "I was attacked."

"Yes, but we healed you," I said, my composure restored.

"In all the war, I was never bitten." Her hand trembled as she studied the blood. "Never were they able to get so close without me sensing their presence."

"Do you remember what happened?" I squatted down, assessing her for signs of how the attack occurred.

Her face contorted into a ghostlike expression. "They ambushed me."

I placed a hand on her shoulder. "How many?"

"Can't this wait?" Merrick's eyes pleaded with me.

"Of course." I nodded. My empathy for her situation, nearly losing her mother, made my agreement easy.

When I moved to help Zabrina stand, she grabbed my elbow. "They used wind to hide themselves."

Impossible. Vampire who had been fae lost the ability to wield magic. My gaze shot to Marius. *How?*

Not now. He sent his reply down the bond. "We should get back to camp. Can you walk, Zabrina?"

"The distance to the camp is fifteen or twenty minutes, but I can vanyshen us if you aren't up to it?" I offered.

Zabrina straightened to her full height, and I saw the same fire in her that Merrick had. "I can manage."

CHAPTER 8
SPIDER WEB
RAIN

When I returned from the search, I found Ari studying the map we'd looked at earlier in the morning. Her eyes were rimmed in a pinkish red as if she'd been crying. I rested my hand on the small of her back and kissed her temple. Dusk had begun to fall over the camp, and general unease settled with it after the events of the day.

"Vampire can't wield elements," I said, unable to believe the claim Zabrina made that the vampire hid their scents and sounds with wind magic. A vampire's previous life died when they were reborn as the undead—undead and with no special gifts or affinities. Zabrina had to be mistaken. The other option sickened my stomach, because if it wasn't the vampire, we had fae traitors in our midst.

"Rain, she is confident that is what happened," Ari said, not looking up from the map where she marked Zabrina's attack and the spot where the dead horses were found. "These strikes happened, not only close to one another, but in a near-perfect line from each other. Do you think that's a coincidence?"

I considered Ari's observation and moved closer for a better look. The soft scent of moonflowers in the evening drifted around me. Wafts of the sweetness arose multiple times since we'd returned to camp. I slipped my hands around the incredible love of my life's waist and rested my chin on her shoulder. "Do you have moonflowers tucked in your pocket?

Ari leaned back against my chest. "No, but I smelled them when Merrick and I healed her mother. It's like the aroma is stuck in the air now."

"I'm not complaining." I pressed my lips against the soft skin of her cheek. "It reminds me of you looking so beautiful in your garden when we first met."

A laugh tumbled out of Ari's mouth. "When I hated you?"

"You mean when you wanted to fuck me?" I nibbled on her lobe. She'd made me think my dick was on fire with low magic, a trick I deserved for trying persuasion on her. I knew in that moment I'd take whatever she offered, whether she stabbed me or stoked the flames between us.

She turned, pressing her breasts against my chest. When she met my gaze, there was love, so much love, staring back at me. I wondered how I'd gotten so lucky to have her for my lifetime and maybe more. Her eyes smoldered, and my dick hardened in response.

"I guess some things never change." She winked at me.

I slid my hands behind her thighs and lifted her onto the map table. Devouring her mouth, I pulled back to remove my jacket.

Ari's eyes went distant. She was present. Her hand rested against my cheek in confirmation, but I knew she was talking to Marius.

"Cyrus is almost here," she said, sliding off the table. Her posture stiffened.

I stepped back, giving her space. "You don't have to speak with him."

Resolution marked Ari's face. "No, but I will. Marius asked me not to kill his brother when he arrives. Does he really think I would kill a unicorn? Especially knowing their reproductive issues?"

I suddenly found a spider's web woven in the corner of the tent very interesting. Ari would defend her family against anyone who hurt them, but she considered Marius family too. She wouldn't wound him by killing his twin. She might inflict some serious pain on his brother, and if I answered any other way, it would be a lie. I kept my mouth shut.

"You too?" She sighed. "I didn't expect you to side with my bonded. I'm not always ready to stab first and ask questions later."

A chuckle threatened to escape my mouth, and I mashed my lips together to stop it.

"Seriously? Does everyone think I just walk around killing everyone I'm mad at?"

I held my hand out to her. She took it, and I pulled her

to me. "Does it make me a horrible fae to admit I like that people think that about you? Your murder eyes make my—"

She slapped my shoulder, though not hard enough to cause pain. I still enjoyed it, but not as much as I relished the smile on her face. "I'm here however you need me."

"Can we take dinner alone in our tent while Marius debriefs Cyrus?"

She hadn't eaten much in days, so there was no way I'd turn her down. If she confronted Cyrus first, she probably wouldn't eat the rest of the night. "Whatever you want, my goddess."

"Apparently, he's brought two vampire children with him."

"What?" My question came out as an unintended roar. "Sorry. Are these prisoners?"

She rubbed my upper arm. "I don't know."

My concern for Ari getting enough food in her to face the battle waiting for us won out over my anger that there were vampire in the camp. Marius was the leader of the unicorn. He could handle that problem, and if he didn't, I'd step in. "I'll get our plates and meet you in the tent."

She stood on her tiptoes and caressed my lips with hers.

Goddesses and gods, her lips are softer than the silk of that flimsy nightgown she wore this morning. She owned my heart. I hoped there was never a time when I didn't want her from a single touch. I grabbed her hips and dug my fingers in. "Keep kissing me like that, and I'll need another appetite satisfied."

"That's what I'm counting on." She extracted my hands from her hips. "I'm going to wash up in that shower tent thing that was set up this morning."

"I could join you there." I raked my eyes over her.

"It didn't look like it was big enough for two." She winked. "Besides, I like it when you're dirty."

Ari using my words from the morning on me went straight to my throbbing cock. "Good. Because I plan on being extra dirty with you tonight."

Starlight danced through her pupils. Her eyes lit up even before her encounter with Nyx, but the twinkle in them now was different in the most exquisite way. Every subtle change I noted since then convinced me she was a goddess in her own right. She certainly was to me, and worshipping her was something I'd do every chance she'd give me...starting tonight.

CHAPTER 9
SPECIAL
ARI

Ipaced the length of the tent while Rain stacked our dishes neatly on a side table. I glanced from the dirty tableware to him. He cocked his head as if daring me to ask the question. I shook my head.

"Why doesn't he just come inside?" I whispered to Rain. The careful, calm demeanor I'd manifested earlier eroded with each passing second. Cyrus didn't want to face me, and I couldn't blame him. I once accused him of stealing Gemma, but my sister and I had just lost our mother. Surely, he understood that it had been the misguided grief of a child. Then again, I'd been pissed when he and Gemma disappeared. Even though I was just fifteen and Gemma twenty, I noted the way her bond changed with Cyrus after their ceremony. Thank the goddesses and gods that didn't happen for me and Marius. I threw up a little in my mouth at the thought and took a drink of the water in front of me.

"Cyrus might come inside if you weren't giving off massive amounts of agitation," Rain said softly. He placed a finger over his lips as if he was hiding the half-smile on his face.

I narrowed my eyes at him, but the voices outside the tent drew my attention.

"We have our secrets." Cyrus's voice carried through the tent.

"This is ridiculous." I stalked toward the entrance and flicked my wrist at the flap. It blew open on command. He looked worried, but I didn't sense it was because of me. Moreover, he appeared exhausted as if he'd been running for days without rest...not hours. "We all do. Get in here before I use my magic to hurl you inside."

Rain laughed a wicked sound like he wanted me to make good on my threat.

"Perhaps we take this meeting in my tent," my bonded said, gesturing to the one equally as large as the one I'd just left. I followed him with Rain at my side.

Cyrus swore under his breath, but he joined us inside. I raised an eyebrow at Marius when he looked like he was about to chastise me. They'd both shifted into their faelike forms, but their expressions couldn't have been more different. Marius smirked, but Cyrus's features creased with defeat.

On the far side of the makeshift room stood two figures that appeared to be teenagers. The girl and the boy cowered in our presence, and their scent hit me. Death with a hint of the sweet decay of the forest assaulted my nostrils. They were the vampire. I rounded on Cyrus.

My bonded invaded my space. "Hear him first."

"Have you lost your mind, Marius? Those are the enemy."

Cyrus positioned himself in a protective stance between me and the young vampire. "They're not. They are different from others of their kind."

The odor coming from them didn't smell like other vampires. I glanced past him and assessed the young man and the young woman. Nothing about them gave off a threatening vibe. Everything about them said broken and lost, and that was something I understood well.

"What are your names?" I asked, deliberately softening my voice.

Cyrus's shoulders relaxed and he moved to give me more access to them.

"Kyle." The young man answered, taking a knee as fae did for their sovereign.

His sister followed his actions. "Jenna, my queen."

"We'll have none of that," I said, smiling at them. They were fae before they turned. "Rise and call me Ari." I extended my hand. "And this is my mate, Rain."

They exchanged confused looks but did as I requested. Rain inclined his head toward them.

"You are special like us," Jenna said, shaking my offered hand. "We'll be proud to serve you."

If she could sense my power, that was indeed unusual for a vampire who'd once been fae.

"My sister and I are here to help." Kyle's voice betrayed his skepticism. He was assessing me in much the same way I was them.

They weren't as innocent as I expected, but their intentions appeared pure. "I believe you, Kyle. The other fae might not be as understanding. How will you deal with that?"

"We'll accept whatever fate has planned for us." His tone was so matter-of-fact that it took me by surprise.

Their behaviors reminded me of Griselda, and the memory pulled on a string deep in my chest. "Were you raised to know the goddesses and gods?"

"Our mother was an attendant in Nyx's temple before we were born." Jenna tilted her head to the side as if waiting for me to make the connection I already had.

Griselda served in the same capacity at Nyx's temple before she'd been made vampire, and I took that as a sign from the goddess herself that Griselda had been accepted in the next realm.

I know you can't answer, Nyx, but thank you for sending these two vampires. Each day you open my eyes more. I studied the brother and sister for a moment and saw them for what they were. Shattered by events of their life but pieced back together into something more. "I think you are indeed correct. We are similar."

"Maybe we should move to the other tent for the rest of this discussion," Rain suggested.

"Agreed." I nodded.

He opened the flap, and I led the four of us to the other tent. Rain opened the flap to our place.

I took a seat at the largest table in the tent and focused on Cyrus. "So, tell me how long you were fucking my sister before you ran off and left her."

"I'm not sure this is a topic I'm comfortable hearing," Marius said for all, but there was a nudge at my mental wall. *Is that really what you want to ask him?*

It wasn't, but he'd left her. He was sworn to protect her, he disappeared, and I was pissed.

I glanced at Marius. "You are in his head. You've certainly been in mine, unwanted. Plus, there isn't enough alcohol in the kingdom to burn the image of you and Amelia fu—"

"Enough, Ari," my bonded said. "You're angry because of your sister's imprisonment, and I know that's triggering for you. Lashing out at those closest to you isn't helping."

I swallowed against the knot in my throat. He was right, but I couldn't let it go. I trained my gaze on the doorway to try and gain my composure.

I'D LISTENED to Cyrus's version of events, and I wasn't convinced he'd done all he could with any of the decisions. A big sigh built up in my chest, and I let it out. "I don't know how I feel about it, but Marius says we need you when we break through to free Gemma." I stood, my glare on Cyrus to drive home what I said. "I trust him."

Marius positioned his body between us. "Why don't you and Rainier go for a walk? I can fill Cyrus in on our plan for tomorrow."

"Tomorrow?" Cyrus asked. Shock skipped across his features before he could mask it.

"Not soon enough for you, or do you need more time to run away?" I asked as I ducked out of the tent.

"I'm not running away," he called after me. I acted as if I didn't care, but I did. He was here for Gemma and Laurel. "I wonder if they have any idea how much alike they are."

Marius and I argued once when he said I was like my sister. Gemma and I were compared our entire lives, but it annoyed me more coming from our bonded unicorns. He'd mentioned that he and Cyrus's twin bond functioned similarly to our guardian and charge bond. They were in our heads respectively, and of everyone they should know how different Gemma and I were.

Rain slipped his hand in mine and led me away from our tent. "I know what you need."

"Some strong alcohol to forget the confirmation that my sister fucked her bonded?"

His face scrunched up in disgust. "Maybe we don't think about our siblings' sex lives for the rest of the night."

"Or ever," I said, swinging our arms.

Rain glanced down and raised an eyebrow. "Did you sw—"

"Don't say it, or I'll cut out your tongue."

"I know that's a lie. My tongue is your favorite part of my body."

Even as hard as this situation was, Rain was still himself when we were alone. His demeanor put me at ease, and I loved him for it. "That is a wonderful part of you, but there is one I like more."

"I plan on using both on you tonight." He stopped and pulled me into a shadow.

My heart sped up, longing to be closer to him...to share the bond that was only ours.

"When you threaten violence, it makes me hard." He pressed his bulge against my belly.

"Okay, two parts." I placed my hand over his heart. "This is my favorite part. I love you."

"Every part of you is my favorite part." He traced his knuckles over my cheek, down my neck, and over the peak of my breast.

His words warm like his skin, I shivered under his touch.

He reached his hand around my waist and paused. He locked his possessive gaze on me. "I will love you until my magic dies and then on into the next realm."

Goddess, he makes me feel alive. Love would never be a strong enough word to describe the depth of my adoration for him. I rested my cheek against his shoulder. "Thank you."

"For wanting to make you scream my name?"

I laughed. "That and for not treating me like I'm broken. For listening to me. For loving me."

"It is my honor to be that person for my mate." He kissed the top of my head and pulled back. "Let's get to the dining tent. I asked them to prepare something for us."

"Don't tell me you requested a chocolate cake out here in the woods." He'd had the cooks make chocolate cake since my arrival in his...our kingdom. In many ways, it was his version of writing me a love letter.

He bumped his shoulder against mine. "Fine. I'll let you discover the truth yourself."

CHAPTER 10
MEMORIES
RAIN

The dining hall buzzed with fae. I hadn't expected most of the camp to eat late in the evening. Curious stares found Ari, and occasional whispers drifted to us with words like "goddess-touched" or references to her mother. I'd sensed Ari becoming overwhelmed with the eyes on her in the makeshift room so I asked her if she wanted to go ahead to get our space ready for the night. There wasn't much to prep for the evening. Our plans were made, but I knew firsthand how difficult it was to sleep before a battle when your loved ones were at stake. She went ahead without even a second thought while I waited for the cake.

I slowed my steps when I saw Ari speaking with Cyrus outside our tent. She appeared solemn, not angry. My mate ducked through the flap, and Cyrus headed toward the other large shelter. I picked up my pace. From just outside Marius's tent, Cyrus watched me with a weary glance. I shot him a giant grin as I walked past. "Cyrus."

He tilted his head to the side. "Is that wise before a battle?"

"It most definitely is." I toed the flap to mine and Ari's shelter open.

Marius exited in his fae form before I could enter. He eyed the chocolate cake and shifted to his natural appearance. We nodded to each other as he walked toward his own tent. Unusual for him not to speak, but the day had been long.

Goddesses and gods, if you are listening, let that be the last of our interruptions tonight. I ducked inside the doorway.

"Who's ready..." My words died on my lips. Merrick sat in my place next to Ari, and they were engrossed in conversation.

Ari raised her gaze to mine and shot a quick glance at the plate holding our two slices of chocolate cake. She gave me an apologetic tilt of the head.

Merrick looked over her shoulder. Her eyes were rimmed in red.

Zabrina? She'd been fine earlier.

"What's happened?" I asked, setting the plate between them and taking the chair opposite Ari.

"Quinn is missing again," she said. Her younger cousin had run away multiple times over the last few years. His power hadn't manifested. It was long overdue, and I suspected it had to do with the pressure of their family.

Merrick possessed some rare skill at finding the young fae no matter what bar or bed he'd found himself in.

"Why aren't you looking for him?" I asked.

"Mother is searching for him, but she said I must remain here."

Her mother's approval held high importance to Merrick, and Zabrina was one of the few people Merrick accepted the word "no" from.

"Surely we can spare one healer," Ari said.

I understood then why she'd been forced to stay. It wasn't fair, and Ari wouldn't like it. "Merrick is the only doctor, or healer, in the camp."

Ari's face twisted in confusion.

"If I leave and something happens to Rain, I'd be executed."

Ari's brows bunched together. "What? Are you serious?"

"She is, and that extends to you now, too, as my mate." I sighed. The chocolate cake dried out like my evening had withered up. "But that is a formality since the throne is yours."

"That's unreasonable." Ari scoffed.

"As right as you might be, it has been fae law for centuries," I said.

Merrick moved to stand. "I'm sorry I burdened you with my family problems. I..." Merrick inhaled and let out a slow breath. "I didn't have anyone else to talk to in the camp."

Despite how she'd all but given up her fire affinity to

pursue becoming a healer, those who knew her before tended to still fear her. She reaped what she'd sown, and what a tough lesson it must have been to realize how hated she was. Plenty of fae respected her strength, but they hated how she treated so many. Unlike those she'd bullied or terrorized before she became a healer, I pitied her.

"You didn't cause any burden." Ari placed a hand on Merrick's arm.

Was Ari trying to make friends with Merrick? Even after what I'd told her? Was she that desperate for friends? It hadn't even occurred to me she was ready for that. She'd been through so much in such a short amount of time. I could try to tell her Merrick wouldn't be a good friend for her, but I was certain that would end in three possible outcomes—me being stabbed, me being told to "fuck off" or similar, or me being set on fire. No, Ari had to navigate a new potential friendship as she saw fit. My lips would stay sealed until she needed me. I could call for a different doctor and send Merrick back, but Ari would most certainly make me pay for that kind of interference.

"Why are you being so nice to me?" Merrick asked, her tone confused.

"I know what it's like to need a friend," Ari said, a tight smile on her face. Goddesses and gods, she was a force in every way, and she didn't even realize it.

"Sometimes I feel like no one sees me as a person." Merrick glanced down at the floor.

Her assessment wasn't shocking, and in my opinion, it

hit the mark. The fae didn't see her as a person because she'd held herself above them for two hundred years.

"I understand that too." Ari's voice held some sadness. I wondered if she was thinking about when we met, and her father was pressuring her into a marriage with almost anyone he considered noble. I'd fallen for her almost immediately, but she'd taken longer to get there. Her world had been upended, and I would have waited decades or centuries for her to work through it. She didn't need that long, though, and I'd thank Nyx for that blessing every day.

Ari stiffened in her chair.

"Are you okay?" I asked, reaching for her.

"Marius is going to look for Cyrus," she said, her gaze coming back to me. "Apparently, he's missing. I tried to tell Marius his brother probably decided to run off like when he'd ditched my sister."

"Ouch."

"Not my finest moment. My anger got the better of me."

"It seems more than that. Is something else bothering you?" I caressed her cheek.

She let out a long sigh. "I'm furious, but it's myself I'm really mad it. Taking it out on Cyrus because of their guardian and charge bond was easier. It's all my fault. I regret what I said to Marius, because he's pretty worried. He can't reach Cyrus mentally...can't even feel him," she said.

I pressed my lips to her temple. "First, none of this is

your fault. That belongs to Albert. Second, is it unusual for Marius not to be able to reach Cyrus?"

"Very. Because they are twins, they can infiltrate the other's minds without much effort. At first, I thought it was Cyrus being Cyrus, but I'm not so sure now, especially with how concerned Marius is."

What could be blocking them? I stood, reaching for my weapons. "This feels like it could be a trap. Tell Marius not to go alone."

"I'm pretty sure he's already in the woods." Ari pushed her chair back. Merrick did the same. Ari strapped her dual Nyx-blessed daggers in place.

Goddess, why was that so hot seeing her holding those blades? She was capable of doing more damage with her magic, but her skill with the daggers made my cock salute her magnificence every time. I didn't deserve her unflinching forgiveness, but I planned to spend our entire existence attempting to make amends. Not for myself but for her...she deserved to have the life she'd thought she had until I had to tell her what Albert had damned her and her sibling to—a damnation for all of us.

A memory of my father's death came front and center. He'd vanyshened across the vampire borders because he'd sensed my grave injuries. While a top warrior in his own right, he possessed strong empathic abilities, similar to those of Laurel. And like my brother, he preferred them over the sword. Laurel had been in what became the Forgotten Forest, administering the passage rights to the next realm for the dead. Father came alone—no guards in sight. He knelt beside me, infusing every ounce of healing power into me. I should have died—it should have been me. All my agony had disappeared by the time he arrived, so I knew I was close. My eyes closed as fresh pain lit up my nerves.

Father gasped, and wetness coated my face. I thought he was crying, but when I opened my eyes, my father's tortured expression met mine. My power hadn't recovered. I'd been spent for days before he arrived. It was probably because a vampire's blade had hit that perfect spot on my side. Father's eyes widened, and I saw the sword, covered in his blood, protruding from his torso. The blade slipped up diagonally across his chest, coming free between his shoulder and his neck. He fell on top of me— dead. A death that should have belonged to me. I struggled to get free, but Casimir positioned herself between me and the masked vampire. She lowered her horn, ready to strike. Then, the masked vampire just disappeared. Justice would be denied for me...for Laurel...for our kingdom.

Fingers grazed my hand slightly, and I flinched.

"Rain? Are you okay?"

I remembered my father's death frequently, but less since Ari had come into my life. I wondered why it chose to remind me of my worst failure. Then I knew—because I had more to lose.

I brought Ari's fingers a hairsbreadth from my mouth and gave her my most wicked smile before pressing my lips to the back of her hand. "As long as you are at my side."

I will live as long as I have you. A silent promise I gave to the goddesses and gods that if I should fail when it came to my mate, my love, my entire world, I would not live another two hundred years alone.

CHAPTER II
VULNERABLE

ARI

I threw the tent flap back to exit, and Rain barged through in front of me. An urge in me wanted to trip him, but I knew this was his way of putting me first —even if it meant he went first through the doorway. "Really?"

He flashed me a grin and walked a few steps ahead. Then he halted abruptly and held his hand out, signaling me to stop.

What had he seen? The open flap obscured my view. *If he thinks that holding his hand out like a parent does a child will stop me, he doesn't really know me.* I took a careful step forward, and in the shadows on the ground was a familiar shape. *Unicorn. No.*

I took another step, my body shaking. *Not Marius.* "Cyrus?" I whispered, scanning the shadows. "Where's Marius?"

Marius? Can you hear me? Cyrus is here.

My bonded's lack of response escalated my unease. I closed the distance to Cyrus. His legs were in a clumsy direction.

Merrick stood beside me. "What could take a unicorn down like that?"

"They're not invincible," Rain said, his voice tense. "I'll check the perimeter around our tents. You two stay here."

"Like hell," Merrick said, fire flickering at her fingertips.

My fear spiked, overwhelming my senses. I didn't see any obvious injuries. If he wasn't lying on the ground in an awkward position, I'd have thought he was sleeping. Even if I was pissed at him, he was my sister's bonded. To hurt him was to hurt her.

"Then stay with Ari until I get back," he said, his tone firm. "Defend your queen."

I ignored Rain's use of the title—a later discussion was needed. Instead, I ran my hand over Cyrus's neck. He was breathing, but it seemed shallow. Not that I was an expert on unicorn workings, but even in sleep, their breaths were deeper than Cyrus's were. "Can you heal him, Merrick?"

She touched my shoulder. Her hand was warm, but her flames no longer burned. "I've had little exposure to unicorn since the war. I don't know if my limited healing power would do any good on them."

I nodded. Cyrus's body jerked under my hand, but he didn't wake. *Marius?* I tried the bond again, but he didn't answer. My fear for Cyrus escalated to terror for my bonded. What if he was out there in the same condition?

He'd want me to save Cyrus. I knew that without a response. *If you can hear me, come back to camp. Cyrus needs you.*

"What do you want to do?" Merrick asked, kneeling beside me. She held a hand in front of Cyrus's nose. "He's breathing in a steady cadence. I don't think he's suffering."

"No, I don't think so either. He just isn't waking up." He didn't seem to be getting worse, but I was concerned he remained unconscious. Marius powered through minor injuries, so this was clearly more. I rested a hand over my stomach and steadied my own nerves. I leaned forward, smelling his breath--no sweetness like found in obvious poisons.

Merrick ran her hand along Cyrus's jaw and around his ears. "There's a knot here. It's almost directly between his ears. At the poll? That spot where the neck joins the head?"

I almost giggled at the reference. "Marius would be offended to hear you say that, and I'm sure Cyrus would too. Horses have a poll. Unicorn do not."

"Then Cyrus has a very large knot. Is this a vulnerable spot for a unicorn?"

"It's like if we were to get hit in the back of the head." *Fuck.* "He wore his glamour when he was hit. The attackers might not have realized he was a unicorn or might have even thought he was someone else."

"They realized their colossal fucking mistake when he shifted back to his real form."

I raised an eyebrow. "Agreed, but I'm still worried."

"Because you can't reach Marius?"

"Yes, and the fact that his brother is knocked out cold, and Rain is out in the woods. I need to go after him, Merrick."

"He'll be severely angry with you and probably fucking kill me. Why don't you try to heal Cyrus? If he's awake and can go with us, Rain won't be so pissed if we show up."

I wanted to help Cyrus, but I wasn't sure I had the right to ask Nyx for help again. What were the limits? She saved me from death and helped me heal both Merrick's mother and Rain. Was it overstepping to ask for more? I guess if it was, surely she just wouldn't respond. So, why not give it a try? I blew out a breath. "Help me like you did before?"

"Me? I'm certain I did nothing, but I'll do whatever you need me to." Merrick held her hands out over Cyrus.

I placed mine on top of hers. "Nyx, I know I've come to you a lot these last few days, but I could use some help here again."

Starlight twinkled around my hands and spread out like a mist over me, Merrick, and Cyrus. To my astonishment, it worked. Nyx had answered me again. A tinkling noise danced around me. *No, not around me. In my head.*

I cannot do this for you, but you only need to look within yourself, Arianna. Nyx's voice flooded in like my bond with Marius. *This is your power. Trust in your ability and open yourself to it.*

Had I hallucinated her speaking into my mind? No, it

was her. Her voice had been as clear as it had been when I almost died. She'd given me the power to save others, and all I had to do was trust her gift.

Thank you. Before I'd even finished sending those two words to her, the tinkling noise was gone. Not sure I was strong enough to heal a unicorn, I put my faith in Nyx. She said to trust myself and believe I could do it. I closed my eyes and thought of healing Cyrus—sending strength to him, healing the injury, and restoring him to who he was when I saw him last.

"It's working," Merrick said, wonder in her voice.

I opened my eyes, and the pale silver light waned as if saying "done." Cyrus's breathing was better, so I released the power. Merrick dropped her hands to her side.

Cyrus opened his eyes, and they widened.

Awestruck and reassured he was awake, I stared at him for a second. "Can you hear me? How are you feeling?" I asked.

"My head has a dull ache, but otherwise, I feel fine."

An intense lightning strike hit in the forest, followed by an equally loud clap of thunder reverberating through me. I jumped, grappling for footing until I was in a standing position.

"Rain," Merrick and I said in unison.

She scrambled to her feet, fire responding like torches on her hands.

"Can you stand?" I asked Cyrus.

He stood without hesitation. "Where's my brother?"

"In the forest too, or at least that's what he said before

I lost contact with him." I checked my blades as I ran toward the tree line. My mate and my bonded were in that forest, and Rain was for certain in a conflict. Another bolt lit up the sky. Desperation drove me faster to the spot it struck. I had to get to them.

Merrick and Cyrus followed, keeping pace beside me.

"He's not responding to me." Concern etched Cyrus's tone.

"Do you know who hit you?" Merrick asked.

"Someone impersonating my brother." He shook his head as if he couldn't quite reach the memory. "Someone impersonating my brother lured me out. I didn't see who hit me, but I have an idea."

"We're under attack," I said, as if that wasn't obvious. Divided and vulnerable was what we were, and we couldn't rescue anyone split up. Zabrina had been bitten and the horses drained. Cyrus's injury wasn't meant to kill. Whoever hit him wanted to temporarily disable him. "It's not vampire, because they wouldn't pass up the opportunity to drain a unicorn." I glanced in Cyrus's direction. "Sorry. Not to be crass, but it's true. Who do you think it is?"

"No offense taken. I think the sprites are here."

"The sprites are siding with the vampire?" The historians in the prison kingdom hadn't taught me much about them—they were old, powerful, and no longer in our realm. "How are they even here?"

"That is a long discussion best revisited when we're

not in danger, but I do not believe they are helping the vampire."

A series of lightning strikes and thunder that rolled so loud my teeth rattled gave Rain's location away. Any argument I had died in my throat. I couldn't run any faster, and it was going to take several minutes to get to him. The kind of power I witnessed would drain him quickly. Minutes would be too late. "Can we vanyshen there?"

"It's risky without having seen the landscape or another fae sending you the view... you know...kind of like coordinates for a map," Merrick said. The flames from her hands cast an orange light around us.

"We're not far," Cyrus said. "But I'm still unable to reach Marius. I don't know if he's with Rainier or not."

"I smell burnt flesh." I glanced at Merrick.

"It's not me." She scrunched her face up as if I'd thrown the worst possible insult her way.

Any other time, it would have been funny. "Rain must be destroying whoever dared to assault our camp."

"There's no question," Merrick said. "He's been taking vampire out along this border for two centuries."

He'd lived so much longer than me, and I was going to remind him of that when we were safe in our bed tonight.

CHAPTER 12

THE CIRCLE

RAIN

Footsteps pounded at my back, and I tapped into the swirling cloud above for another bolt of lightning. I spun to aim and drew up short. Ari, Cyrus, and Merrick emerged into the small clearing. My tired muscles relaxed with relief, but the power building in me begged for release. I pivoted back to the group of frenzied vampire, letting the bolt fly like a spear. Three more exploded, adding to the pile of remains. Another ten or so emerged from the other side of the clearing.

"No matter how many I end, more keep appearing," I called over my shoulder.

"Where are they coming from?" Merrick asked over the dull roar in the air.

"I don't know, but it must have something to do with wind, because those gusts aren't me. They haven't let up since I came upon the vampire." I gave Ari a once-over. She wasn't hurt. *Thank the goddesses and gods.*

"Marius isn't here?" Worry filled her voice, but Ari drew her daggers and took her battle stance like the badass she was.

"No, I haven't seen him." Knowing he was unaccounted for would be a distraction, but I wouldn't lie to her. I met her determined gaze. "Want to give me a boost and see if that stops them?"

She studied me with weary eyes, and I knew she was remembering how I'd expended my power in the city.

I held my hand out to her. "It won't be like that. There aren't as many."

She mashed her lips together and placed her hand in mine. "Don't overdo it. There's no need for theatrics. Make it quick."

I chuckled. Cyrus took up one side and Merrick the other as if we needed protection. Ari was damn near invincible, and she could take these vampire out without me. She just didn't know it yet.

"Ready?"

She nodded. Her power surged through me like the strength of ten thousand sprites.

Exhilaration coursed through me like a high that could never be reached again. I extended my other hand to the sky and found the line of power I wanted to pluck. The ultra-charged lightning blasted the space where the vampire kept coming from, lighting it up like daylight. I squinted at the distant shadowed shape, but I couldn't make it out. I didn't see any more vampire, but I didn't know what I was looking at either. "What is that?"

"That is something from sprite lore," Cyrus said. "And I'd know because I was just in one a few days ago."

"What does it do?" Merrick asked, studying the circle enclosure from the vantage point of where we all stood in a line.

The stones were placed with precision and roughly the same size. Magic radiated off it like a star powered it. The only magical strength I'd ever sensed like it was from Ari. She was studying the area with a skeptical look.

"It depends on the intent, but beyond that, I'm not sure. We were shown various things," Cyrus said.

"How did the vampire get it?" Ari raised an eyebrow.

"And can we destroy it to stop them?" I asked.

"I do not know the answers. Sprite magic is strong, and there could be repercussions for destroying something so sacred," Cyrus said.

Fuck. That's not a choice. "At least it looks like they stopped coming, but we can't leave this unguarded again."

Ari's hand shook in mine. "We still haven't found Marius."

"If he were no longer with us, you and I would both know, Ari," Cyrus said.

"Then where in Nyx's name is he?" Ari asked. "And where is the impersonator?"

I pulled Ari closer to me, keeping an eye on where the vampire had been. No movement came from the dark space. "Impersonator?"

Cyrus stepped forward and peered into the darkness.

"Someone appeared as my brother and then I was hit in the head."

"Vampire?" I asked, even though I hadn't heard of any bloodsuckers who possessed that kind of skill.

Cyrus shook his head. "No, it wasn't vampire."

"But you have a suspicion?" Ari asked.

"Sprites. Although the last ones I met were on our side...I think," Cyrus said.

"That knock to the head must have messed with your memory. Sprites haven't walked among us in a thousand years," I said.

"Longer. Until Leana and I met them with Drew."

Ari stiffened at my side. "What does my brother have to do with this?"

Cyrus hesitated. "I'm not sure this is the place to have this conversation."

Even though I suspected it was a stalling technique, I agreed with Cyrus. Vampire roamed the forest and surrounding areas too freely. Then again, we were on their border.

Ari's gaze drifted to the pile of ash that was once far too many vampire. "Let's find Marius, and then I want answers and to rescue my sister."

Cyrus went rigid then.

"If you say 'unicorn don't answer to fae,' like your brother does, I will cut out your tongue." Ari tapped one of her blades.

Goddesses and gods, I love this woman.

"I wasn't going to say that." Cyrus turned his attention

to me. "How do you propose we guard the sprite circle and find my brother?"

"You've been gone a while." I smiled, extending my arm. Lightning shot across the sky in short, controlled bursts. My soldiers were trained to recognize the signal and find me. I'd originally thought of it to let them know when it was safe to return to my side. Being too close when I let out the destructive force of my power was a death sentence. My control wasn't as strong wielding at the top end of my magic. There was a cost to everything, and that was the price of controlling the weather—especially the destructive side of it.

"You really met sprites?" Merrick asked, studying Cyrus.

He stared at her with contempt. "You hurt Gemma. I owe you no explanations."

"That was a long time ago, Cyrus," Merrick said, her voice barely a whisper.

Oh shit. Merrick's remorse wouldn't be enough for my beautiful and quick-tempered mate when it came to her sister. *This is either going to be fun to watch or I'll have to intervene and then Ari will be mad at me the rest of the night.* I didn't care for the latter option.

Ari watched the exchange, and I noted the subtle shift in her standing position. She was no longer relaxed from the brief battle. Her feet moved into her fighting stance, and she raised the single brow that meant she was ready to pounce. "How did you hurt Gemma?"

"It was years ago. I was engaged to Laurel when she

arrived." Merrick's face dropped as if she had lost her only friend, and there was a good chance she had.

Her recollection wasn't entirely wrong, but she painted a different picture from the facts. Laurel was the nicer of us, and I wouldn't be as gentle in my contradiction.

"Not exactly," I said, tracking my love's movements. She'd inched away from me and closer to Laurel's ex.

Merrick swiveled toward me. Flames danced in her eyes. "Our betrothal had not been officially called off."

"You know the only reason he hadn't ended it publicly was because you agreed to do it to save face," I said, softening my tone a bit.

"Skip to the part where you hurt my sister." Ari crossed her arms over her chest.

Merrick blinked a few times like she was choosing her words carefully. She swallowed hard and glanced at me.

"She knows that part," I said.

Merrick raised her chin. Humble was never going to be used to describe her. "I ran into your sister in the hallway outside Laurel's room. Tensions were high, and we... tussled. We both used magic and had injuries."

It wasn't a lie, but she left out a key part—Merrick started it by denigrating their mother's memory.

"That is one way to describe it," Cyrus said.

"Gemma had you on the ground, beating your..." Cyrus nudged my arm, and I stopped mid-sentence.

Ari cut her gaze at me and back to Merrick. "You fought over Laurel? That doesn't sound like my sister."

Merrick swallowed again. "I provoked your sister. I was angry and said some hateful things I shouldn't have."

That was the first time I'd actually heard Merrick take responsibility for her actions that day. Maybe her developing friendship with Ari meant that much to her.

"I see," Ari said, her words mild but her tone deadly. "And what did you say?"

No matter what Merrick said, it wasn't going to end well. Normally, I wouldn't interfere in Ari's form of justice, but Merrick wasn't the same person she was four years ago. "Ari, things were different. It was years ago."

Merrick reached her hand out but dropped it. "I can speak for myself, Rain."

"Cyrus, you were there for it. What say you?" Ari studied him.

"I didn't see it, but your sister did feel remorse for her part," Cyrus said, his tone factual.

"As do I, even after half a decade," Merrick said.

The love of my life wore a thoughtful expression on her face as she weighed her next move. With her goddess-given power, she could eviscerate Merrick where she stood. I edged between them enough that I could either absorb the power or pull Ari away if needed.

Ari let her arms fall to her sides, but her feet remained in her fighting stance. I moved a fraction closer. Cyrus sidestepped toward Merrick. He met my gaze and gave one nod, signaling we were on the same page. He didn't like my brother's ex-lover who'd attacked Gemma, but he would pull her out of the way of Ari's magic if it came to it.

"Then we'll let this one go." Ari dodged me and stood toe-to-toe with Merrick. "If you ever harm my sister or anyone I love again, our friendship will be over, and I will make you pay ten times over for whatever you do to them."

Merrick's shoulders dropped. "That will not be a problem. I have no intention of harming anyone other than vampire."

Ari studied Merrick for a second. I couldn't tell if my mate was going to hug her or hit her.

I held out my hand. Ari reached for it and stumbled toward me. Her hand, missing mine by a hairsbreadth as her eyes rolled up. I dropped to my knee, catching her before she hit the ground. "Ari? Are you okay?"

She'd fainted out of nowhere. Her cheeks were flushed like she had a fever. "Marius..."

"Ari, are you hurt?" I scanned her for injuries, but there wasn't anything. She hadn't used that much power with me, so it had to be something else.

Merrick lowered herself down in front of me and touched Ari's face. "Her skin is hot to the touch. Has she been ill?"

"No, she's been fine." I looked up at Cyrus. His eyes were unfocused.

"He's trying to reach out. It's faint, but I hear him," Cyrus said. "I can't quite understand what he's saying."

Ari shuddered in my arms. I stood, lifting her with me. "Why is she like this?"

"I don't know," Cyrus said. "I think we should take her

back to the camp. If Marius is in range, that's where he'll be headed."

"I agree with the unicorn. I don't have anything for a fever with me, and we need to get her temperature down. She's burning up." Merrick brushed the damp hair away from Ari's face.

The others were on the way to guard the place where the vampire had been. They could handle it, but what if vampire came through while no one was here? *Gods-dammit.* Ari was the most important thing. *Fuck the vampire.*

CHAPTER 13
SLEEP
ARI

Exhaustion covered me, but I refused to let go of the thread that connected me and Marius. I had to know he was safe, because the people I cared about seemed to be in increasing danger. There was one person to blame, and that was Albert. I channeled my anger at the fae responsible for one-half of my gene pool into maintaining contact with my bonded.

Marius? Where are you? He seemed so distant like the faintest shadow cast in the last light of the day.

*The sprites…*His words cut off like there was interference or a block.

He'd said sprites… *I'm going to kick their asses for kidnapping you.*

A rough chuckle, almost imperceptible, danced down the bond in a broken cadence. I took comfort in his laugh. If he was finding humor, he must be safe.

Can you free yourself, or do I need to come get you?

Not...prisoner. Be...by morning.

I let it sink in that he was unharmed and on his way. My body relaxed as the tension released. The exchange drained me in a way our communications never had. I needed rest, and he said he'd be here in the morning.

MY BRAIN WAS CLOUDED with the fog of sleep. I was in my bed in my tent, but the other half of it was empty. No minty scent. He'd left me alone, and I was surprised he wasn't here waiting for me. Rain must have gotten up early to check in before we left to get my sister and his brother.

Warmer than usual in the mornings, the tent felt steamy. A thin layer of sweat coated my forehead. Awareness of someone in the room with me set me on alert. I steadied my breathing. I didn't smell heavy perfume, so it wasn't Merrick. *Who is here?*

"I know you're awake," a woman's voice said. "And we don't have much time."

I opened my eyes.

"There you are."

She sat at the table with her hair as red as flames blowing in nonexistent wind. She appeared very fae-like and not at the same time. Her nearly translucent skin glimmered in waves around her, causing a slight blurring effect. She glamoured her appearance similar to how unicorn did.

"Who are you?" I sat up in bed, still dressed in the same clothes I had on last night. *Where the fuck is everyone else?*

"We'll get to where your companions are, including your bonded unicorn."

I hadn't asked that out loud.

"While I speak so it's more comfortable for you, I can hear your thoughts when I choose." She smiled. "As to who I am, I'm Neala." Her smile broadened.

"You're a sprite." Marius had said he was with her kind. I hadn't imagined it. How was she here? I thought they were no longer in our realm. Cyrus was telling the truth.

"Your thoughts are erratic, but yes, I am a sprite." She crossed her legs, and I noticed she wore an outfit similar to what Zabrina had worn, right down to the boots.

"What do you want with me?" I scanned for my daggers only to find them on the table where she sat. Nyx's power ran in my veins, and though I was unsure how to fully control it, I'd use it if I had to.

Neala dropped her gaze to my blades. Surprise flitted across her features. "Nyx gifted you these?"

"She did."

"Before or after you met her?" Neala asked.

While many knew I was blessed by the goddess, it wasn't common knowledge I'd met Nyx. Neala could be more powerful than she appeared. Or did Nyx speak with her too? "Before but I'm not sure why that matters."

"No need to become irritated. I was only curious as I cannot see when you came into possession of them," she said, her tone curious.

"Is that unusual?"

"Nyx is our goddess. She can shield what she doesn't want seen, so no." The corners of her mouth turned down in a frown. "Today is going to be a difficult day for you."

I tensed, a knot forming in my chest. "If you are about to tell me we will fail to save my sister today, I don't want to hear what you have to say. I know what we, my family, are capable of."

"Her bonded has already left with the two young vampires."

"He what?" I hopped out of bed, looking for my boots. "Does that idiot not know he's risking their lives?"

"Cyrus will succeed," she said, her voice solemn. "Your father will elude you, and his machine to bleed magic from a fae soul will still work."

My sister and Laurel would be free. A mix of joy and frustration joined in my chest. Tears burned my eyes, but I held them back. "Why tell me this?"

"Because you will be torn between going to save your sister and chasing down your father."

"There is no question. My sister's safety will always come first." I walked toward the table and tapped my fingers on it. "Stop calling Albert my father. The man I knew wasn't real. He never existed."

She inclined her head. "The healer is waiting for you, but the others have gone ahead after realizing what Cyrus's decision was."

"I need to go," I said, my voice sounding disconnected from my body. The tent blurred.

"Live, Arianna. While you can't do it alone, this realm needs you to survive." Her hand rested on mine, and a cold heat like ice radiated out from her touch. "Now, wake up."

I jolted, still in bed. The aroma of a meadow in spring with fresh flowers, not moonflowers but wild blossoms blowing, floated in the air. Merrick sat in a chair beside my bed. Her hands were clasped in her lap.

She looked concerned. "How do you feel?"

I wiped my hand across my brow. It came away damp with perspiration. Had that been a fever dream? "Fine. Where is everyone?"

Merrick sneered. "Cyrus snuck those little blood-suckers out before any of us realized he was gone."

Just as Neala predicted in my dream...it could be a coincidence. "Like ran away?"

"No, your bonded showed up with another unicorn, Cleave. They left about twenty minutes ago, tracking him. Rain and a few others went with them."

My hands shook as I slipped my daggers into their sheaths. If Neala told the truth about the events, I'd face an opportunity to stop Albert, and I'd walk away from it to secure Gemma's safety. There was no decision to make. Gemma would do the same for me. "A sprite visited me in my dreams."

"Wh—"

I cut her off. "We don't have time for that discussion. I think she was telling me that if I'm not there my father is going to get away today. She said Cyrus would succeed in rescuing my sister."

"And you trust this dream?"

"I do because she was the one Cyrus spoke of."

Merrick nodded. "Very well. I will go with you."

"You're a healer. You should stay here and tend to any wounded who may get hurt."

Since Neala had seen our mission as successful, I assumed that meant we all survived. She didn't explicitly say that, but it stood to reason.

"I was a warrior for centuries before I became a healer, and you need someone to have your back." Her resolve was impressive, but I didn't want to get anyone else involved if it wasn't absolutely necessary. Merrick's fire would be helpful against the vampire, and she hadn't given me a reason not to trust her.

"If that is your decision, I will not try to stop you. Do you know which way they went? Can we vanyshen there?"

"It's too deep into the vampire lands to vanyshen, but I do know the direction they went to access the palace."

I held my hand out toward the tent flap. "Lead the way."

CHAPTER 14
CUT A PATH
ARI

Merrick moved fast through the trees, and I caught whiffs of Rain's minty scent along the way. Every step brought me closer to him, and I needed sight of my mate to ground me in the success of freeing our family...even at the cost of letting Albert escape. Marius had said he himself was free, and I wondered if he had gone with Rain or Cyrus since he wasn't with me.

Marius?

Ari? You're awake. Relief enveloped our bond.

And you're okay?

I'm fine, but my brother needed me. I thought you'd be out longer.

Because of the sprite?

She needed a way to get into your dreams from a distance.

Anger spiked in my spine, and I tried to let it go before it passed to Marius. *You could have warned me.*

I tried, Ari. I was so far away that it was difficult for my communication to reach you.

Don't let anyone else in my head without my permission. Never again.

She doesn't ask for permission, but I'll do what I can. Can we have this conversation when I get back? We've reached the palace.

I'm on my way.

No, stay back. Today is not for you.

The bond cut off like he'd shut me out. It wasn't unprecedented. We'd both kicked the other out at times. So why was I so nervous this time? Because Neala had warned me about the events of the battle. I stumbled over a root.

Merrick caught my arm and steadied me. "You're quite clumsy for a fae, especially compared to your mother."

My chest constricted, and I gasped for air. Grief flooded in on me like a drowning wave. "Why would you say that?"

She stopped. "It's the truth. Your mother was a graceful fighter. It was like watching poetry in physical form on a battlefield."

The tightness in the upper half of my torso loosened. "I'd like to hear about that sometime...when we're not walking into a potential battle of our own."

"It's already in progress." She paused. "Sssh. Listen."

I stood still, straining to hear what Merrick did. Swords clashed with a metallic clank, and I flinched. We were closer than I'd estimated. "This way, right?" I pointed toward where I thought the sounds came from.

She studied the tree line. "Maybe a hundred yards ahead. If we remain unseen until we get to the edge, we could vanyshen from there to any vantage point we see."

Merrick and I trekked with careful steps through the trees. We remained silent, communicating with eye and hand gestures. A chaotic scene came into view. Vampire and fae grappled, but I didn't see any unicorn. Expecting Rain to be with Cyrus, I thought finding a unicorn on the field would be quick. I was wrong. Recalling the maps Whit had laid out in the camp, I scanned in the direction of the door closest to where we believed Gemma was. The entrance wasn't visible from our location. I didn't know where any of them were, and it frustrated me.

A familiar warmth drew my attention. I surveyed the area until I found the deep blue eyes that could drown me in their depths. He sank his sword into the neck of a vampire without even looking. His gaze locked on mine. To him. To my mate. There was no other decision to make.

If my father was on the field, I hadn't seen him. I suspected he was in the palace, hiding like the overconfident ass he was. A few days ago, I'd been ready to become like him to defeat him. The sprite's visit made me think differently. She said I needed to live, and while I wasn't certain why, I had this sense of knowing that my father's path wasn't mine. No matter how the day ended, I wouldn't allow myself to be like him—not even entertain it as I had a few short days back. My family, the ones I'd chosen, would walk away from this field.

"There are so many. How did they get enough of their tonics, the ones that allow them to walk in the sun, for all of them?" Merrick's voice was grim.

I inhaled and let out a steadying breath. There wasn't time to think about how the vampire were here. That was a topic we'd need to analyze later. My mate fought alone, and that wouldn't do. If the sprite was right, and it seemed she was, it would take all of us to free Gemma and Laurel. "I'm going to Rain's side."

"Where you go, I go," she said. "There are too many to try to vanyshen to his location, so we'll have to cut a path to him."

"Fine by me," I said, drawing my daggers. The emblems emblazoned by Nyx glowed like silver moonlight.

Merrick ran side-by-side with me. As we plowed into the first line, we turned back-to-back, balancing off each other as we took down vampire after vampire. I'd lost sight of Rain, but we were close enough that I could sense him as my mate. He was near...so close. I just had to fight through a few more members of Albert's army. I drove one of my blades through the skull of a vampire, and the other dagger into the neck of a different one. They fell at my feet and turned to ash.

My revenge and need to make Albert pay wasn't the most important thing today. The top priority, the only thing that mattered from the events unfolding in front of me, was to get my sister and her mate to safety.

CHAPTER 15
GODDESS BLOOD
ARI

Vampire flesh was tough. Fatigue ached in my biceps and shoulders, but I pushed forward. Merrick moved through the field as if she'd done it many times, like a true warrior. Her practiced fluidity highlighted how different our lives were.

The air was heavy with the nauseating odor of old blood and ash. I held my breath as much as I could, but I needed air to breathe and more to fight.

Where had Rain gone? "Do you see him?"

"No," Merrick said. "But I'd wager he's in the middle of those large bloodsuckers."

I followed her gaze to three massive vampire, but I couldn't see who or how many fae they were in combat with. My mouth dried at the thought he might be there alone.

Merrick pointed out a gap to one side of them, and we made our way there, cutting down the enemy as we went.

I was close enough to see Rain but still had dozens of vampire between us and him.

The three huge vampire loomed over Rain. They towered over everyone. Why wasn't he using his magic? … because I was too close. So were a lot of others, but his stupid promise I hadn't asked for was what was stopping him now. I summoned the earth and wind magic to me. A vampire's head rolled to my feet, and I looked up to see Merrick smiling. I punted it like the Moirai players did in the game we'd watched in what seemed like a lifetime ago.

"I'm going for my mate," I mouthed to her.

"Ari!" Merrick shouted, running toward me.

Pain exploded from above my wrist. A vampire latched her jaws down on me. I jerked my arm, trying to pull free, but her grip was stronger than I expected. She took long, languid draws. As if a switch went off, the vampire's bite sharpened into frenzied pulls. Fighting against the fear and agony, I kicked my foot against her head, but her grip was too tight on my arm. I grasped the back of her hair and yanked so hard that a wad of strands came off in my hand with bits of scalp still attached. A woozy feeling hit me. Panic struck me in the gut and mixed with the light-headedness. I thrust my palm against the vampire's fore-head. Her eyes widened into a vacant stare. A milky film formed over her irises. She released her bite. *Thank the goddess.* Relief cleared the fog in my mind, and I reached for my double swords gifted from Nyx. I drew back to slice her head from her shoulders, but she erupted into flames and cracked apart into tiny, disgusting pieces. What the fuck?

The other vampire staggered away from me.

Merrick made it to my side. "What did you do?"

"Nothing," I said. "Was it you?"

"No." Merrick studied me with an amazed look on her face. "Goddess blood."

Rain. There wasn't time to process what she'd said. "My mate. Where is he?"

"He was handling the three giants last time I saw him," Merrick said.

If I knew anything about my mate, he was either looking for me or searching for a vantage point. Because while he might not strike with me on the battlefield, he would know I'd find him. That is when he would rain down all hell in the form of his storms. I scanned the highest points and saw nothing. *Fuck. Where is he?* I focused on the rooftop of the palace and let out a breath. *There's my mate.*

We lost Albert, Ari. Marius's voice filled my head, but keeping my focus, I sliced through the vampire on my way to Rain. Merrick stuck to my side.

As in, he ran like a coward? My father was a sadistic bastard, but he wasn't spineless. Always one step ahead, he had a plan we didn't know about. My stomach dropped, but I kept moving forward. *He's got a trap set for us somewhere, Marius. Tell everyone to keep their eyes open.* "Merrick, use all your senses. My father is trying to snare us. Prepare for an ambush."

"I'm not afraid of any man if you haven't figured that out." With vampire blood smeared on one side of her and covering her opposite arm, Merrick looked fierce. She winked, and a wicked smile grew on her face.

"This is why we're friends." I returned her smile, and we fought our way across the field into the palace courtyard.

CHAPTER 16

THE PLAN

RAIN

I'd vanyshened in small, calculated movements, taking out as many vampire as I could along the way until I made it to the high point I'd planned. From the palace roof, I could see Ari's location better. She and Merrick were the best fighters on the field. Their motions were spectacular in coordination as they moved in tandem. Wishing it was me fighting at my mate's side, a hint of jealousy stung in my gut. There was no denying that neither of them needed magic to take out a horde of vampire.

My fear was realized as I surveyed the open field and courtyard. The fae were too scattered for me to safely call upon the storms at my fingertips. Even after how I used it last night, it was itching to escape. Being around a vampire spurred my power to near uncontrollable heights and the catalyst that made me lethal on the battlefield.

The magic built into painful arcs inside me. It begged

for release, but the strategy had gone to hell. My people had scattered about on the battlefield like misplaced chess pieces, and worse, Ari and Merrick were right in the middle of the clusterfuck. How had it gone wrong so quickly? Cyrus and his misguided plan to sneak out with the two abnormal vampire, that's how.

He fucked every bit of our plan.

Unicorn or not, I'd make him pay for endangering Ari. No way to shield the fae from my strikes, I found Ari and prepared to vanyshen to her.

A wall of raw power slammed into me from behind. The sheath of my sword dug into my back. I stumbled forward, slipping on the clay tiles. Fingers grasped my upper arms in a painful hold and hauled me back from the edge.

"Not yet, Rainier. I have other plans on how to kill you," the deep voice of pure evil said over my shoulder. I'd used my changeling power to lure him here and wished I could have seen the surprise when he realized it was me and not Ari on the roof.

Albert. On the roof. Tell Marius. I sent my thoughts to Casimir, unsure if she would hear it from this distance given that we weren't bonded in the traditional sense.

At least this part of the plan, the part Marius and I had agreed not to tell Ari, worked as expected.

CHAPTER 17
FOREVER CHANGED
CYRUS

With the path opened by Kyle and Jenna, Marius, Cleave, and I entered the underground torture chamber. The stench of death made the air rotten. My fear intensified at the putrid scent. A vampire lunged at us in front of the entrance to the stairwell. I didn't hesitate, stabbing my horn through him. He fragmented into pieces of ash.

"Surprisingly few of them here," Cleave said between the sounds of flesh meeting horn behind us.

Marius hummed his agreement. "Albert always has a plan. If Gemma and Laurel are not here—"

"They are." I reached down the mate bond and felt for them—weak but still alive. Violent anger engulfed my anguish like I'd never known before, and it was only due to my mates still being in this realm that I did not act on it. Once they were free of this dreadful place, I would have revenge for their suffering.

The pressure as we descended to the lowest level suffocated my magic. Memories of my own recent time in a similar cell increased my anger tenfold. Unicorn were stronger than fae even without magic, so anyone we countered at this level would be outmatched in brute force alone. Tension rolled off Marius and Cleave.

"I feel like I'm being strangled," Cleave said.

"It's the fucking stone. We're close." A door where the hall dead-ended stood open as if beckoning us forward. My connection, the only magic still available this deep, was like an invisible string pulling me to them. "There."

With the door wide open, the only conclusion I came to was that we were expected. I'd suspected we would be. The stone prevented me from sensing anything other than Gemma and Laurel. There were no sounds other than our steps, and even those were muffled despite not having elemental magic to cover them. My brother and friend had to know the same—this was likely a trap. Cleave and Marius walked in step with me to the end.

I peered inside from the edge of the door and glimpsed two unmoving forms hanging on the wall by chains. Overjoyed to see Gemma and Laurel but terrified of the condition they were in, I was hot and cold at the same time.

Darting toward them, I glamoured into my faelike form. I landed on my knees in front of Gemma and Laurel. My head even with Laurel's waist, I wrapped an arm around both my mates. Relief fought for space against the elation building in my body. My heart raced as my chest tightened. While happy to finally be near them, touching them stole my breath.

"You're here," Gemma said. Her weak and broken voice shattered my soul. Laurel didn't open his eyes, but his chest rose and fell against me. His lip was split, and bruises marked so much of his body that it was difficult to tell where they stopped.

I wanted my mates closer, but I had to free them first.

The wretched black stone nullified all of my elemental powers, but there was one gift from Erebus the stone couldn't take. "We're going home."

My honor was already ruined, and I didn't hesitate to give the purest form of my magic for their freedom. A tear ran down my cheek, and I caught the golden liquid on my finger. Placing it on the chains binding them to the wall, the metal dissolved, freeing their hands first, then their throats, and finally their ankles. I'd pay for disclosing that ability, but it was a price I'd pay a thousand times for my two true loves.

Gemma and Laurel bent forward, embracing me and each other.

"Cyrus..." Laurel's knees buckled as he fell against me. Gemma kissed the top of my head. I let myself go in the euphoria of having them near. Love and desperation over-whelmed our bond, and I dove into it like a bottomless pool of water. I'd pay whatever the cost was owed to make sure no one ever hurt them again.

"We need to go," Marius said, placing a hand on my

shoulder and squeezing. "Albert has Rain on the roof. Ari will unleash the power of the goddess on this entire land if we don't get out there."

I hugged my mates one last time and stood. Gemma and Laurel struggled to stay upright in their weakened state. My life forever changed by them, I didn't hesitate to shift to my natural form and drop to the ground. Each point of contact with the stone resulted in excruciating pain as I fought against its drain.

"You can't carry us both." Gemma's voice came out in a rasp that didn't sound wholly like her.

"I assure you, I can. Get on." Having them back made me whole, and anyone who tried to stop our escape would find the sharp end of my horn.

My brother helped them both on my back. I bit the inside of my jaw, tasting the metallic flavor from the blood. When I got to the standing position, Cleave and Marius flanked me.

"I'll go first," Cleave said, leading us out the way we came.

The stairs were clear, and I expected resistance at each corner, worrying if Jenna and Kyle had retreated as instructed.

Sunlight and no vampire greeted us at the exit. Kyle and Jenna had done their part, and the distraction worked.

Marius turned toward the sounds of the battle. "Cleave, escort them back to the camp. I have other business to attend to."

"Thank you," I said to my brother.

"No thanks needed. This is what family does."

I nodded and using my magic to hold my mates in place, I ran in the direction where I'd instructed Kyle and Jenna to wait.

CHAPTER 18

ASH

ARI

A unicorn form appeared in my periphery. A black coat with white mane and tail, and the white around his ankles that looked like socks—I'd know my bonded anywhere. None of the others were with him.

I paused, afraid to ask the question—afraid the answer wouldn't be what I wanted to hear. *Did you get Gemma and Laurel out?*

We did. He stabbed vampire after vampire with his horn. Ash rained down around him like gray snow.

Gemma and Laurel would be reunited with their daughter. Phina would have her parents. *Thank you, Nyx.* The day wasn't done though. Vampires outnumbered us, and Albert wasn't going down without a fight.

Merrick and I have this. You don't need to plow your way here.

Unicorn don't answer to fae.

I bit back my tears and smiled. *Thank you.*

Have you seen your fa...Albert?

No, but I have this feeling he's going to show up. Rain made it to the rooftop, so if we clear the battlefield, he can...

Thoughts died on our bond. I froze in place.

"What are you doing, Ari?" Merrick asked from my side.

I heard metal clank against metal and the whooshing sound as she used her fire magic. I couldn't look away from the roof of the palace. Rain. Albert and Rain, held in place by two vampire that made the three giants from earlier look minuscule. How?

Marius...

I see him. You can't use your magic on Albert if that's what you're thinking. You have the power of the goddess running through you and little training on how to control that intensity with precision.

It hadn't even crossed my mind. Nothing had. I was paralyzed in terror for my mate.

"Ari?" Marius called my name.

I blinked and became unstuck. My training kicked into place. "I'm not letting him leave here with Rain, Marius."

"Rainier would want you to be safe."

"But my mate knows I'm not built that way," I countered, knowing Rain would respect my decision, but he'd ask me to save myself too. He wouldn't consider what I was about to do the safe choice.

"Rain wouldn't leave you either," Merrick said, frying a vampire off to the left like he was dry birchwood.

"Do you want to hear my plan, or are you going to do whatever you want?" Marius asked.

"Both." I drove a dagger into the skull of a vampire coming up on my side.

Marius came to my side. "Do you think you can channel your magic to bring the palace down?"

I broke eye contact with Rain to look at Marius. "What?"

"This palace is his seat of power as it was before the war. He won't want it to fall. If you distract him by trying to save it, that gives Rain time to get free and unleash his own force."

"And how do either of us do that without killing everyone in the vicinity, including ourselves?" I asked.

"Rain has excellent control over his ever since the tornado he accidentally unleashed on the city."

I glanced at Merrick. That was definitely a conversation for when we got out of this disaster of a rescue attempt. *At least Gemma and Laurel are safe.*

She shrugged. "It was a long time ago."

I didn't have a better idea, and there wasn't time to think. Marius' suggestion had to be it. I turned my face up to where Rain was perched with Albert and the two vampire. "Okay, let's do it. How is Rain going to know?"

"He'll get it once you start."

I inhaled and cleared my thoughts, focusing on how to bring down this palace with the power Nyx had bestowed on me.

Whatever you are thinking, my love. Don't do it. Get your-

self out of here. Rain's voice drifted in like the gentlest breeze on a starry night.

Just get ready to unleash your wrath and vanyshen away as fast as you can. I love you.

You, my incredible goddess, are my heart. When my lightning strikes, know that it's the beat of my heart for you.

Say that again later. I closed my eyes and grounded into my power—Nyx's power. It occurred to me that I had one of the most formidable elements at my command and didn't have to use the goddess's glorious gift every time. I opened my eyes and held my arms out. "Earth."

The ground beneath us trembled. Screams came from all around me. Unsure if they were fae or vampire, I was concerned I'd caused harm to our people. Marius and Merrick stood strong and steady beside me. I took that as a sign that the fae on the field were fine. My gaze lifted to Rain, and his mouth curved in the most wicked grin.

"Do you have me?" I asked Marius and Merrick.

"Yes, always," Marius said.

"Nowhere else to be," Merrick said, turning away to head off any incoming vampire.

I closed my eyes again and envisioned pulling pieces of the palace down, starting with the gallery where my fath-- Albert had put me on display and had me lashed for not agreeing with him. My power retreated at the memory, but I doubled down with determination. Battle noises rang out around me, and I tuned them out. My hearing narrowed until I heard the sound of destruction, probably walls falling, but I didn't look for fear of breaking my concentration.

"Ari," Marius shouted my name.

A body smashed against me, and I fell. Was it a vampire? The body landed on top of me. When I opened my eyes, it was Marius and Merrick both covering me. I pushed, and they rolled off me.

"Did we do it? Is Rain free?" I sat up.

Albert towered over us. *This is my chance. The sprite was wrong.* Wind swirled. Dust and vampire ash coated me—in my eyes, my mouth, everywhere. I swiped at my eyes to clear them. A funnel dropped down on him, picking him and slinging him so far he looked tiny from the distance. I could just make him out as he stood for a moment and disappeared completely. He must have vanyshened away.

I shook my hair, freeing more of the soot. The fucking sprite had been right after all.

As I maneuvered to stand, a hand thrust in my face. I followed the line of the familiar arm up to the handsome face with the perfect scar along his jaw. Grateful to see him this close, my heart expanded to radiate all the love I had for him. His hand was warm as I slipped mine into his.

"Hello, love," he said, pulling me to my feet. He took my hand and placed it on his chest. "You truly are a goddess, and my heart beats at your command."

Merrick and Marius got to their feet. I didn't see any obvious injuries.

"Are you both okay?" I asked.

"Other than being covered in vampire remains, I'm fine," Merrick said.

Marius shook his body, and dust flew everywhere, including on Merrick.

Disgust passed over her features, and she tried to brush it off. "I know you two like your reunions, but we should get out of here. I already sent word down the ranks for the others to head back to the camp."

I quickly took in the damage I'd done to the palace. It wasn't as vast as I'd imagined, but there was an entire wing destroyed. I assumed that was the one where my punishment was administered. No one would be the featured show in the gallery again, and I took some satisfaction in knowing that. I hoped Griselda could see from the other realm.

"Ari," Rain's voice was soft. "Save it for another day. We accomplished what we needed to."

I let out a long sigh and extended my hand to Marius. "Up for a ride?"

Marius huffed but glamoured to his faelike form and took my hand.

"I'm assuming you can vanyshen?" I asked Merrick, recalling the power of her arrival a few days ago.

She flicked her ash-covered hair over her shoulder. "Of course."

The vampire around us looked disoriented, which made it the perfect time for our exit.

"Back to camp," I said, holding onto Rain and Marius.

I made an easy landing in the middle of the camp. *Yes!*

Thank Nyx, I didn't land us in one of those sticker bushes or the fire pit. "I want to see my sister first."

Merrick motioned for me to follow her to the tent set up for the healers. The anticipation of seeing my sister outweighed the fear I had for what Albert had done to her. I could hear Marius and Rain's footsteps close behind me. Their siblings were out of danger's path too. For once, we were all safe. Merrick flipped the flap of the tent.

Cyrus sat in his fae form between the cots Gemma and Laurel were on. The bruises on each were too many to count, and in various stages of healing. My stomach roiled. Deep crimson coated Gemma's ear, and her beautiful red hair was matted with dried blood. My sister and her mate had been tortured, and anger swelled in me. My hands glowed, and I boxed up the anger in my mind to unpack when I saw Albert next. A healer attended to their injuries, but what caught my eye was Cyrus held Gemma and Laurel's hands. It was the most humble I'd ever seen a unicorn, and tears stung my eyes.

I witnessed love in a true and pure form—the kind written about for the ages, like Nyx and Erebus. Their love was beautiful and magical and could only be the kind they carried from this realm to the next. The moment was real and intimate, and I hated to interrupt it.

My sister's tear-stained face met my gaze as I approached. "Thank you," she croaked out in a voice that sounded like sandpaper on stone.

I leaned against the bed, taking her free hand. So many bruises marred her beautiful face, neck, and hands, and I imagined other parts of her I couldn't see. Yet, she'd survived. Beaten but not broken, because it took something larger than our father to break the strength my sister possessed. "I'm not the one to thank. He is sitting between you and your mate."

Cyrus raised his head and gazed at Gemma with enough love for ten thousand lifetimes.

"He is my mate. They are both my mates." Gemma's tears flowed as she turned her gaze to Cyrus. "And we will never be separated again."

The adoration in her words held a promise, and their love was beautiful. I didn't know what happened to make Cyrus leave before, but it was clear the three of them belonged together. *Nyx, please give them your blessing.*

Cyrus kissed the back of Gemma's hand. Then, he pulled Laurel's to his mouth and pressed a soft kiss on it too. Laurel hadn't moved, but there was my mate standing by his brother's side. I could heal our siblings thanks to my goddess-given power. It was my fault they were taken, so their healing should rest in my hands too.

Merrick waited by the opening, and I turned to her. "Can you clear the tent?"

She nodded and started ushering the others out.

"Merrick, you can stay. I'd like your help." Gemma's hand tensed in mine, and I looked down at her. "I know you have a reason to hate her, but she has helped me. Can you trust me this one time?"

"I always trust you, Ari." She squeezed my hand. "You

are my sister, but I would choose you even if we weren't blood."

"Don't make me cry or I might grow you an extra arm when I heal you." I tucked her hand to her side.

Marius and Cyrus chuckled.

"You can heal others now?" Gemma's eyes widened, and she winced. Both her eyes were purplish black.

"It's kind of a new thing, but it seems to work well." I glanced at Rain.

He'd pulled a chair over next to his brother and whispered in his ear. Laurel didn't respond. He looked thin and pale where he wasn't bruised and swollen.

"I'll take care of Gemma and then I'll help your brother. Okay?"

Rain gave me a tiny smile and nodded his head.

"Cyrus, can you let Merrick through over there?" I asked.

His eyes narrowed on her.

"I can just..." She vanyshened to the spot in front of Cyrus and between the two cots.

She held her hands out over Gemma, and I placed mine on top of hers. The power flowed in a misty glow, and my sister's bruises began to disappear. It took longer as I tried to control the power. Healing could be painful, and Gemma had enough torment from Albert. Pain he would receive back in droves. My sister flinched, and I eased back on the magic.

When I sensed no more places to heal, I let the power retreat. My sister sat up, and outside of the dirt and matted hair, her body appeared restored. All the bruises were gone at least. My firsthand experience showed me the inside...the mental part would take much longer. Guilt penetrated deep into my heart. Gemma had been living a happy life until our father was released, and that was because of me.

"How do you feel?" I asked, pushing past my own remorse.

"As if I'd never been..." She swallowed hard, and I understood the aftermath. I'd lived it at the same man's behest. "Tortured."

"He's a cruel, power-hungry bastard, Gemma, and he will receive the punishment he deserves." I moved to go see to Laurel.

Gemma grabbed my hand. "Ari, don't lose yourself to our father. You don't have to be like him to defeat him."

My sister knew me so well, but the sprite had just said I needed to live. She didn't say how or who the version today would make me. After watching Albert disappear on the battlefield, I realized I had to become stronger and embrace all the power to defeat him. No one remained unchanged from that kind of consumption. It would remake me, and I feared who I would become. I only gave my sister one nod and then healed her mate.

CHAPTER 19
FINALLY
RAIN

My brother had woken with strength I hadn't expected from him. As an empath, his healing was often slower than others. I didn't pretend to understand it, but I gave credit for his incredible recovery speed to Ari. She looked radiant, even with ash stuck in the dried blood spatter coating her. I held my hand out. It was an act that had become so natural between us, and I planned to never take it for granted. "Want to take a walk and give them some privacy?"

Ari smiled and nodded, slipping her hand into mine. "We'll be back in a little bit."

Marius and Merrick waited outside the tent. While they were covered in similar muck from the fight, they both looked unharmed. I had no injuries, but my muscles, sore from the battle, protested with every movement. Even so, I looked forward to time alone with Ari. Time I wouldn't get. Since Merrick and Marius walked with us until we were out of earshot, we were about to get some news from Ari's bonded.

"Albert was seen outside the city. We should return as soon as possible," Marius said.

Ari clutched her hand to her throat. "Do you think he's going to retaliate for what I did to his palace today?"

I was less shocked than Ari. I understood her concern, but we'd immensely weakened Albert's forces today.

"No, reports say he doesn't have enough vampire with him...at least for now," Marius said.

I expected that to be the case. "He's lurking, looking for ways to rebuild his army."

Merrick clasped her hands in front of her. "There are other healers here now. I can go back and monitor things."

"Thank you. Will you check on my brother and my niece?" Ari took Merrick's hand in hers. "They are with a unicorn named Leana. Tell her I sent you."

"Of course," Merrick said, smiling at her. Ari brought out a different person in Merrick, but then again, my mate was the best of us.

Ari's gaze turned to Marius. "Will you let Casimir know to grant Merrick access to the children? And to not give her a hard time?"

I snorted. "She won't like being told what to do."

Marius glared at me. "Your existence isn't necessary, fae."

"Harsh." I raised my hands in surrender. "You know it's true."

Ari positioned herself between me and her bonded. "Maybe you should go with Merrick. Rain and I can stay until Gemma, Laurel, and Cyrus are ready to return."

"It's a bad idea to leave you here," Marius said.

Ari's gaze had that slight haze they took on when she spoke through their bond.

Marius's eyes narrowed at her. "Fine. I'll see you there shortly." Marius glamoured to his faelike form. "Merrick?"

She held a hand out to him. A breeze kicked up around us, and they were gone.

Finally. All I need is her. I pulled Ari into my arms. The scent of moonflowers floated in the air around us. "Alone at last."

She rested her head against my chest. "I'm ready for a real bath."

I laughed, letting it vibrate through us. "What I need doesn't involve a bath." I considered my words. "But it could."

"Two things can be true at the same time." She leaned back and smiled at me. "I don't want to ever sleep in a tent again."

I kissed her forehead. "I didn't mind it, but I'm happy just to be in your presence."

"Just my presence?" She raised an eyebrow in challenge.

My cock responded in kind. I pressed my growing hardness against her. She gasped in that way I loved, and I covered her face in gentle kisses until I reached her mouth. She parted her lips, and I obliged, claiming her. I ran my fingers over her collarbone through her tunic and trailed my hand down until I was cupping her breast.

"I want to wait until we get home. I don't want to fuck anywhere near the vampire lands. Seeing Gemma brought it all back. I thought I'd dealt with it." Her words were a whisper and like the icy waters of a mountain stream in winter for me.

How could I have been so insensitive? She'd been tortured in the vampire lands and not far from where we stood. I wanted to erase those memories, but they were hers to deal with in her way and time.

I placed a soft kiss on the tip of her nose. "Of course."

CHAPTER 20
REUNIONS
ARI

As the camp was packed up the next morning, Rain and I made sure the forest was left the way we found it with no sign of our stay visible. I used the very first gift my mother taught me in our garden to restore the vegetation that had been trampled. My first lesson resulted in me turning an entire bed of flowers brown. Mother had stepped in to save them. I'd picked up on the magic with ease in a few short weeks. Now, it just took a brush of my fingers or a flick of my wrist, and the plants responded like they'd been waiting for me to ask them to bloom.

After we made certain all of the fae vanyshened back to the city and to their appropriate spaces, the sun had long since set. Rain and I traveled with our family—Gemma, Laurel, Cyrus, and Marius—to the unicorn area of the city. As we walked into the space on the far side of town, I hid my surprise at the building shapes. They looked like horse barns. I chanced a glance at Marius, but he looked unfazed. He'd clearly seen them before today, but that shouldn't surprise me since he'd had people here all along.

Cyrus led us to the very last one that stood a good distance from the others. At first blush, the homes looked like barns, but up close, fine finishes adorned the outside. The structures were as modern as the rest of the buildings but made to not look so. The oak was reinforced with a thick metal, and the door was heavy wood with a metal-framed transom window above it. The windows around the building were some kind of glass that prevented curious onlookers from peeking inside. All I could see was my reflection.

Casimir waited outside. A flicker of warmth came down my bond with Marius and shut off as I turned my head in his direction. His gaze was fixed on Casimir and her shiny white coat.

Casimir bowed in the unicorn way. "Marius."

"Rise, Casi," he said.

Casi? I questioned him down the bond, but he had me blocked from his thoughts and feelings. For good reason, it seemed.

"I believe I owe you details of events," she said.

He nodded. "Yes, shall we go somewhere we can discuss unicorn business in private?"

Please go far away where someone doesn't accidentally walk up on you. I gagged.

Stop. Marius sent the single word down our bond before he shut me out again.

"As you wish. I have a private area that should suffice." Casimir swung her head in a direction away from the house.

"Lead the way," he said.

I watched them walk away in utter disbelief. Not only did he know her, but she wasn't just one of his random fucks like the day I found him with Amelia...*Goddesses and gods, that image is going to be stuck in my head forever.*

Cyrus opened the door, and Leana greeted him. The vibrant colors of the rainbow flowing around her disappeared as she glamoured into her faelike form. Her beautiful mane transformed into white-blonde hair with streaks of the same colors. When she moved aside, Drew and Phina ran out the entrance. Gemma knelt down for Phina, and I expected Drew to go to her as well. Instead, he barreled toward me. I bent and lifted him in my arms.

"Ari." He hugged my neck. "I missed you."

"I missed you too. You've grown so much." Joy and relief filled my heart. I ruffled his hair.

"I'm a big boy, and I do big boy magic now."

Leana hovered close. Surprise flickered in her eyes at his declaration, and I suspected that wasn't the only one that had been made. The glamour around her faelike form shimmered as if it was hard for her to hold the form. I assumed she was tired from taking care of the children.

"You'll have to show me," I said to Drew and held an arm out for Leana. She leaned in to hug me, and her scent was off. I was certain she'd declared Drew as her charge. "Thank you for taking care of him and keeping him safe. Do we have something else to celebrate?"

Shock skated across her face. "A couple of things, but let's start with the fact that I declared my oath for Drew. He will have unicorn protection for the rest of his life."

"You do him a great honor," I said, having hoped for her declaration to him since she started working with him after Gemma left our old home.

"The honor is mine."

"I think I need to do a reintroduction between my siblings." I sat Drew on the ground and took his hand. He kicked an acorn, and it ricocheted off the building, eliciting the cutest laugh from him.

Leana walked with me, and I wondered if she'd be the shadow to Drew like Marius had been to me when I was a child. Phina leaned toward Laurel, and he took her from Gemma. He and Cyrus entertained Phina, but both males kept a watchful eye on Gemma.

"Drew, this is our sister, Gemma. You probably don't remember her, but she gave us both so much love before she had to leave." My brother had barely been a toddler when Gemma left, and I didn't expect him to remember much, if any, of his time with her.

Drew's eyes lit up. "I remember." It was like a memory just came to him. He couldn't remember that time, could he?

She held out her arms. "Can I have a hug?"

He embraced her with one arm, but his other was

firmly holding on to me. It was a start. We'd be a whole family.

Just one more thing to take care of...Albert.

I sat down on the ground with the others. Phina came over to hug me.

"I'm so glad you came back," she said.

"Me too. I still owe you that unicorn show."

She giggled, sitting beside me with a little doll that looked almost identical to her. "There's a new episode tomorrow."

"Then we shall watch it together."

Phina smiled. "Drew hasn't watched it either. He can join us."

Drew yawned. It was late and had been a long day for all of us.

"Are you sleepy?" I ruffled his hair, noting it was a little darker.

He patted his hair down. "Yes, it's past my bedtime, but Leana let me stay up. She knew you were coming home tonight. I did too."

CHAPTER 21

THE BITE

ARI

After working out the sleeping arrangements for the kids, Rain and I headed back to our room. Drew would stay with Phina in Gemma and Laurel's suites. Cyrus said he'd see them in the morning. He had unicorn business to attend to and get the two vampire, Jenna and Kyle, settled. I got the impression he wanted to talk to Leana alone. Although he'd mentioned in the camp that she knew about his relationship with Gemma and Laurel, I was sure that conversation would be rough. Gemma had looked disappointed but hugged him goodnight with the promise of tomorrow, as did Laurel. Phina told him everything was going to be fine. I smiled at how thoughtful she was.

"What are you thinking about?" Rain said, opening the door to our suite of apartments.

It was like we never left, and as I stepped inside, it felt safe. Everyone important to me was mostly under the same roof, and that made it home. I wanted to find Val, because she was somewhere in the kingdom. My thoughts drifted back to my sister and her mates...two of them, and Leana. How did they begin to untangle and live their lives?

Rain unfastened his sword and sheath, laying the weapon on the table.

I undid my blades and passed them to him. "What a mess Gemma, Cyrus, Laurel, and I, guess Leana too, have to sort through."

"Life is complicated." Rain pulled me against his chest and flicked his wrist to shut the door. "That never changes, no matter how many years we live."

"I'm just glad we are all safe and whole." I wrapped my arms around his waist.

He brushed the hair from my face and tucked it behind my ears. "I love you with all that I am. Every part of me is yours for this lifetime and the next. The realms cannot contain the love I give to you."

My chest heated, and I melted. "I don't know what brought that on, but I love you with everything I have to give."

He brushed his lips across mine in featherlight touches. "Shower or bath?"

I smiled. "I believe you owe me a bath."

"So I do." He scooped me up and carried me through the room to the bathing chamber. The maids had cleaned since the day Albert attacked the city. The creams and perfumes were lined up neatly on little trays along the marble counter. The pattern resembled the swirling clouds when Rain evoked storms. Candles with magic for flames lit up around the bath. Setting me on the cool stone, Rain shifted to reach the bath. "We're going to make some filthy water."

His hair still had flecks of ash in it, and some fell into the tub when he turned the faucet on. I twisted to look in the mirror. My hair was the victim of a similar fate. While we'd changed clothes and sponged off any blood at camp, the vampire ash was difficult to get out. I wasn't sure which was more unbelievable—that the kids weren't frightened of us or that we thought we looked better than we did.

"Do you think one of the unicorn glamoured our appearances while around the kids?"

"I don't know," he said, pulling his tunic over his head. The soot had worked its way into his tunic, as evidenced by the ash mixed with sweat and smeared across his chest and abs.

I pulled my shirt out and looked down. I had the same issue. "Would it be awful if we did a quick rinse in the shower? I'd like to be able to soak in the tub with you, but vampire remnants are in places they should never be."

He chuckled, and the sound rumbled deep in his chest. "I can't make any promises once you're naked."

That wicked look I loved so much gleamed in his eyes. My core heated with need and want. "I don't care if it's in the shower or the tub or on this fucking counter, but I want you."

Rain reached in the shower and flicked the water on. "I'm claiming all three."

I worked out of my clothes and piled them with his on the floor. "We should burn those. I don't want them on my body again."

He stuck his hand under the shower water and tested it. "We can throw them in the fireplace after you are thoroughly satisfied."

"Then you'd better get started." I passed him and stepped into the shower.

Rain turned off the bathtub and stood at the open glass door.

Gray ran down my body into the drain. "Aren't you getting in?"

"Only you could make crusty vampire ash look sexy as fuck." He climbed into the spray and walked me back to the wall. Water flowed over both of us, washing away the past few days.

"What are you going to do about it?"

"Make you scream my name, because that's what you owe me." He traced the back of his hand down over my chest, my nipple, and down to my belly.

My heart fluttered, and I arched my back and reached for his cock.

He thrust his hips back. His eyes glazed with desire. "Not yet. You first."

Goddess, I loved the way he looked at me. Rain circled his fingers over my bundle of nerves. Heat lit like a fire in my core.

I leaned into his touch, and he rewarded me by inserting one finger in me, and I trembled. He added a second and used his thumb to maintain contact on my clit. My breath came in pants. I rode his hand seeking more friction as my need intensified.

"Say my name, Ari," Rain whispered against my ear. He nipped at the skin. "I need to hear my name from your mouth." The desperation in his voice brought me to the edge.

A moan slipped through my lips. I pressed one hand against the wall and gripped his arm with the other. Rain flicked his thumb over my clit in time with the increasing pace of his fingers, and it sent me over the line into ecstasy. I tumbled into starlight, and my vision erupted in the brightest moonlight.

"Rain," I called his name like a curse. "Gods. Rain."

He kept thrusting, and the aftershocks rocked my body. I trembled with pleasure. When he withdrew his fingers, I opened my eyes, feeling so satisfied. Rain lowered his head until his mouth met mine.

"That was a good start, but we're going to have to practice how you scream. I want the entire kingdom to hear you." He kissed my neck. My desire notched up again.

"Counter or bathtub next?" I grabbed his cock in my hand and stroked back and forth.

His head fell back, and he moaned, a low, feral sound. "I don't care as long as I'm inside you."

My insides were fire and starlight, and he did that to me. I needed him as close to me as possible.

"I'm going to come in your palm if you don't stop," he said, his voice lower than usual. His cock twitched in my hand.

Watching him unravel from my touch was one of my favorite views. Rain lifted my arm. His lips close to my skin, he stopped. "Ari, what happened here?"

I glanced at my arm. "A vampire bit me during the battle." I'd forgotten about it. "The vampire exploded, and Merrick said something about goddess blood."

Rain held my wrist and skimmed his other hand over it. "This doesn't look like it's healing."

"I used a lot of energy on other people today and brought part of a palace down. I'm sure that's why." The bite did look ugly, but it didn't hurt...much. "I don't want to repeat that."

Rain studied it. "I think a healer needs to look at the wound."

I pulled my arm free, annoyed a small injury was keeping him from taking me to the counter and fucking me. "You mean a doctor."

"No, I mean a healer," he said, his tone serious. "We need to go see my brother. Now."

INFECTION

ARI

"Call Merrick instead. We shouldn't disturb Gemma and Laurel tonight." I tightened the belt of the fluffy robe I'd grabbed from behind the door. Having someone else see me in the robe, or anything else for that matter, wasn't how I'd envisioned the night.

Rain blew out a breath and dialed Merrick. He put the phone on the speaker setting where we could both hear.

Merrick picked up on the first ring. "What?"

"I need you in my room." Rain sounded flustered.

I widened my eyes at him.

"Sorry. I mean Ari needs you. There's something wrong with her arm."

Merrick made a disgusted noise. "What did you do to her? Never mind. I'm on my way."

She hung up the phone so fast I couldn't even tell her we needed time to get dressed.

"Better throw some clothes on. She'll be here in a few minutes."

"FUCKING VAMPIRE. It looks infected to me," Merrick said, her voice concerned. "Infections are rare for fae."

I'd never had an infection, but I had seen a couple. The bite didn't look like those—their wounds were...red. Since leaving the shower, the bite had become inflamed.

Rain's face looked like he'd been struck with a jolt of panic. "What do we do for it?"

"I'm not the right healer for this. You need someone with more than a few years' experience to handle an injury this serious." She picked up her phone.

How can it be that serious? Infections might be rare, but no one I knew had died from one. "Who are you calling at this time of night?"

Merrick shrugged. "The healer I trained under."

"Hang up the phone. I'll call my brother." Rain punched the keypad on his phone and walked into the other room.

"I should go," Merrick said.

"No, I want you to stay." She was my only friend here, and she was a badass by my side on the battlefield. "Please."

Merrick dropped down onto the couch. "They won't be happy I'm here."

I gave a smile for encouragement. "They will be fine."

"Ari, you heard what I did. They might not want me dead, but they don't want me anywhere near them."

"We're going to try to fix that. Maybe not tonight but soon."

Rain handed me a pair of boots. "Laurel said to meet him in the medical room."

Glad I'd changed from the robe into real clothes before Merrick arrived, I slipped the shoes on and laced them. Maybe this bite was worse than I'd thought. Did fae actually die from infections? Were they going to have to cut it out of my arm and then heal me? I do remember that happening to a guard when I was a kid. It took multiple healing sessions and left a rough scar. A scar didn't scare me, but remembering his screams the day I'd been near one of the sessions frightened the hell out of me.

"I'll walk you there and then head home," Merrick said, standing. "Laurel is much better equipped to handle your arm than me.

Two guards were stationed at the end of the hall. It was an order Rain issued before we left the camp to have them everywhere that allowed access to our quarters or Gemma and Laurel's. Soldiers in the palace, even personal guards, weren't unusual. The sheer number of them to cover the different areas we frequented was.

Rain led us around the final turn to the medical room. The doors opened, and my sister was seated on one of the beds. Laurel stood in front of her. Merrick stopped when she saw them.

"I'll say goodnight to you here," she said. "I'll check on you later." She walked away quickly.

Not wanting to make the situation any more awkward for Merrick, I didn't try to stop her.

"You're keeping bad company with her, Ari," Gemma said.

The times I'd disagreed with my sister, like really, wholeheartedly disagreed with her, could be counted on one hand, but I didn't agree with her about Merrick. "She's had my back since right after the attack on the city, and she proved herself trustworthy on the battlefield."

"You don't know who she really is. She hasn't shown you her real personality."

"Are you saying my judgment is bad? Because it kind of sounds like you are." I wanted to give her grace for what she'd been through at our father's hands, but I wasn't going to let her tell me how to think either.

She flicked her gaze away, then back to me.

Rain stepped into my path. "Let Laurel look at your arm. We need to make sure that doesn't spread."

I met his gaze and saw his raw fear. He was afraid for me, and I wondered if he had more experience with an infection like the one on my arm.

"Have a seat." Laurel's voice was gentle as he gestured to the bed opposite my sister.

I hopped up on the weird mattress and held out my arm.

Laurel pushed the sleeve up. "You definitely have an infection. Merrick was right to tell you to call me." He shot an annoyed glance at Rain. "I would have expected to be the first call."

I didn't want there to be animosity between them over me. "That was my idea. You and Gemma just got home, and I didn't want to disturb you."

"How would it get infected so quickly?" Rain asked, stroking my back.

"I'm assuming it's been a while since this happened?" Laurel asked.

Gemma's face had softened, but she remained silent. I glanced at Rain, and he gave me a nod in agreement to tell them.

"Merrick and I were in the middle of taking down every vampire we could as the distraction." *But we weren't the real distraction, were we, Rain?* I didn't know how much made it down our mated connection, but he mashed his lips together. "My focus was split, and the bitch latched onto my arm. She went into some kind of weird frenzy. When she finally pulled back, her eyes went vacant, and she exploded. End of story."

"Except it's not," Rain said. "Merrick made a comment about goddess blood. Does that mean anything to you, Brother?"

"Not really. We know Ari was changed from her visit with Nyx, but we don't know in what ways."

I had a pretty good idea how. "You mean other than the fact that I can heal people now." I studied the bite mark. "But apparently not myself."

"That's not unusual. A healer is typically immune to

their own magic." Laurel crossed the room and opened a drawer. He dropped some tools on a tray. "I'd like to take some blood and a scraping of it before we try any treatment."

"Sure." I held my arm out.

Gemma rose from her bed and came to sit by me, taking my free hand in hers. "We're going to figure this out."

"For now, no one speaks about goddess blood outside of our group," Rain said, retrieving his phone from his pocket.

Everyone already stared at me. They didn't need another reason.

Gemma huffed. "You'd better tell your buddy, Merrick, the same."

"Already on it," Rain said, walking to the front of the room and out of earshot.

I wanted peace for us, and I wanted everyone I cared about to get along so we could all be in the same room without having to fight battles from within. Marius had taught me enough about strategy to know that a kingdom divided, especially among the leaders, was a sure way to lead to our downfall. We were finally all safe. Well, we were as safe as we could be until we caught Albert. He'd been the danger I didn't know to fear growing up, and now he was the monster trying to destroy the most beautiful parts of our world.

"You'll feel a slight pinch and a bit of sting." Laurel held up a syringe.

I didn't notice the needle, but Albert's betrayal stung, so Laurel had been right about that sensation.

Gemma squeezed my hand. "Look, Ari, I don't wish Merrick dead or anything tragic, but I don't want to be around her either."

Was she worried about Merrick replacing her? There was no way in all the realms that would ever happen. Gemma was my sister and the person who held me during my deepest grief when Mother died. She was the strongest person I knew, and I'd never put anyone in her place.

"You are always going to be a priority to me, but she's the only friend I've made here. Can you give some grace?" Even as I asked, I wasn't sure I would be able to do so in the same situation. If my sister said she couldn't, I would accept her answer.

Gemma's gaze went to the floor, and she let out a long sigh. When she looked up, she squeezed my arm. "I can, but don't expect me to become her friend. That is never happening, and I would caution you to watch your back with her."

"All I ask is that you just don't go after her."

She cocked her head to the side. "Maybe you should make that request to her."

Laurel held up a tool that looked a lot like a scalpel. Every muscle in my body tightened, and I pushed back.

Rain was at my side in seconds. "Can't you see she's terrified?"

"I haven't done anything yet," Laurel said, holding up

a medicinal-smelling container. "I need to clean the area before I do the scraping."

"What are you going to do with that?" I pointed to the instrument that looked like it could slice open the wound, and not just a sample off the top.

Laurel looked at it and back at me. "I'm going to take a small section of the infected area. It will hurt more than drawing blood, but it shouldn't be too bad."

I inhaled and held it in, gritting my teeth. "Do it now."

He held a towel under my arm and poured the liquid over it. The medicinal odor intensified. I held my breath. The cool metal hit the inflamed skin, and it sent spikes of pain radiating up my arm. I ground my teeth together to keep from crying out.

Rain, on the opposite side of the bed as Gemma, took my other hand in his and placed a kiss on the back of it. "Almost done."

I couldn't look, but it felt like Laurel dug around in my arm. "Done."

Rain ran a finger along my cheek, and it was damp. A tear had leaked out before I could stop it.

"I'll flush the wound and dress it. Then, you can go rest."

"Thank the goddesses and gods. I don't want to do that again." I did want to get out of here and pick up where Rain and I left off earlier.

Laurel patted my foot. "I don't blame you." He shook a small, slightly opaque container.

"I've had wound irrigation done before, and you might prefer the scraping over it." Gemma's face paled.

Rain squeezed my hand. "I have to agree with Gemma on this one."

"There is some numbing spray I can apply, but we don't know what we're dealing with, so I can't predict the reaction." Laurel handed a small metal pan to Gemma. "Hold this under her arm."

"Just get the flush-out over with." Goddesses and gods, what had I done to deserve this torture? I flashed to the real torture I'd faced at my father's hands. He'd ordered me tied to a post and whipped in front of a crowd. His demented ass would know what that was like one day. I'd rip his head from his shoulders.

"Done." Laurel patted my leg. "You did better than Gemma and Rain."

I hadn't even realized he'd started. A quick glance at my arm revealed a bandaged wound. It was like my father continued to steal moments from me, but he could have that one. "When will we have answers?"

"It will take a few hours for the tests to run, so you should go get some rest. I'll call you when they are ready."

Patience. I needed it in droves. *Nyx, if you can offer any help in that department, I'd take it.* I didn't expect an answer and none came. I inclined my head toward my sister's mate. "Thank you, Laurel."

Rain helped me off the bed and tucked me against his side. "We're going to see Whit at first light. Do you think you'll have the answers before we leave?"

Laurel tilted his head. "Maybe. I'll see if I can get them wrapped up by then. I'd like to hear what Whit says."

"Me too," Gemma said.

"Whit? The historian?" I asked. Rain hadn't mentioned the visit to me.

Gemma smiled so brightly that her face lit up. "You met him?"

"Briefly. He was one of the advisors when we…came for you."

Panic flashed across Gemma's face, but it disappeared fast. "You're going to love him after you spend more time with him. He's the kindest person, and he knew Mother, so he has stories about her from long before we were born."

I wanted to hear what Mother's life was like here, and I wanted to learn about how she led the forces.

"Should I be jealous?" Laurel kissed Gemma's cheek.

She looked him up and down. "Probably.

Rain leaned next to my ear. "Should I be jealous too?"

"He is what some would call a silver fox." I studied Gemma and turned to Laurel. "You know she's always had a thing for older fae."

"Ari," Gemma said, her voice going up an octave.

I laughed it off, but my sister had once dated an elder fae she nicknamed "silver fox." My comment had hit the mark. She couldn't chastise me without owning up to it. I relished the rare moment of having something to hold over her.

"It's a good thing I'm older then," Laurel said, smiling. He turned his head toward me. "You should let your body do some healing. Try to sleep for a few hours if you can."

"We'll meet you in the courtyard at first light," Rain said, placing his hand on the small of my back.

CHAPTER 23
SILVER FOX
RAIN

My goddess was sick, and Laurel's initial thoughts, or lack thereof, were worrisome. I scooped Ari up and carried her through the doorway and headed toward the bedroom.

"I can walk, Rain." She giggled and kicked her feet. "And I'm not sleepy."

"Your body needs rest," I said, setting her on the bed. "Doctor's orders."

She fisted my shirt with both hands and tugged me toward her. "That word is so weird."

I pressed a gentle kiss to her forehead. "What word?"

"Doctor." She ghosted her lips over mine. "Healer fits much better. It's their job to heal people."

"True." I planted my hands on either side of her for balance. "I have no argument against that."

"I'm shocked, Rainier." Her eyebrow quirked up in a challenge. "You argue everything."

My cock twitched. I rested my forehead against hers. Laurel said she needed to let her body fight the infection since that was all we could do at the moment. I pulled back.

Ari, still holding onto my shirt, yanked me down. I tumbled on top of her.

"Still no argument in you?"

"You know I don't like it when you call me Rainier." I was used to doing what I wanted, but that was before Ari. Her well-being outweighed any of my own needs. Whatever it took to keep her safe was what I'd do. I'd take the bite and transfer it to my body if I could. She'd only been where she was on the field because of a stupid decision to keep her in the dark on the distraction plan. I'd confess my transgression as soon as she was healed with the hope her forgiveness was as generous with me as it was with Merrick.

I rested my forehead against her. "Why must you make it so hard?"

She slid her hand between us and rubbed the bulge in my pants. Fuck, it felt good. I hardened for her, and I couldn't imagine a time when I didn't react to her like this. Whether asleep or awake, I wanted her body as much as to know every thought that went through her head.

"Because I like when it's hard," she said, her voice raspy with desire. "Rain."

Godsdammit. I wasn't built to be a good fae, much less a good male.

Ari licked up the side of my neck and nibbled on my ear.

I rolled off of her and covered my eyes with my arms. Her body needed to heal, which meant not using up energy on other things. "What if we watch some TV?"

"Seriously?" She flipped over to her side and propped up on her elbow. "Are you really not going to fuck me because your brother said I need to rest?"

No, I wasn't going to fuck her because of what Laurel told us. She needed to let her body heal. It went against everything my body wanted—I wanted. "I'm telling you I want to be inside you more than I want to breathe, but I respect my brother's opinion and your health."

"I don't recall him saying we can't have sex." Ari sighed, and it was the most dramatic thing I'd ever heard. "What are we watching on that horrible, brain-rotting device?"

I chuckled. "Your description is on point." I stood and pulled her up with me. "I have no idea what is on this time of day. I'm usually sleeping."

I'D FLIPPED THROUGH CHANNELS, and it turned out our people watched the news in the earliest hours of the day. Most of the shows were covering our events at the vampire border. Thank the goddesses and gods, one blessed channel was covering a children's art festival.

"Drew would have fun there. I wonder if Gemma would want to take Phina. It would be nice to do something normal. We could all go together," Ari said, her tone wistful.

When Albert was dealt with, I'd make sure we had many days to enjoy art festivals and all the things Ari deemed "normal" days.

"I bet we could arrange that," I said, avoiding the obvious issue that we still had to find her father. Some of our guards reported he'd made an appearance in the city, and that was dangerous. I'd upped the patrols and had the specialists turn all the cameras on. With any luck, we'd capture him quickly, given that most of his forces were destroyed. Treks outside the palace needed to be limited until he was no longer a concern.

Light peeked through the balcony window and cascaded across the floor. Whit's text said he'd be at the museum to meet us by the time the first light pierced the sky. "We should be going soon. Anything you need to take care of?"

"Give me a few minutes, and I'll be ready." Ari popped off the couch and headed to our room.

I picked my phone up off the table and texted Laurel.

BE IN THE COURTYARD
IN ABOUT 10 MINUTES

"Ready?" Ari said.

I looked up from the phone, raking my gaze up over her. Only my mate could make black boots, black pants, and a white sweater look that sexy.

"If you keep looking at me like that, you are going to fuck me, and we'll miss our appointment."

I closed the distance between us, cupping her face in my hands, and devoured her mouth. When I leaned back, we were both breathless. "The next time I take you, expect to scream my name so loud the guards will knock down our door."

"But?"

"That's not going to be until Laurel says you are clear for..." I searched for the right words. "Other activities."

She narrowed her eyes at me. "Then let's go see what this silver fox has to say about goddess blood."

I held my hand out to her. "What does that mean?"

"It's a long story and probably better told by Gemma." She slipped her hand into mine. "But let's just say it's an extremely good-looking older fae male for now."

I cleared my throat. "You'll have to tell me if Whit lives up to that name."

I was genuinely curious if he would satisfy the description. In my opinion, Whit had aged well, but I wasn't the best judge of fae males. I'd have to ask my brother if he thought so.

"Do you think Whit will know what Merrick meant? Or do you think this is a futile trip?" Ari asked as we descended the back stairs that exited to the door Laurel and I used when we wanted to leave unseen.

"Whit is a historian of our people. If anyone knows, it is him." I didn't tell her he'd said he'd been waiting for the call when I texted him. He definitely knew something, and I hoped it was news to help us and not another blow. We all needed a break.

Armstrong, one of my most lethal and trusted guards, met us with one of the large autos in our collection. Many fae had adapted to them in the city, but many more hadn't, and even fewer had in the outlying areas. I wasn't particularly fond of them, but if we ever lost our magic permanently, it beat the hell out of walking twenty-five miles in the dark.

Gemma and Laurel emerged from the same door we'd exited.

"Armstrong," Gemma inclined her head at him.

"Princess G," he said.

Ari's head practically swiveled at her sister. "Princess G?"

"Armstrong gave me driving lessons, and he said I drove like one of the racers. He gave me the nickname, so I'd have a name like them. There's a track near the stadium." Gemma's smile faded as soon as the last sentence left her mouth.

A tremor ran through Ari's body, and I hugged her to my side. "We're safe."

"I'm not getting in that thing." She grimaced, pointing to the auto.

"Your sister isn't driving, and Armstrong is not only a skilled driver but a decorated member of our guard."

Ari studied me for a minute. I'm not sure what she was looking for, but she must have found it because she walked toward the door Armstrong held open.

"This feels like a coffin on wheels," she said, sitting on the forward-facing seat.

"They are actually a lot of fun." Gemma patted Ari's knee as she took the seat next to her.

I didn't like Laurel and me both being in the rear-facing position, but I'd concede this for the sisters. They'd missed years together only to be ripped apart again by their father once they'd found each other.

Armstrong pulled the car out of the gate and sped up. Ari gripped the armrest on her side until her knuckles turned white.

It's fine, my love.

So you said.

I promise.

If I die in this thing, I'm going to stab you.

You know it makes me hard when you threaten to stab me.

Her gaze turned to me, and she held mine. *You had your chance to fuck me earlier.*

I'm going to make love to you and fuck you and make love to you again.

Ari's face flushed on that, and she stared out the window. Having that reaction on her was what I dreamed of at night. At least she wasn't worried about the bite or what we were going to hear from the historian.

THE CAR STOPPED in front of the modern building. The sun glinted off the glass facade in a near-blinding light and gave the patinated metal positioned in random angles a rust-colored cast. I brought Ari here for answers, but I hoped what she discovered wasn't more pain. She'd had enough of it, and she wasn't afraid to meet it on a battlefield. Damn me if I didn't want to protect her from any more hurt though.

Whit waited at the door and opened it as we neared. His silver hair shone in the morning light, and I presumed that's why Ari and Gemma called him a "silver fox." He shook Laurel's hand and gave him a warm smile. Gemma embraced him like an old friend. She'd spent many hours with him learning about her mother and the fae past.

"Hello, old friend," I extended my hand to Whit.

"Rainier." Whit gave my hand a firm shake. "Always a pleasure."

Natural light poured into the museum, casting a warm glow around Ari. "You met my mate a few days ago, but let me officially introduce Arianna, General Daphina's youngest daughter."

"Ari is fine," she said, extending her hand to his. "It's nice to meet with you here versus in a forest."

He grasped hers and smiled. "It's wonderful to make your acquaintance again. I can see the goddess has blessed you immensely."

"Whit is a gifted empath," Laurel explained. "He can often recognize what we cannot."

"That is quite generous, Laurel. I've just had more years to practice." Whit held his hand out, gesturing to a hall. "I have one of the private rooms prepared for us. Shall we?"

"You have our undivided attention," I said, praying to the goddesses and gods that our trip would give Ari the knowledge she sought.

CHAPTER 24
BLOODLINES
ARI

The room Whit led us to was the farthest away from the others. The walk reminded me of the trek across Rain's palace when Albert had been imprisoned there. I shuddered, letting the memory fall away. Rain pressed his hand against the small of my back, and the warmth of his touch grounded me in the moment. I was in a museum with a master historian, and he offered knowledge no one else had access to.

A thick wooden door opened. It was framed with rubber along the edge, so when the door was shut, no sound could penetrate it. There were several screens lining the walls, like the computers and TVs in the palace. A larger, dark wood table was in the center with matching chairs all around it. Numerous books had been placed on the table and opened to various pages. Most of the texts looked ancient. The pages were brittle in some, and others were written in a language I didn't understand. The hope in my gut wanted to believe this wasn't a waste of time.

"I found a few references to goddess blood in these texts, but none specifically about vampire reactions." He punched his fingers on a keyboard. "I did find this one of particular interest concerning General Daphina."

Rain pointed to one of the screens. It looked like a handwritten entry. The penmanship was familiar, but it wasn't Mother's handwriting. "Where is this from?"

"Your father's journal."

Surprise trickled across my neck. I thought all his journals were either with me or in the study in the prison kingdom. I read the paragraph.

> *Her blood is that of Nyx, and I don't think she even knows it.*
>
> *The power in Daphina's veins could cure me. I have to find a way to get her to freely give blood I can test with. She will be my salvation and my path to the throne.*

The words read like Albert's, and I cringed as I heard them in his voice. He'd used Mother as he'd intended to use me and Gemma. The more I learned of who he'd been, who he still was, my disgust for him expanded.

"I don't understand," Gemma said.

"What did he think she could cure him of? His madness?" I asked.

"That I don't know, but I suspect when he says 'her blood is that of Nyx,' he is indeed speaking of goddess blood."

If Mother had goddess blood, then there was something we shared. My eyes burned that I had something like, and I carried a part of her with me. Refocusing, I recalled my belongings that travelled with me from my former home.

I'd brought some of Albert's journals with me in the trunk from the prison kingdom, but I hadn't read through them all yet. They'd remained untouched since the day in my father's study when I read the entry about Gemma being alive. "This is obviously written when Mother was still alive. Was it during the war?"

"No, this was before the war. Around the time he..." Whit paused, looking between Rain and Laurel as if he needed their permission to finish.

I crossed my arms over my chest. "Around the time he what?" Gemma and I said at the same time.

"It was near the same time he found out King Veran was his father."

"King Veran?" Gemma whispered.

I looked at Rain. My stomach dropped, and I touched my belly as if I'd have to catch. My mate appeared not to be surprised.

Marius? If you can hear me, I've got a question for you.

"Then that makes Ari and me..." Gemma's brows scrunched together, and she looked at Laurel.

"Part of the royal family," I supplied. I wasn't sure how

Gemma had felt, but I'd been relieved to no longer be royal when I found out my home was a prison for a false king. I wasn't eager to step back into the role. "But...does that mean Albert is the rightful heir to the kingdom's seat?"

"No," Rain said. His eyes narrowed on Whit, but I got the sense it wasn't from the actual information but about how Whit had told us.

"I'll explain," Whit said. He pulled a family tree out of the book.

Pages had been magically sutured together, but the lines where the pieces met were visible. I wondered if it was intentional.

"The throne passes to one who was chosen. While it could be the oldest child, it's not always." He pointed down through the line that led to King Veran's reign. Most of them were women. Then, one generation only had male heirs, and that was when King Veran ascended.

Gemma pointed to the same line where I'd been looking. "And how is one chosen? Especially in this situation. King Veran's siblings are all male."

"There is another story there which is pertinent to today's discussion. Wind passes down the male line—the only elemental magic that does. But when it came to King Veran, he was unusually gifted. He could cast wind for miles, even beyond where he could see."

"That sounds like a gift from beyond this realm," I said. "A very dangerous one to wield blindly."

Rain came close to me and placed his hand between my shoulder blades and letting it trail down in a slow descent to my lower back. I let the warmth seep into me, willing it to calm my already battered nerves.

"If used inappropriately, yes, but no more so than wielding the weather." His gaze fell on Rain and then me. "Or bringing down a building with earth."

I cast my gaze down to the floor. Never had I felt so much remorse for not having better control of my gifts. I'd had so little faith in my abilities. What an insult that was to Nyx. I would learn to flourish in my power.

"So, Rain is the chosen one for our generation?" Gemma asked. "No one else can control the weather."

One by one, all heads turned my way. *Fuck me.*

"What if I don't want it? Can I just give it to someone else?"

Whit laughed. "Unless Nyx has offered that or the Fates come to intervene, no."

"What if I refuse it?"

"Then, we'll likely see a failure in our society similar to one that occurred around two thousand years ago."

Marius, I'm going to kick your ass. Because I know you knew this was going to happen.

"I just want to live my life," I said. "That's all I've wanted, and yet, I keep being forced to a throne that isn't even mine."

"It's a lot, but these decisions are made with the realm's best interests," Whit said.

"Wait…" Gemma glanced between Laurel and Rain. She swallowed hard. "We're not…"

My stomach roiled, and I placed my hand over my belly. *Nyx, goddess, tell me that we're not related to them.*

You are not. Her voice rang through my mind like the sweetest melody. The goddess herself would answer me, but not my bonded.

Thank you. My stomach settled. "We're not."

"How do you know?" Gemma asked.

"A friend told me but go ahead and let the others confirm it for you."

"We're not," Laurel said. "Our father, mine and Rain's, was the brother of a queen who bore no children with King Veran."

Whit pointed to another line of the family tree. "His first wife died in childbirth, and they told everyone the babe died as well. However, I believe that child was sent to live elsewhere, and I believe that child to have been your father."

Why would he be hidden? If he was the rightful heir, he should have been raised to succeed his father. "When did he find out?"

"We know it was before the war," Rain said. "In fact, we believe that is why he started the war. He wanted to dethrone his father and rule in his palace."

"But he wasn't chosen even though he was the king's only living child?"

Whit shook his head. "No, and the throne would have sat open, but Rain and Laurel's father received a missive asking him to hold the seat of power for the next ruler to be born. When he left us, the missive appeared on Rain's bedside."

I touched Rain's arm. Goosebumps covered his skin. He hadn't expected this role either. "And you held it for whoever would become the chosen?"

"For nearly two hundred years," he said, hanging his head.

This was an impossible situation. If I don't take it, Rain is stuck with the role until another one of us comes along. It meant we were as tied to the throne as our mate connection. *This is absolute fucking horseshit.*

Why are you stringing so many profanities together? Marius's voice came in a way as to calm and relax.

The images of him in the field rolled through my mind. Eww. *Fuck you, Marius. You knew all this time and didn't tell me.*

It's fae dealings, Ari. It wasn't my history to tell.

It affects the entire realm, so I'm calling that a lie.

When we meet up later, I'll share why that can't be handed down from me.

If I'm talking to you later, we can. For now, fuck off and get out of my head. Even though I knew he'd have some kind of rational reason as to why the events needed to unfold as they did, I didn't have to like it, and I had no plans of doing so.

Cyrus hadn't told Gemma either, but he might not have known, so at least he'd have a good reason not to tell her. Marius admitted he knew. I threw all my anger down our bond like a dagger. It probably wouldn't hurt him, but it made me feel better.

"Ari, you shouldn't be forced into a position of power you don't want." Gemma met my gaze, then Rain's and Laurel's. "None of us should be."

No matter what anyone did, there was no going back. "As much as I'd like to agree, we've all been forced into positions we didn't seek. Nyx saved me for a reason, and it's time I accept why I was given a second chance." I looked at Whit. "What's next? How do I take my place and what is expected of me?"

The screens around us flickered and went black, along with the lights turning off. Was this what the fae depended on so heavily in this city? My eyes adjusted to the dark. I reached for Rain's hand and accidentally grabbed his crotch.

He cleared his throat and entwined his fingers with mine. Faces cleared in the darkness, and I could see everyone blinking as they adapted to the change.

"I hope no one is scared of the dark," Laurel said. Gemma leaned against him.

Whit fumbled in his pocket and pulled out a small ball. He tossed it into the air. The sphere glowed like the moon and illuminated the space better than the other lights.

"How long before the electricity comes back on?" Gemma asked Laurel.

"I don't know. This hasn't happened before that I'm aware of. Rain?"

Rain shook his head. "I've never experienced it."

I studied Whit waiting for his thoughts.

He rubbed his chin. "It's highly unusual. I don't think it's happened since the early days."

"We should go check on Phina and Drew," Gemma said.

"See you back at the palace." Laurel vanyshened them out before Rain or I could respond.

"I think we should be going too. I know there's more to discuss on my ascension to the…" I didn't even want to say the word. "Me taking the throne, but I'd also like to hear how you knew my mother."

The historian's face lit up even under the light of the orb. "General Daphina was one of my dearest friends, and I look forward to sharing many stories with you about her life before the prison kingdom."

"Thank you." I shook his hand and blocked out the memories of my former home.

"I hope you'll come to dinner this week," Rain said. "We've missed you at them. Let Armstrong know he can return the car to the garage for us?"

Whit nodded. "Go. I'll take care of that."

Rain wrapped his arms around me. "Conserve your energy. Let me lead this time."

"Only because you asked so politely."

He vanyshened us back to the courtyard in the palace.

PERFECT

RAIN

Ari and I made our way to the house Leana had taken and found Gemma and Laurel with the kids there. Everyone seemed fine without the electricity. The kids played with toys, and Phina had the doll I'd given her. She took it everywhere she went. Ari used a spark of her fire magic to heat water for tea. Leana helped her prepare everything, including a snack for Drew and Phina. Leana returned from giving the kids the cookies and milk when Ari set the tea on the table.

"I didn't burn the palace down, so I consider this a win," Ari said, pride in her voice.

Laurel wore a confused expression but didn't ask questions. I held my palm out to Ari. She slipped her hand into mine, squeezing it.

"Everyone here drinks coffee," Gemma said, smiling. "It's nice to have tea."

The power flickered back to life with a little buzz. Phina cheered from her bedroom.

"Do you know where Cyrus and Marius are hiding?" Gemma asked Leana.

I didn't know they hadn't checked in, and I glanced at Ari. She lifted a shoulder that she didn't know either.

"They are with the two young vampire, trying to determine what should be done with them."

The vampire couldn't stay in the city. Not only was I unsure if I wanted them here, but I wasn't sure the fae people would accept those they'd only seen as an enemy. It might create an unsafe situation for them and others in a position to protect them.

Ari rested a hand against her throat. "Jenna and Kyle helped us. I hope they aren't thinking of ending the young vampire. I will not hesitate to interfere—"

Leana held a faelike palm up. "No, not anything like that. They need a place to stay and whatnot. I don't think either of them is sure the city is the right place for vampire though."

I agreed with the unicorn. Fae accepted all kinds in the realm with one exception, and I didn't know one fae who would want a vampire in our kingdom, much less the city. My phone buzzed in my pocket. A text flashed on the screen from my personal guards.

THE OUTAGE WASN'T AN
ACCIDENT. WE BELIEVE
IT WAS ALBERT.

Every muscle in my body tightened. I stood from the

table and walked to the window by the door and surveyed the area in front of us. Fae milled around on the streets past the courtyard. The world moved on with the day as if we hadn't experienced an electrical outage. Meanwhile, Ari's father planned his next move right under our feet.

Laurel followed me. "What is it?"

"Nothing definitive," I whispered. "Maybe we should take this outside."

ONCE OUTSIDE, my brother and I walked to a small hill on the edge of the city where we could see for a decent distance in all directions. The rolling hills, beautiful meadows, and the Forgotten Forest made up three sides, and the city the fourth. The city had come alive in the short time it took us to find our position. Not satisfied there was no one lurking around, I spun a wall of wind up around us to keep the conversation private.

Laurel eyed the sound-blocking technique. "It's Albert, isn't it?"

"My guards believe so, but they don't have proof yet." I faced the house where most of the people we both cared about sat without the knowledge I'd just shared. There wasn't much to be done without more information, and Ari and Gemma deserved some good moments before their father tried to shit all over their lives again.

"What are we going to do?"

"That should be Ari's call," I said, picking up a rock and tossing it as far as I could. My magic sliced through the barrier as if it didn't exist. "We need to be ready when he comes for us. I know I once said I would never evacuate the city, but I think we need to have the guards on alert to facilitate should Albert attack again. Ari holds the guilt for every death, and I don't want to add to it."

"The price of leadership is the burden of life," Laurel quoted a line from the talk our father had given us at the start of the war.

I tossed another rock at the wall of wind. "Did you find out anything on the bite?"

"I did, but I think we should discuss it in my lab." Laurel's solemn tone wavered.

"Is it better or worse than the news that Albert is in the city?" I braced myself for the worst, knowing I would sacrifice myself if it meant she'd live. Nyx heard my request once, and I'd reach for her again for Ari to survive and thrive as the leader of the realm.

"That might depend on your perception, but I would say better than any encounter with Albert."

My brother was a terrible liar but an incredible optimist. I patted his arm. "Let's get this over with. Nothing gets better by letting it sit. It just spoils until it's rotten."

Ari? I sent the question down the bond in a gentle breath, sensitive to the fact she had two of us in her head all the time. I kept my barrier firmly in place unless I was specifically speaking to her to cut down the noise.

What are you two doing outside?

Laurel has the results of your tests, but he asked if we could come to his lab.

It's bad.

She assumed the worst, and with the way the secrets of her life unfolded, she'd learned to assume outcomes would not favor her. In time, I intended to shower her with only goodness to reset her expectations of life. *I don't know, but he wants to discuss what he found.*

On my way.

"Goddesses and gods, I want to give her the moon and a perfect life, but there has been nothing perfect so far," I said to my brother.

Laurel squeezed my shoulder. "It won't always be like this."

The door opened, and Ari walked out with Gemma right behind her.

"Leana will watch the kids for us," Gemma said, her voice wavering.

Ari wrapped an arm around my waist, and I slung one over her shoulder.

It's going to be okay. No matter what he says.

My life is perfect, Rain. Even with the heartache and struggles. It's perfect because I have you and our family. She glanced over at Gemma and Laurel, who held hands.

Five years had made a difference in my life. My brother and his mate made me an uncle to a child that I'd protect with my last breath. I wasn't even sure I'd have children of my own and then Ari entered my life. If she wanted to have little versions of us someday, I'd give her as many as she wanted. I couldn't imagine a greater legacy to my love for my mate than to have a part of her live on with a part of me.

"Shall we vanyshen to the courtyard?" Laurel asked.

My gut tightened. He didn't want to waste time. "We shall."

I pulled Ari against my chest. It was wholly unnecessary to hold her that tight, but I wanted her close. "As you like to say, hold on."

INSIDE THE LAB, Laurel pulled one of the big monitors over and plugged his laptop into it. "Before I show the findings, I want to preface this by saying I've never seen this before, so most of what I'm going to say is speculation."

Ari swallowed so hard I could see her throat bob. "I'm not afraid of the truth, Laurel. Not anymore."

I wished I could take the nerves and worry away for her. My love was fierce and strong, and she wouldn't face whatever he said alone.

Laurel tapped his fingers on the desk. "We still need to look through the texts with Whit too."

"Just tell us, Laurel. No one needs this buildup," Gemma said, crossing her arms.

Laurel took a breath and let it out. "Your blood isn't acting like normal fae blood, Ari. It's similar but very different in some ways."

"I kind of figured that when the vampire exploded into a million pieces," she said, her tone flat.

I coughed to hide my smirk. At least my love still had her personality.

My brother punched on the keyboard, and a screen popped up. "This pic on the left is how regular fae blood reacts to vampire venom. It fights against it, but eventually, if not healed, it succumbs."

Ari gasped, and I pulled her tighter to me. Death wasn't a fucking option. Neither was turning into a vampire. It was no secret that the rest of us would either die or turn when bitten. Most vampire couldn't stop drinking once they tasted blood. The only way to stop them was to end them.

"And mine?" Ari whispered.

Gemma wrapped her arms tight around herself.

Laurel punched some more buttons. "This is yours. It destroys the vampire venom and seeks the source."

That sounded like good news, but it puzzled me why Ari wasn't healing.

Ari looked down at her arm. Blood spatters soaked through the bandage. "So, what is happening with the arm?"

"That's what I'm not sure about, but I have a theory. I think your blood has isolated the small amount of venom the vampire injected with the bite, and I suspect your natural healing properties are at war with the part of your blood that's different."

"How do I stop it?" Her voice wavered.

"There has to be a way to reverse it," I echoed her.

"Please don't say you need to cut my arm off above the bite." She grabbed her forehead.

"No." Laurel hesitated. "I don't think so."

His lack of confidence was not reassuring, but my brother always looked for alternatives. "I know you, Laurel. You want to try something radical, so spit it out."

He nodded. "This is the part I'm very unsure about, but I think it could work."

I motioned him with my hand. "Give it to us."

He punched on the keyboard again. "This flower is normally poisonous, but when we mix it with these other properties, it seems to at least slow the progress."

I squeezed Ari's hip. "What do you mean by slow the progress?"

"Back up." Gemma clasped her hands together. "Is this advancing on her body?" She looked at Ari with terror.

Ari let out a deep sigh and undid the bandage. "It is."

I choked on how far it had spread in such a short time. It had gone from a reddened bite mark to double in size, and her skin was pink up to her elbow. I refused to lose her...not now...not over this.

"Ari..." Gemma closed the distance and took Ari's arm in her hands, examining the growing wound.

Laurel moved closer, studying the flesh. "That's why I believe you should rest and not use any magic. Any exertion, especially power, drains your body's ability to do other things."

She wouldn't be able to train, and that put her in more

danger knowing Albert was near. Ari and I wouldn't be practicing for babies while she was like this, but that was the least of my worries. The infection was spreading faster than most poisons I'd seen work. She needed whatever Laurel could do to slow it down while we figured out how to eradicate the venom.

"Like healing," Ari said, her voice sounding defeated. "Do you really think this elixir you are testing will work?"

"With enough time," Laurel said, "yes, I do."

Time was never on our side. It hadn't been since the moment we met, but I was going to fight with all my power to make sure Ari survived this.

"So, what do you need from me?" she asked.

"Some more samples, if you can take them."

"Do I have a choice?"

That might be the worst part. Her only request of me had always been that she have her freedom to choose, and this situation was out of my control. She didn't really have a choice.

CHAPTER 26

CONTRADICTION
ARI

By the end of the third day after Laurel told me how different my blood was from other fae, there were three things I hated—needles, scrapers, and being told test results failed.

I decided to spend the day at the museum with Whit in hopes he might have some ideas or texts to examine, and if that was a fail, then I'd ask him for stories about my mother. The guards had woken Rain up before sunrise to see to urgent court business, so, the only person I invited along was Merrick. She wouldn't coddle me like the others did, and I was tired of being treated like a broken doll.

"Ari?" Whit called from the door of the private room.

"I'm in here."

"Merrick is here. I wanted to make sure you approved her visit."

I smiled. "Yes, she's welcome to join me."

He cocked his head. "But not the others?"

I pointed to the phone on my table. "They can reach me with that annoying thing if they need me."

Whit chuckled and held his hands up. "Very well. Is there anything else you need?"

The glass of water he'd brought earlier was empty, but I hated to ask him to refill it for me. "Where can I get more water?"

"I'll bring a pitcher in for you," he said.

"I can get it myself," I said, moving to stand.

He shook his head. "You are doing important work, and it won't take a second."

He disappeared, and Merrick walked through the door. She was dressed immaculately in gray slacks and a cream-colored sweater, but the dark circles under her eyes said she hadn't slept.

"You look like your best friend died," she said, taking a seat beside.

Val. I hadn't thought about her in a while, and guilt washed over me. She and Theo were taken to the lands on the coast for safety, and I wondered if I'd ever get to see her again.

"I take that back. Now, you look like your best friend died," Merrick said, her voice firm but soft at the same time. "That didn't really happen, did it?"

"No, but she is on the farthest side of the kingdom she could be from me."

Merrick placed a hand on my uninjured arm. "You know I'm not the best person for kind words, but you are a fucking badass, Arianna. You are going to get through this and be the leader our people need."

I blinked back tears and met her gaze. "I don't usually cry, but this..." I gestured around us. "All of this is too much."

"It would be for anyone," she said. "Anyone but you. Dry those tears and straighten your face. We're going to figure this out."

Whit stepped in with the pitcher and another glass for Merrick in one hand. He set them on the table and picked up an old book. He passed it over to me. "Might I suggest looking in this one. I've been drawn to it, which can be a sign, but I haven't found anything useful in it yet."

"I can't read this language," I said, studying the page. It was a beautiful text with scrolling letters, but I'd never seen this writing style before.

Merrick leaned over and surveyed the words. "I can. Give it to me. I'll take this one."

I DOWNED my third or maybe fourth glass of water, flipping the page of the latest book from the stack. *Why am I so damn thirsty today?*

"This is interesting," Merrick said.

"What?" I leaned toward her.

"Whit? Can you come in here?" she called out down the hall.

"How can I help?" he asked as he entered the room.

"I think I found something, but the interpretation seems off for me. Can you take a look?" She passed the book over to him and pointed to a paragraph.

He scanned the page and then seemed to scan it again. His eyes narrowed and widened as he traced the words with his fingers. "Those word choices seem off for the time period."

"Right," Merrick said. "Almost like they had been written by Nyx herself."

Nyx...would she do that? Could she have done that?

"Hmm. I'll need to look into this." Whit started out the door with the book in hand.

"Is anyone going to tell me what it says?" I asked, taking another drink of my freshly filled glass.

"Sorry." He turned around. "Sometimes I get so into a mission and the books I forget where I am."

Disbelief turned into amusement at how nice it was to be forgotten instead of the one everyone stared at all the time. I let out a completely inappropriate laugh. "It's fine, Whit. One of you just let me in on your secret."

Merrick covered her mouth, but her eyes said she was smiling and probably hiding a laugh.

"If we are interpreting it correctly, it says that Nyx will be reborn in this realm, but also that she can never return to the realm. They seem to be in contradiction of each other, but Nyx was known for texts that made others dig deeper for meaning."

I almost wished I hadn't asked, because the text made

no sense. I thought back to my time with Nyx and how the space itself felt—there but not—and that sounded like the text. "When I visited the goddess in her realm, it was like mist and moonlight and stars. I had the feeling of floating, but I wasn't."

"She's often referred to as darkness personified, so that would be consistent with what we know," Whit said. "Do you remember anything else?"

"There was this feeling or sense maybe of ..." I struggled for the word—not prison, like my former home, but something else.

"Peace?" Merrick asked.

"Yes, peace, but something else too. Like it wasn't entirely her choice to be there, and she didn't want me to be committed to the same existence."

Whit squinted his eyes as if he'd find the answer by narrowing his vision. "That's certainly interesting and not something I've heard before from any other near-death experiences, but there might be something to that. I'm going to pull some more texts for us."

Us. I gazed at Merrick, and she smiled. I liked being part of a team and having friends who supported me. With Rain and Gemma, it was different. They treated me like a piece of crystal that had been broken and put back together. I knew it was from love, but there were times I needed someone to not filter things to protect me from the broken parts.

"You're not going to cry again, are you? There are limits to the number of tears I can handle in a day."

A laugh rumbled in my throat until I couldn't contain it. "I'm glad I met you, even though you're rude."

"You like me because you are similar."

She was right. Part of the reason I liked her was because we shared the "stab first, ask questions later" mentality. As much as I tried to reform myself, that was part of my personality. "I think you and I are going to get into a lot of trouble once we get the kingdom settled."

"I know we are," Merrick said, winking at me. "And I'm looking forward to introducing you to shopping. Your wardrobe needs a serious overhaul."

"These are pieces I brought from the kingdom," I said, glancing at the black pants and black tunic I had on. I laughed. "This isn't what most people are wearing here, is it?"

"Maybe people from my mother's generation." She eyed me.

My throat felt dry, so I sipped some water. "Fine. When the safety of the kingdom is secured, we'll find me some new clothes."

I flipped the pages of the book in front of me, not seeing the writing on them. A heaviness had settled over me because if I survived this bite, there was still Albert to resolve. Somewhere between or after, I had to figure out what to do with the seat of the kingdom. I wasn't the leader of this group. My sister was. Rain was. Even Merrick carried herself like a leader. Not me. How was I going to lead so many people who didn't even know me?

But I was getting ahead of myself because that was all

predicated on whether I survived the vampire bite I'd originally dismissed. We'd had limited knowledge in my former home, but I knew not all bites resulted in turning or death. I'd been meant to turn. If I did turn, I couldn't stay here. I wasn't even sure I wanted to live without magic, but then I thought of Griselda. She hadn't been a bad vampire, and she'd given her life for me. In my soul I knew, I was never meant to be a vampire. That's what Laurel's tests showed without him saying it...the bite should have made me a vampire. My weird blood was the anomaly holding it off, and none of us could predict for how long.

"Look at this," Merrick said, pushing the book I wasn't reading out of the way and putting hers in front of me.

The same beautiful language I didn't understand stared back at me from the page. "Once again, can't read that language."

She smirked. "You need to learn it. A lot of the oldest texts are written in it."

I groaned. "Just tell me."

She pointed to where a symbol with swirling marks was. "This symbol is the ancient symbol for eternal life and is often used in reference to Nyx's realm."

"I've seen that somewhere before, but I can't recall where." I finished my glass of water.

"There's a more modern version most of our people and spiritualists use, so it probably wasn't here unless you saw it in one of these books." She gestured to the growing pile on the table. "Anyway. The paragraph talks about Nyx's fall from grace."

I choked on my water. "Her what? Nyx is The Goddess."

"According to this, she was sent to live among the fae like her other siblings, but she didn't like taking orders. Good for her."

"So, she wasn't the original highest?"

"No, I wonder if she led her own little coup?" Merrick pondered, flipping the pages. "Sadly, it doesn't say here. Maybe Whit can find us something on this."

The benevolent goddess I'd met didn't seem the type to start a coup, and I had a hard time imagining her in battle. "Why does no one talk about it?"

"Would you want to risk being smited?"

"I don't think Nyx is the smiting kind of goddess. She seems so full of love." She'd refused to let Rain sacrifice himself for me and gave us a second chance. Everything about her seemed kind, as if love radiated off of her.

"You can say that because you've met her. The rest of us haven't. I don't think the average fae would risk it."

Whit clamored through the door, covered in dust, with a cobweb in his hair and several books in his arms. "I found something that I think will help."

"So did I," Merrick said. "I hope this is the Fates nudging us."

Whit eyed the book in her hand and smiled. "Indeed. I believe it is."

PART TWO

THE GENERAL'S DAUGHTERS

I had a dream last night where a sprite
visited me. It wasn't the first time. When I was a
child, one visited me. She hadn't looked like more
than a child herself then, but I wondered if that
was her last night too. Sprites disappeared from
this world before my birth, and the only thing I
knew of their power was what I'd been taught by
the historians or found in texts. The sprite, ethe-
really captivating, told me that I would have two
daughters and together they would change the
world. Sadly, she said I would not live to see

their success. If that is what it takes to find the root of the diminishing magic in our world, then it is a sacrifice I willingly make for the children I haven't met yet. I decided not to tell King Veran of the sprite's visit. It hasn't even been a year since he lost his wife, but I sense his growing affection for me. Though the sprite didn't say I'd marry him, she had said my daughters would rule the kingdom. A king couldn't be crowned without a queen under our laws, but a queen can take the throne on her own. If these two daughters were indeed ruling our realm, then I'd likely have to return King Veran's affection at some point. The visit confirmed to me why I'd been doodling two names over and over—Gemma and Arianna. I can't wait to meet them both.

CHAPTER 27
FEVER
ARI

Whit placed a book in front of me...again in the language I couldn't read. I sighed. *Nyx, if this is part of your plan, it would be helpful if you gave me the knowledge to read this.*

A soft, tinkly laugh whispered through my head. *Granddaughter, learning to accept help is an honorable trait.*

My independence says otherwise.

Her smile radiated in my mind with the silver glow of the stars as if she were right in front of me. *Trust me.*

Then she was gone. Annoyed I didn't get the chance to ask her if she could heal the bite, I took that as we must be on the right path. "You both keep putting books in front of my face in this language you know I can't read."

A knock at the door drew our attention. Rain stood there. His eyes were a storm as if he'd been through a battle to get here. "May I join you?"

He looked like he would bring down lightning on the building if I said no. "Of course, you can."

He glanced at Merrick. She started to move to another seat. She didn't cower in front of anyone except my family, and I didn't want anyone to feel that way unless they were an enemy.

I touched her arm. "You don't need to move for him. He doesn't always get what he wants."

She looked between me and Rain. Rain's gaze was locked on mine, and I could almost see the wheels turning. The corners of his mouth turned up.

"Merrick, my mate is not one to be challenged," Rain said, and I waited for him in my head. He didn't send anything to me.

Merrick dropped back into her chair.

That sounds like a challenge to me. I whispered my thought into his mind.

Thank you.

For what?

Giving me what I wanted.

I picked up one of the books and threw it at him. He flicked his wrist, and it hovered there. His smile broadened. I sighed and shook my head.

"Whit and I are working. If you two are going to play, maybe take it elsewhere," Merrick said, not raising her head from the book.

Whit cleared his throat. "I was just about to share the tales of this book with Ari and Merrick. Won't you sit, Rainier, while I do?"

Rain took the chair across from me and bit down on his lip. What was he thinking?

Whit showed us pictures from the book. Erebus was shrouded in Nyx's mist. While the goddess was clearly depicted in power, Erebus was hidden in a position similar to where bonded unicorns would be placed. "There is more to the story of Nyx and Erebus than what is taught to fae today."

"There is more to Nyx and Erebus's union than what is told by fae historians." Marius leaned against the door in his faelike form.

Was everyone going to show up here? Not that I was unhappy to see them, but the constant interruptions weren't productive. I glared at him, a bit agitated he'd disappeared with Cyrus. "Decided to come out of hiding and face me?"

"I waited until the time was right," he said, pushing off the door and walking over to the table. He flipped the covers to see what books we had. "The real history behind their story is one the unicorn have kept unspoken since long before they departed from this realm. Passed down to only a few each generation."

"What do you mean? They aren't the first charge and guardian bond?"

"No, they are, but it's how that came to be," he said, flipping through pages. "Before Nyx ascended into her role of Goddess, she, like all of the goddesses and gods, was required to live a fae lifetime in fae form without her goddess powers."

I had to consciously close my mouth. I'd never heard any of this before Merrick found the reference earlier, but this was the second time. Fates were at work, it seemed. "She lived as one of us?"

Marius tilted his head to one side and then the other. "For all intents and purposes, she was one of you for that brief time in her long existence."

Rain leaned back in his chair. "So, Nyx met Erebus while she was living as fae?"

Marius flipped a page in Whit's book to a depiction of Nyx and Erebus looking very much in love. Mist floated around them like when I was in her realm. "She did. He was a unicorn, and unicorn were unable to glamour to present a form like human or fae."

"Say that again...unicorn couldn't glamour into a form like ours?" Merrick asked, disbelief in her tone.

"No, in fact, there was very little interaction between the two species." Marius shrugged.

"That's hard to imagine," I said. Our lives were so entwined...at least they had seemed that way in the prison kingdom. In the city, they seemed far less symbiotic.

Marius nodded, seemingly to agree with me. "It was possible, of course, but neither did much to intermingle."

Fate or love or mates. Something changed with them. "Until Nyx and Erebus fell in love?" I asked.

Marius took the seat next to Rain. "Yes, precisely. Nyx wanted to be able to hold Erebus. As the goddess eternal, a difference that set her apart from others of her kind, she was able to summon her powers. She used her goddess magic, with Erebus's permission, to grant him the ability to change form."

I gasped. Nyx was the reason why unicorn could glamour to faelike forms, and not only that, she'd done the forbidden to be with him. It worked out for them though. They lived eternally together in their realm.

Every choice has a price, my child. Her gentle voice carried a warning.

I wanted to ask her what her price was, but that felt too personal. The warning though...what was it? *What should I be concerned about losing?*

Everything. Her answer shook me. My body trembled. *Don't make the same mistakes as I.*

"Ari, are you okay?" Rain asked from over the top of me.

"I'm fine," I said, wondering how he got behind me so fast. "Why?"

He cupped my face. "Your eyes rolled back in your head."

You were communing with the goddess? Marius asked down our bond.

Yes.

Keep that for you for now, Ari.

They already know she's spoken to me.

Everything doesn't require an argument. For this once, keep that conversation to yourself.

If Rain asks, I will tell him.

Marius huffed down the bond. *Of course, you will.*

"Can you all give me some space? I'm fine. Really. I just

need a glass of water." My throat was so dry it was like sandpaper.

"You're running a fever," Rain said, pressing the back of his hand to my head. "We need to go see Laurel."

"There's a healer in this room. Merrick can tend to a fever," I said. *That's why you didn't want me to say anything. They would dismiss it right now.* I sent the thought to my bonded.

See. I'm not a total idiot.

This time. You're not an idiot this time.

He grumbled down the bond. Rain and Merrick were arguing over whether or not to take me to Laurel.

"I don't have anything to treat her here," Merrick said, showing her empty hands.

"Rain"—I held my arm out to him, wanting to end the argument—"take me to your brother." Then I pointed between Merrick and Marius. "You two meet us there."

My mate wrapped me in his arms like a cocoon. I rested my head against his chest. We spun like a tornado through the beautiful colors and the short distance to the courtyard. The stones, soft but unsteady under my feet, were a reminder of so many things in my life.

"Do we have plans tonight?" I asked, unable to recall if we did, but hoping we didn't.

Rain took my hand and led me through a door that had become so familiar with its understated look but bold carvings. "Not that I know of. Why?"

"I'd like to go to the garden. The big one dedicated to my mother," I said, daydreaming of how beautiful the flowers had looked and the stunning view of the night sky. Even though life was completely and utterly askew at that time, the garden had given me peace and an unforgettable moment. I looked up at Rain and saw love and concern in his eyes. I thought about how things had changed in such a short time.

"If you haven't figured it out yet, my love, I will give you anything you want." He stopped at the top of the stairs. Brushing the hair off my face, he traced the line of my jaw. "All you have to do is ask."

The asking was the hard part. I didn't like depending on anyone...even him, but I was getting better at it because I trusted him. "Thank you."

He kissed my forehead and slipped his hand in mine as we walked the rest of the way to Laurel's lab.

CHAPTER 28

THE TEA
RAIN

Laurel administered some of the herbal tea to reduce fevers. When he pulled the bandage back, my heart constricted. I wasn't prepared for how much the infection had spread. Half of Ari's forearm looked like a mottled mess. The only time she complained of pain was when he scraped some of the infection.

My brother's brows knitted in a concerned expression. "Have you been using your magic?"

"No, not that I recall." She studied the ceiling and then looked back at Laurel. The sweet smell of moonflowers scented the air, but I hadn't seen her use her power. "No, I'm sure I haven't."

"Why is it spreading so fast?" I asked.

"It could be several things," Laurel said, his tone frustrated. "Her metabolism, Nyx's blood, the age of the vampire who bit her. There are so many factors, and we need time."

Time was the one thing we seemed to be in short supply of.

Marius and Merrick entered the lab.

"I think we might be able to find a cure, but I'm missing something...a key."

"What did you say?" Ari asked, sitting up.

I reached out to steady her, but she didn't need my help.

Laurel opened his mouth, but Ari waved a hand at him.

"Never mind. Whit showed us a journal of fa...Albert's where he referenced using Mother for a cure. Maybe there is something in that journal."

"On it," Merrick said, heading to the door.

"I'll go with her," Marius said. He held Ari's gaze with a pensive expression on his face, and I could almost feel him speaking to her down their bond.

A low laugh rumbled in the unicorn's chest. Ari lifted one eyebrow in the way that said she was about to get stabby.

"As I was saying," Laurel said, and I wondered if I'd missed something. "I think this combination is our best chance."

"We'll wait to see what Marius and Merrick bring back." I studied Ari. She looked calm considering the diagnosis. "If you agree."

"You're being too nice," she said. "But yes, I agree."

The door opened, and Gemma came through. "I

wondered where everyone was." She studied her sister. "Why do you look so flushed?"

"She had a bit of a fever, but I've already given her the fever-reducing tea," Laurel said in a soothing voice.

"I'm fine, Gemma."

"Says the person who is in an infirmary bed." She pulled a chair up beside me. "You look pale."

Ari took a long drink of water. "I'm just tired and thirsty."

"That should get better when the fever breaks," Laurel said.

"I can have some food sent up if you are hungry." I pulled the phone out of my pocket.

"Enough of this. You're smothering me." Ari gestured with a sweeping arm. "Hovering around me like I'm a delicate piece of art you are protecting. I see your acts of love, but I need you to all behave normal."

"This is normal, Ari," Gemma said, taking her hand.

"No, it's not." She shifted her gaze to me. "And we have plans tonight."

A genuine smile spread across my face. She must be feeling better to comment on our garden trip. "We certainly do."

Her lips parted in a stunning grin. That was what I wanted to see. Her happiness was everything to me.

She turned her gaze to her sister. "How is Cyrus? I haven't seen him since we returned."

Gemma looked at Laurel, sadness drooping both of their faces. A regretful look filled Ari's features.

"He's still working with Jenna and Kyle," Gemma said.

"But we think he's avoiding us," Laurel added.

Ari nodded. Cyrus's duty and honor were his entire personality...and probably his stubbornness too.

Gemma wiped a finger under her eye.

Ari looked at both like they'd drunk one of the tonics at the old taverns that made fae hallucinate. Her gaze settled on my brother. "He is, because he thinks that is what his duty demands. As an empath, you should know that. If you want him to be a part of your life...your family, he's going to need some encouragement."

"He not only returned for us, but he saved us," Gemma said.

"Maybe you need to go to him this time," I added.

One side of Ari's mouth turned up as if she were proud of me. I'd changed in the short time since I'd known her, and I'd never wanted someone's approval the way I desired hers.

"We could invite him for dinner tonight, so he could get to know Phina better, and talk to him after she goes to bed." Laurel lifted his gaze to Gemma's.

She squeezed his hand. "I like that idea, and I think he would too."

A smug expression took over Ari's face. She'd diverted the attention from herself.

Damn. She's impressive. Well done, my goddess.

The door opened, revealing Marius and Merrick.

She waved the journal in front of her. "Whit said to keep it and use it however you need."

CHAPTER 29

BEGONIAS

ARI

The soft grass muffled the sound of landing and was a welcome change from the gravel that normally greeted us in the courtyard when we vanyshened. I inhaled, taking in all the sweet aromas on the breeze. The sun set on the horizon, and it was that perfect time many called the golden hour, with cascading oranges and pinks falling over everything.

"This was what I needed." I bumped my shoulder into Rain's.

He wrapped his arm loosely around me, guiding me down the paths. "So did I. What I really wanted was time with you here."

I tucked myself to his side. Goddess, he made me want to live forever, but if our time was short, I wanted to make every memorable moment possible.

"What kind of flower is that?" I brushed the delicate

petals with my fingers. They were shaped like purple butterflies, lighter, more violet, in the center of what would be the wings if it were a real butterfly. The edges were trimmed with a darker purple, and where the torso of the butterfly would be, the purple was almost black. "It's so beautiful."

"It's a moonlight butterfly begonia," Rain said. "Or as the people have named it—Arianna's Moonlight Butterfly Begonia."

"They what? Why?"

"You are beloved by your people. They know your rightful place and what you've sacrificed. This is how they have honored you."

If they knew I might not be around or that I wasn't a leader, would they still think so much of me?

"I don't know what to say," I said, running a finger over the soft petal.

"Nothing is required," Rain said. "But if you are moved to, you can always issue a statement of thanks for the gift."

"Yes, I'd like to do that. Can we do it tomorrow?"

"If you are up to it, of course," he said, tapping a finger on his lips. "There's something else I want to show you."

He took my hand, leading me down the smooth, winding path past moonflowers, roses, and many beautiful flowers in shades of blues, pinks, purples, yellows and reds. Their sweet scents floated through the breeze. Tall trees with graceful branches sheltered random portions of the trail to a waterfall. More of the flowers named after me were planted around the base of it. The garden teemed with beauty and life and nudged the part of me that desperately wanted to know what it meant to be present in every moment and enjoy those seconds with Rain.

"Breathtaking. If paradise existed in this realm, I'd declare it to be here." I trailed my fingers through the pool at the base. "We didn't see this last time?"

"No, I had it installed while we were at the border of the vampire lands." He waved his hand over my shoulder. Numerous fae walked toward us carrying chairs, a small table, and, by the scents drifting my way, dinner.

My stomach growled, and I realized I hadn't eaten all day. I'd been so consumed with thirst that it hadn't even crossed my mind to eat food.

"You did this after I asked if we could come here?"

"The flowers were already planned, but I added the dinner when I knew for sure we were going to be here tonight." His tone sheepish, he rubbed my shoulders.

The fae set up with little effort, giving quick bows and making a hasty exit. I didn't miss the sweet smiles on their faces and thanked them.

"It smells delicious," I said. "What do we have?"

Rain lifted the cloche to reveal meat and potatoes. A tureen held vegetable and rice soup. The aromas prompted my stomach to growl in approval.

"No wine?" I asked, teasing but disappointed. A glass of wine would be great after everything I learned today.

"I figured you would want water, considering how

much I've seen you consume today. The fever dehydrated you, I'm assuming."

"Nothing seems to quench the thirst. So, I think you're right," I said, cutting into a large potato he put on my plate. The vegetable melted in my mouth, and I savored the way the juices of the meat it had been cooked with added extra flavor. "Why is the food so much better here?"

"I could say it's the technology." He laughed. "But everyone knows it's Mabel's cooking. She's been cooking for my family since before I was born."

"She's the one who should have a plant named after her." I dipped my spoon in the soup, and an explosion of flavors hit my tongue so fast I thought I might have an orgasm.

Rain stuck his fork in a piece of meat and looked just as pleased when his utensil came back clean. I slipped one of the red heels he'd talked me into wearing off under the table. Letting my elemental connection guide me, I found his ankle with the side of my foot. The instep was always particularly soft, and the hair on his leg tickled me as I moved up and down in a painfully slow gesture.

Rain froze with his fork in front of his open mouth. "What are you doing, my love?"

"Seeing if I can tempt you." I slipped the other shoe off and let it fall to the ground, hoping it would inspire him.

"Being near you in the same realm, in the same universe with you, is a constant temptation," he said. "But I can restrain myself with great remorse."

I studied him. His expression was serious. Drastic

measures were needed to persuade him. I waited until he had a mouthful of meat and gathered my thoughts. "I feel like I'm on restriction, and it makes me want to rebel."

When I stood from the table, I undid the buttons on my top and tossed it aside.

"What are you doing?" Rain's gaze darted around us.

"Not doing is a better question." I removed my pants and tossed them at him, leaving me in the red undergarments that matched the heels he'd picked. "I'm not going to walk around like I'll break if I live my life."

"Ari..."

I hopped up on the edge of the pool and stepped into the cold waters. They were beyond frigid, but I summoned my friend fire to me to warm my skin.

"I can see the flames licking your skin," he said. "You shouldn't be using your magic."

I shrugged. My blood was the issue...not my magic. I'd come to understand that. Nyx had said to trust her, so I did. "I'm fae and Nyx's magic runs through my blood. Do you think she saved me just to let me die from a vampire bite?"

He opened his mouth and closed it. He had to know I was right. Was I afraid? Yes. But I was done not doing the things I wanted or fucking the man I loved because I might die one day. We were all going to die, so whether my time was today or a thousand years from now, I was going to live my life with joy.

I unclasped my bra and held it up, tossing it at him.

The soaked fabric hit Rain in the face with a wet smack. I laughed.

He pulled the lacy item from his face and tossed it aside. Then, he reached for the hem of his tunic and pulled it over his head.

This was going to work.

When he stripped down to his underwear, his defined abs were exposed down to the deep V of his hipbones, but his scars were too. I cherished every line of his body, including the battle marks. The one under his pec was the one I'd noticed when I first saw his bare chest in the kitchen of my former home...the night he taught me the proper way chocolate cake should be eaten. He met my gaze with intense heat. His thumbs rested in the band. "You first."

"Gladly," I said, reaching for the two little straps holding the fabric on my body. I slid them off and tossed them to him. I felt free...so truly free.

Rain caught them with precision. "If these weren't wet, I'd put them in my pocket for later. I might still do it."

He dropped his underwear to the ground. His glorious cock, hard and with a little precum on the tip, glistened in the last of the sunlight. If I was descended from a goddess, then surely he was part god. He eased into the water and came toward me. "I didn't realize we'd be doing this when they asked me how deep to make it. I'm glad I answered with five feet in the shallow."

"How deep is the deep?" I asked.

"I'll show you." He devoured my mouth, and I opened

for him. His kiss burned with his love, a promise and a claim that he would never let me go. He leaned back, studying my face. His steady mask was gone, and adoration and desire replaced it. "Are you sure you feel okay? I don't want to hurt you."

My wantonness ached to be free. "I'm sure. I've never been more positive about something in my life."

His hardness pressed against me, and I reached between us, stroking him from head to base and back.

"Fuck, Ari," he whispered against my cheek.

"That is the plan." I smiled against his skin and sucked on his neck.

Rain smoothed his thumb over the hollow of my throat, and I leaned back, giving him access. His lips burned a trail from my chin to where his palm rested. A moan drifted from low in my throat, and I fisted my hand in his hair.

His fingers drifted to my breasts. Rain rubbed the back of his knuckles over my breast in a swirling motion until he reached my nipple. My skin pebbled under his touch. He worked it between his fingers until the peak hardened. "I love you."

"I love you," I said, my voice breathy. "But if you're not inside me in five seconds, I'm going to drown you."

A husky laugh in Rain's chest vibrated against me. "Patience."

Heat pooled in my throbbing sex. I rubbed his dick in long, quick motions. His lids lowered, and he bit down on his lip. His pleasure brought me closer.

He ghosted his hand over my skin until he reached my folds. "Touching you like this"—he slid his finger over, back and forth, in a torturous touch—"gets you and me both ready."

"I'm ready. Trust me," I rasped out.

"Let me see." He thrust a finger inside me and added a second one, stretching me.

My desire ratcheted up, and I wanted him inside me. I pushed my hips toward him so close and craving more friction.

"Mmm. Warm. Tight. Slick. I think you are ready." He withdrew his fingers and sucked them.

I nearly found release from his thick baritone voice and the shameless way he made every word a sexual symphony. Rain grasped the back of my legs and lifted me. I wrapped my legs around his waist. Rain captured my mouth in a demand. I couldn't get close enough to him. His familiar minty taste coated my tongue.

"Rain."

"If you want it, take it," he said, his voice rough.

I reached between us and guided him to my entrance. The tip of his cock entered, and he held still.

"Do you want it?" Lightning flickered in his pupils.

"Yes." My need spiraled up.

Rain pushed into me inch by delicious inch, filling me. I gasped. My head fell back.

He stopped, digging his fingers into my hips.

I wanted him to move faster and pressed against him.

With his other hand, he grabbed my neck and lifted.

"Look at me, Ari. When you scream my name for the entire city to hear, I want to watch you."

My core turned molten from his words. Goddess, he was too controlled, and I wanted him undone. I locked in on his gaze, and he thrust into me.

"That is deep," I said, maintaining eye contact and saw how feral he was behind that mask of restraint. He wanted to see me, and I him. Broken on our own, we were made whole together.

Rain drove deeper and faster until his strokes became erratic. I swirled my hips. He slipped his hand low below the water until his thumb found the bundle of nerves at my apex. My view narrowed to only him. He rubbed slow circles on my clit, increasing the pressure with each pass. Stars erupted in my vision.

"Say my name, Ari," he grunted out.

"Rain." My whimper turned into a cry of pleasure. "Rain...Rain."

"That's my mate," he said, thrusting hard. My toes curled, and I squeezed my thighs around him.

My climax soared to the night sky, but all I could see was Rain's face. Warmth filled me from his seed and in my chest with our connection.

Rain buried his head in my neck, placing soft kisses against my skin. "How are you feeling?"

My mate made me realize what it was for two fae to be undisputedly intertwined without giving up our individual identities. I'd feared losing myself to the crown and to a husband who would be looked to lead, but it would never be like that with Rain. He wouldn't stand in front of me or behind me. Instead, I knew I'd always find him by my side, supporting me. There was only one word that could name devotion like he showed me.

"Loved," I said, noticing the chill. My body was tired, but the weariness was a reminder of how I chose to live the day. "Cold but loved."

He walked toward the edge of the pool area, my legs still wound around him. "Loved is what you were meant to feel. You are the reason the moon rises in the night sky."

"You already had me. You don't have to make me feel special." I smiled against his cheek and pressed a kiss to his damp skin.

"If there is one thing you should always know, it is that you are special." He sat me on the ledge while he climbed out. Moonlight reflected silver where the water ran down his torso. Leaning forward, he brushed his lips across mine and lifted me. "I'd rather stay here all night, but we should probably head back before someone sends the guard to find us."

"Are you going to cuddle me?" I winked at him.

"I'll do that and more." He pulled on his pants and held up my red bra and panties. "These are still soaked. I don't think you want to put them on." He tossed them on the table.

I snatched them up. "I can't leave them here for the others to find."

"I'll take them." He took them from me and shoved them into his pocket.

"You're going to look like you had an accident on the way to our rooms."

"It won't be the first time you made me walk around looking like I pissed myself."

I laughed, pulling my pants over my hips. "At least this time I'm not using low magic to make you think your dick is on fire."

CHAPTER 30
OUR CITY
ARI

Rain and I didn't bother to use magic to dry ourselves. When he vanyshened us back to the courtyard, since we couldn't go directly into the palace, our clothes and hair were fairly dry. I patted my hair down, but I could tell it was wild. Rain, for his part, looked perfect and unrumpled. "That is not fair."

"What, love?" he asked.

"That my hair is uncontrollable, like I've been skinny dipping, among other things, and you are the epitome of perfection." I gestured to him.

"Magic, my goddess. We have it. Remember?"

While I'd been perfectly willing to use it for warmth to live the beautiful moment at the waterfall, asking magic to make me look presentable seemed to cross a line. A quick glance at my wound revealed it was still spreading. I tugged my sleeve back down. "But I'm not supposed to use it."

Rain flicked his wrists, and my clothes were wrinkle-free. He frowned. "I don't know how to do hair."

"I've never really cared what people thought," I said, smoothing my hair back as best as I could and twisting it into a knot. "Until now...with you...in our city."

He slipped his hand in mine and led us toward the door. "My heart swells every time you call it our city. This is your home. Our home."

The two guards opened the door and bowed to us. I'd been raised to ignore them even though I didn't always do it, but that wasn't what I wanted the future of the kingdom to be, so I inclined my head toward them. Rain did the same.

I took the stairs two at a time, and Rain matched every step. He tugged me around a corner and pulled me against his chest. His lips were hot on mine, and I couldn't get enough of him.

"Still want to snuggle?" he asked.

"No, not at all." I shook my head.

"Good." He scooped me up and carried me the rest of the way to our room.

I reached for the doorknob and turned. The power went off. All of it—electrical and magical.

CHAPTER 31
NO POWER
ARI

No lights. No phones. And the scariest part...no magic. We had nothing but our senses. Rain and I jogged straight to Gemma and Laurel's room. Albert had taken them once to get to me, and I could see him attempting it again because he thought I wouldn't expect it.

Marius? I called down the bond, but received no response. *Where are you? What is happening?*

Rain pounded on the door, and without the noise from TVs and the hum of the other electrical items, the sound was almost deafening.

Laurel opened the door, and thanks to our fae vision, we could see his bewildered face. "Again?"

Rain leaned to one side of the door. "It appears so, but it's our magic too."

"I can tell. I feel heavy," Laurel said. "And slow."

"Are you all okay?" I asked.

"Yes, everyone was asleep." Gemma appeared over his shoulder, a groggy expression on her face.

Laurel shifted aside. "I'll make us some coffee...No, I won't."

He turned. "Anyone want water?"

Thirst hit me as soon as he mentioned the liquid. I raised my hand. "Me, please."

"Are you still running a fever?" Gemma asked.

Laurel crossed the room and felt my forehead. "You feel warm."

"I..." I sighed. "There might be a reason for that."

"We went for a swim," Rain supplied.

Gemma frowned and turned her narrowed gaze on Rain. "The water had to be freezing this time of year."

"No, it was fine," I said, drawing her attention back to me, and seeing how concerned she was. "I needed a break from all the...noise."

Laurel retrieved one of the orb lights like Whit had used from a drawer. He tossed it into the air, and the room was illuminated as if the moon was granting us an audience. The similarity to the night sky comforted me, but it didn't extinguish my uneasiness.

"Mommy?" Drew called down the hall.

My heart shattered into so many pieces. I knew what it was like to wake up looking for your mother to only discover she was still dead and nothing you did would bring her back. I met him halfway and crouched down, holding my arms out.

"Ari," he said, a smile in his voice. His blond hair was a mess from sleep, but he looked ethereal. "You're here."

"I am," I ran a hand through his hair. "Shouldn't you be in bed?"

"Mommy told me to wake up," he said.

Oh, this sweet boy. I pitied his loss. I understood those dreams that seemed so real. "Your mommy isn't here. Remember?"

"She whispered into my dream and told me to get out of bed. I have to warn everyone."

Fear skated up my spine, and the others gathered around us. Gemma rubbed Drew's back.

"Warn us about what?" I asked.

"He's coming for you, Ari," Drew said.

Albert's face flashed in my mind. My gut roiled. I didn't have to ask, but I did. "Who, sweetheart?"

"The bad guy."

I held my profanities inside, but I wanted to scream them. "Our father?" I hated even using that term, but it was how Drew knew him.

He nodded. "He's not our father anymore."

I knew it, but I hadn't planned to tell Drew the truth for years. He didn't deserve to have those memories destroyed at such a young age. My heart broke into a thousand pieces for the grief he would experience for years after this moment. "No, you're right. That man is not our father."

"Drew?" Phina called from the room. "You left, and we were in the middle of the game."

"Game?" Gemma asked, picking Phina up in her arms.

"Yes, we were playing with Neala," Phina said, patting Gemma's face. "Drew's friend from the mountain."

The same name as the sprite who visited my dreams before the battle...that couldn't be a coincidence. "Neala?" I lifted my brother's chin. "Who's Neala, Drew?"

"The sprite who let me see my mommy," he said, pointing in a direction that I was sure meant to be far from here. "In the mountain."

"I see. And does this sprite come to your dreams often?"

"No, just since we met her."

That was pretty frequent by my count. Either the sprite was preparing them for something or interfering. "What do you do in your dreams?"

"Play games." Phina cheered.

"What games?" Laurel asked.

"I was the healer this time," Phina said. "I had the power to heal everyone from any injury. It was fun to help."

I looked at Gemma, and her face wore a shocked expression that matched my astonishment.

The power flickered like it tried to come back on. I looked around and back at Drew. "Is this you?"

He shook his head. "It's the bad man...the not-our-father man."

If this was Albert, then he was too close. We were all in danger.

"And you are sure, Drew?" I asked one last time. "The not-our-father man is doing this?"

Drew nodded.

Fuck. The power roared back to life around us. I sat Drew down, and Gemma did the same with Phina.

"Go play in your room and let us do some adult talking," Gemma said.

I didn't want to assume they would be safe in there, but it wasn't any riskier than them being with us. The kids happily padded off. "We need to get to Leana and get the children out of here. If Albert is behind this, he's already in the city even if we can't pinpoint his location."

"We haven't been able to confirm the reports," Rain said. "But, with the reported potential sightings, it does seem like everything is pointing to him."

Did you know he was here? I stared my mate down.

Not with certainty.

We'll discuss that later. "I trust Drew," I said. "His words were his."

Gemma surveyed the hall. "Phina has never lied, so we have no reason not to believe them."

"Why haven't the cameras picked him up?" Laurel asked.

Rain pulled out his phone. "I don't know, but he is powerful. It's possible he's found a way around them."

"I think we make a stand," Gemma said, turning to me. "I'm tired of living in fear of the man who caused our mother to die a slow death."

"Interestingly, I told my mate the same thing earlier

this evening," I said, running a hand over my hair. Albert was never going to stop coming for us, and more fae would die the longer he was out there. It might be one of us, and if I was going to die, I wanted to take out as many of his followers and, with any luck, him too.

"We can't go after him without a plan," Rain said, resting a hand on my lower back. I leaned into him.

"Albert is cunning and a master of strategic warfare. He was difficult to defeat because he thinks of a problem from every possible angle and anticipates outcomes with precision."

"Careful, Rain. You sound like a fan," Gemma said.

His posture went rigid. "Not at all. My father is dead because of him. I want Albert's head hanging as a door knocker on our front door."

I stared at Rain, blinking through a haze. I'd seen his fierce demeanor many times, but this was a whole different persona. How had he come to the court in our prison kingdom and stood face-to-face with my father without killing him on the spot? How did he love me in spite of my parentage?

Laurel patted Rain's shoulder. "We lost many in the war, and none of us is to blame. We simply tried to survive until General Daphina figured out how to trap him."

Rain gazed down on me, and tears pooled in the corners of his eyes. His hurt went so much deeper than I realized. Even though our grief was centuries apart, we were the same. "I'm sorry," he said. "I wouldn't have you if it wasn't for him, but I still want him dead."

I wrapped my uninjured arm around his waist and patted his chest over his heart. "I see you, Rain. I know you. You don't need to apologize," I said. "I want my father dead too."

It sounded horrible, probably made me more like Albert than I wanted to admit, but my top priority was ridding the world of his evil.

"First things first," Rain said, pulling me so close I felt confined. "We need to figure out this cure for Ari. Then we go after Albert."

Gemma looked at me almost apologetically. "Agreed. I don't think we can defeat him without you."

I sighed. An attack could be imminent, and they were still hoping for a cure. There wasn't time for that. "Was there anything in Albert's journal?"

Laurel's eyes widened. "Maybe." He started toward the door and turned like he'd forgotten something. "Wait here. I'll get it from the lab."

CHAPTER 32

LOVESICK

RAIN

Ari, Gemma, and I gathered around the dining table as Laurel opened the journal to the paragraph we'd already seen. "There are some key indicators here." He pointed to it. "But there are some points before it on what he was testing." Ari looked stoic, like she didn't expect us to get any kind of helpful answers.

She didn't have to say it. I could see in every action she took, especially after what she'd said in the garden, that she'd made her mind up. She didn't believe she'd survive the bite and was going to do what needed to be done to defeat Albert, even if it caused the infection to consume her.

"Such as?" I asked, crossing my arms to keep from taking the book. My brother was methodical, and while I appreciated his thoroughness, my patience disappeared an hour ago.

"He was searching for goddess blood. He knew there was a descendant of Nyx in their generation, but he didn't know who. He wrote this paragraph after he'd learned it was General Daphina, and he was already in love with her."

"So how does that help us?" Gemma asked.

"Because love makes people sloppy, especially in the early days when they are—"

"Lovesick," Ari said, her tone flat.

I'd take another battle scar to be in her head and know what she was thinking, but I wanted to respect her privacy.

"Exactly." Laurel's excitement would be contagious any other time, but I didn't understand why he was so happy.

"Not following you, Brother."

He flipped to almost the end of the journal and read it out loud. "She is my everything, and I can't bring myself to tell her the truth of what I am."

"Wait," Ari said. "What he is? Isn't he fae?"

"He is," Laurel said, grinning.

"I don't understand," Gemma said. "If he's fae, then what truth is he writing about? How evil he is?"

Laurel tilted his head. "Maybe, but I think he meant this." He flipped the page. "The infection had grown. I injected her blood into my veins, and an overwhelming sense of peace came over me as if I'd found my reason for existence."

"Mother was his mate," Ari whispered. "I think I'm going to vomit."

"Me too," Gemma said.

That couldn't be true. The Fates shackled the greatest general of our people to a monster...

"It doesn't end there." Laurel flipped the page. "One week later, there is no sign of infection, but my blood still carries the marker."

"Marker for what?" I asked.

"I think he was bitten by a vampire," Laurel said. "And his mate's blood healed him."

Ari gasped, and I picked her up, hugging her to me and swinging her around in a circle.

"My cure has been in front of me the entire time," Ari said, squeezing her arms around my neck.

I set her down on her feet and looked at my brother. His expression turned skeptical, and I wondered if we celebrated too soon. "How do we do this, and how much blood do you need?"

"And we're sure this will work?" Gemma asked. "Sharing fae blood has consequences, too."

"I don't want to think about Albert seeing Mother's memories..." Ari's voice trailed off.

Having the General's blood, explained how he evaded our efforts. He must have tricked her out of it, and that made me hate Albert more.

Laurel nodded. "I need to do some testing with the tissue I scraped off. I'd like to take a blood sample if that's okay with you, Brother."

"Whatever you need," I said. "Do we need to go to your lab now?"

"The sooner we do, the sooner we'll know."

Ari kissed my cheek. "We'll need to go back to the waterfall to celebrate," she whispered in my ear and then used her normal tone when she pulled back. "Since there are already a ton of samples, I'm going to hang out with Gemma and the kids."

"Of course, my goddess," I said, cupping her cheek. I leaned against the door. "Come on, Laurel. You know how much I love needles."

My brother grinned at Ari. "He passed out once when we were young after—"

"Now," I said, opening the door.

A PINCH

ARI

Gemma made us some tea and handed me a cup. The steam drifted off it as I inhaled the bergamot scent. I sat on the overstuffed alabaster-colored couch. My sister sat close to me at the bend that made an L-shape

"How are you?" I asked. My mind flashed to the torture I'd endured at our father's hand.

"Physically, I'm fine. Laurel is back to his old self." She set her cup on a coaster and focused on the window. "I dream of it every time I close my eyes. The pain, of course, but more his words. He no longer saw me as a person. I was a means to obtain the power he wanted. Laurel, on the other hand, is doing all the things he'd normally do as if it never happened."

"Laurel and Rain have lived a lot longer than us. They have seen much more than we have. Survived a war that was fought two hundred years before we were born.

Besides, Laurel is an empath. You can't judge yourself by how he copes. We each deal with pain, loss, and healing differently."

She gave me a small smile. "When did my little sister become the wise one?"

I stared into the swirling tornado in my tea. I wasn't. I'd made so many mistakes. It was my fault that my sister and her mate had been taken. "I'm sorry, Gemma. He came for me. If we hadn't gone to that Moirai game—"

She put a hand on my knee. "Stop it. Right now. As was said earlier, none of us is to blame for Albert's actions. There wasn't anything you could have done to stop him. If it hadn't been that day, it would have been another."

If I'd stayed when Albert came for me the first time or if I'd ended him when I was a captive at his palace, I might have been able to prevent what happened to her. Nothing she could say could really erase that from my mind.

"I wanted to console you," I said, tears thickening my voice.

She took the cup from my hand and set it on the oval table. My sister held her arms out. "When was the last time we had a proper sister hug?"

After our mother passed, Gemma often gave me a proper sister hug. She asked for them when I was depressed. Her own sadness the excuse, she would say she needed one, and maybe she did. As I matured, I realized she'd done it for me.

"You are trying to make me cry now," I said, leaning my head over onto her shoulder.

"No, beloved sister, I want you to be happy." She rubbed her hand up and down my back like she had when she consoled me after Mother died. "There's something I wanted to tell you that I'd noticed about Rain years ago and forgot it until I saw you again."

"What's that?"

She studied me as if she were reading me like a book. "You and Rain have the same aura. It's like a twin flame that burns around both of you."

My chest warmed with contentment. Rain and I were so much alike that my sister's revelation didn't surprise me. The Fates might have played a part, but I don't think the goddesses and gods themselves could have kept us away from each other if they had tried. "I wonder if that's a mate thing."

She shook her head. "It's not. My aura is very different from Laurel's."

"I guess it's another sign from Nyx." The goddess seemed the most obvious answer, but my heart told me love like what Rain and I had could only attract someone who could handle the kind of fire that grew between us.

"Don't make too much of it. I just thought it was interesting, and it's one of the reasons I didn't give Rain too much of a hard time for pursuing you."

Leaning back against the cushion, I stared at the ceiling. Gemma, who had kicked a fae's ass for hurting my feelings, gave Rain a pass to court me. That alone was blatant Fate interference. "Why?" I asked. "Why do you think we were given this destiny?"

"Why not us?" she asked. "We are strong, Ari, and I'm not just talking about our powers, but inside. Look at what we've overcome and survived, and we're still able to love. I don't know if Nyx selected our souls specifically, but I do know that there is no one better to lead the fae people than you."

The disquiet in my chest sat there like the weight of ten unicorns and urged me to deny my sister's proclamation. I sat up and studied her face. Her expression was serious, but I didn't see in myself what she saw. "I don't feel like a leader. Most of the time, I'd rather give the world a rude gesture and do my own thing."

Gemma scooted over and leaned her head against mine. "For as long as I can remember, you have been a leader. It is because you refuse to walk a predesigned path or fit into a mold because someone told you that you should. Those are the actions of someone who will not be afraid to challenge old laws or break rules for the betterment of the realm."

"It's not like I have a choice anyway," I said, hating the bitterness in my voice.

"You always have a choice." She straightened, tugging on the knot in my hair until it fell loose. "And your hair is definitely a choice. Maybe you should go take a shower. You can use one of ours if you want. The kids should be asleep for hours, so we could watch a show while we wait for our males to get back."

Unable to concentrate on the show, my mind drifted to the future. I wanted Drew to live with me and Rain, but he seemed so happy with Phina that I wouldn't separate them. That felt wrong. If the cure Laurel was brewing up didn't work, then it wouldn't matter anyway, and I wouldn't want him to face that kind of upheaval and loss again.

"You might need to point me in the direction," I said, forcing a smile.

A SHOWER WAS what I needed. Gemma had even put fresh clothes out for me. I heard low voices in the other room, specifically Rain's. A pit in my stomach twisted into despair. The news wasn't good. I couldn't hear the conversation, but the word repeated in my head was "no." I knew on a subconscious level it hadn't worked. The infection had spread and covered most of my forearm. I was either going to die or turn, and neither of those options suited me. *Nyx, is this really what you saved me for?*

I didn't expect her to answer. She'd given me a second chance, and the rest was up to me. The mark where she'd healed me from the poison arrow tingled. I turned to the mirror to look, and it sparkled like the stars. *What are you trying to tell me? I don't understand.*

The mark twinged like a pinch. *Fuck.* I kicked my clothes from the evening across the room. The release of my anger helped. I'd forgotten, in such a short time, what it was like to get my frustrations out by sparring. If my fate was sealed by this bite, then I was damn well going to do the things that reminded me who I was.

Marius? I need to spar. Where are you?

In the courtyard. I just left my brother. What's wrong?

Relief warmed my chest that he responded. *I'm pissed at you, at my family, at the realm, at Nyx...You name it, I'm mad at it.*

I wondered when you were going to get to this point.

Fuck you. Meet me at the sparring building.

I'll be the one on four legs.

Are you fucking kidding me? Was that supposed to be a joke? I didn't even want to think about what had him in such a good mood, especially when I was in about as foul a one as I could remember.

I still had to get past the room full of my family. There wasn't a back door. The balcony was off the living room. *Fuck every last second of this day.*

Straightening my clothes, I proceeded to walk out front. Everyone stopped talking as soon as I entered the room—a sure sign I'd been the topic.

"Ari—" Rain said, his voice solemn.

"You don't need to verbalize it. I already know the tests failed. Marius is waiting for me. I'll be back...whenever we're done."

"Arianna," Gemma said.

I didn't dare stop or turn around or glance over my shoulder, afraid I would lose my shit or worse, say something I didn't mean. Space. All I needed was to go stab something.

CHAPTER 34
A THREAT
ARI

Marius leaned against the wall of the training center in his faelike form. He looked far too relaxed. His easy demeanor flooded our bond, and I wasn't in the mood to be cozy.

"I thought you said you'd be on all fours." I smiled, faking a punch at him and pressing my hand to the entrance pad.

"You seem better," he said. "But I can tell it's an act."

I wasn't, and he was right. My magic itched under my skin to be unleashed, and my emotions only made it worse. "I want to destroy things. Like I want to burn down buildings and call the earth up to bury the ruins."

"Where is this coming from?"

"Can't I just have a bad day?" I asked, looking around to find the building completely vacant. I didn't want to rehash failed serums and my impending vampirism. All of those things could fuck off to the depths of the most loathsome realm.

"You can, but I know what your bad days look like. This isn't it." He eyed me with a face full of skepticism.

I let out a long breath, debating whether to tell him, but he probably already knew. The bandage itched. *That's new.* I pulled up my sleeve and ripped the gauzy shit off, dying to scratch it, but that would just make it bleed. "The vampire that bit me and exploded left a calling card, and it's infected."

"Ari," Marius said, looking at my arm. "Have the healers not been able to draw the venom out?"

"No, and my blood, or should I say Nyx's blood, is part of the problem." Apparently, goddess blood and being a goddess worked differently.

"I can't here," he said, lowering his voice. "But let me try when we are somewhere that isn't watched by a camera."

"Great," I said with sarcasm, because I knew it wasn't going to matter. "Fuck. I forgot there were cameras in here. Now, everyone will know."

"There's no sound and the images are not clear enough," Marius said, letting my arm drop. "They will assume you are wounded but won't know how exactly."

"I want to break some shit. Can we kick some ass?" I asked, walking backward toward one of the enclosed rooms. The frustration inside me set its sights on one outlet. No other fae was as powerful as I, so I could hurt them. Marius could handle anything in my arsenal, and he knew my moves. "If I don't break something, I am going to burn this entire city down."

"I'm at the service of my charge," Marius said, dipping his head.

"This nice side of you is new, and I absolutely do not want to know any details," I said, opening the door. "I still have nightmares about you and Amelia."

Marius huffed, following me, and I hit the panel to close us in.

"I don't like this. It feels like a cage."

"Is it wrong that I'm glad it makes you feel uncomfortable?" I stretched my arms above my head and cracked my neck from side to side. In the time he'd been my guardian, I'd never had the upper hand. *I'm going to enjoy this.*

Marius chuckled. "It is, but since when has that stopped you?"

I smirked. "Ready, Daddy Marius?"

"You are still young, fae, so you better be careful."

A wall of wind rushed over me. I held my position, but I slid backward until I slammed into the wall.

"Oh, that was a mistake." I turned in a circle and released fire. The flames rolled from my fingers with ease. A twisting column of burning tornado flew toward him.

Marius opened his mouth and blew a puff of wind at it, extinguishing it like he'd pinched the flame of a candle between his fingers.

Stunned he was able to snuff it out with little effort, my mouth fell open, and I had to think about closing it. "You've been holding back all these years."

"You weren't ready for everything I can wield until now."

"I had to die and come back for you to show me your full strength? That's something a unicorn would say." I spied a pitcher of water out of the corner of my eye. Ignoring my thirst, I snapped my fingers. The water soaked him.

"I believe we had this discussion about me and water."

"Oh, you don't like for your hair to get messed up." I laughed.

Marius's horn appeared, and I knew whatever was coming for me was going to be rough. The table in the room came flying at my head.

I threw my hands up, summoning anything that could prevent the pain I was about to feel. Silver light shot from open palms, and the table splintered into a thousand pieces like the vampire who'd drunk my blood.

"What the fuck?" I whispered, watching the tiny chips rain down on the room.

A deafening sound like cats being slaughtered rang out. Were we under attack? Marius's startled expression made my anxiety rise.

"What is that?" I shouted over the repetitive tone.

"Alarms," Marius shouted back. "Apparently, these rooms can't handle us."

"Alarms?" I'd never experienced such a terrible screeching noise, and if I never heard them again, it would be too soon. "Let's get out of here."

I pressed my hand to the panel, but nothing happened.

I tried again, but it didn't respond. One more try told me we weren't getting out via my hand. I covered my ears again. "It's not working."

"Let me try," Marius said.

I moved aside, and he put his hand on it. The panel lit up red like blood.

"It must think we're a threat," I yelled.

Marius let his glamour go and kicked his back foot to the panel, busting it. The panel shattered, but the door didn't open.

"Now it really thinks we're a threat."

He glared at me. "I've called Cyrus and Casimir to come get us."

"Or we could just break the glass."

I summoned the same power I'd used on the table.

"Ari," Marius said, his voice landing between the pulsing sound. "Don't. They'll be here in a moment."

His gaze settled on my arm. I glanced at the bite, and it had taken over more of my flesh. *If I turn, Marius, promise me you'll end whatever I become.*

I will do all I can to save you. It's not just my oath to you as my charge but my word as your friend. A tear formed in the corner of his eye, but it never fell. The evil alarm cut off. I scanned for the source and saw Casimir at a panel on the opposite side of the building.

My ears throbbed, but I was thankful for the noise to be gone. She glanced over her shoulder at us and punched some keys on the keyboard in front of her. I surveyed the room for Cyrus but didn't see him. His absence was very noticeable, especially since Marius said he had called both of them. Unicorn didn't refuse their leader if they were able-bodied. The door opened. Marius and I exchanged a glance that said what we couldn't say out loud or in our thoughts, and he nodded in the direction for me to go first.

"Thank you," I said to Casimir.

"You two shouldn't be in here," she said, but not to me. She looked straight at Marius.

Unicorn didn't speak to him like that.

"Close your mouth, Ari," he said, without looking at me. My mouth was, in fact, wide open.

"My sister showed me this training center and said it was for anyone's use."

Casimir turned to me, and the dispassionate anger in her eyes made me take a step back. "For fae, yes." She turned back to Marius. "You are not fae." Then she looked at me. "And you are of Nyx's descent. You two should not be in here."

"It's fine, Casi," Marius said, using a particularly sweet tone.

"Don't Casi me, you idiot."

I stifled a laugh. My first impression of Casimir had been wrong. I liked her.

Her stance was a strong posture to take in the company of their leader. She was a good match for Marius, even if she looked ready to fight him. "The others come. No doubt notified of the horrid alarm ringing like a death toll."

As if she summoned them, Rain entered, followed by

Gemma. My sister's expression was disbelief. Laurel wasn't with them.

"Is everything okay?" Rain asked, looking me over.

"No one is injured," Casimir answered for us in a biting tone.

"Ari?" Gemma asked, ignoring Casimir's response.

"We're fine. Marius and I were sparring and then that incredibly annoying sound started blasting."

"Laurel wants us to meet him in the lab," Rain said, his tone defeated. "If you are up to it."

"I am." I turned to my bonded. "Thank you." I smiled. "And good luck."

Ari, I still want to try to heal you.

If Laurel doesn't have good news, we'll try. He wouldn't be able to. I didn't need special powers to know that answer.

CHAPTER 35
A SEER

ARI

Laurel sat at the desk in his lab, punching away on his computer. Papers, tablets, and instruments were scattered about on the desk and surrounding tables. He was so into his work that he didn't hear us come in.

"Brother?" Rain asked.

Laurel looked up, surprise on his face. "Oh, good. You're here."

"I already figured out the cure didn't work for me." I dropped into one of the chairs in front of his desk. Rain took the other seat.

He looked at me apologetically. "No, it didn't, but I think I know why."

I crossed my arms. "I'm listening."

"You're..." He thought for a moment. "Albert doesn't have goddess blood. It was your mother who did."

"Yes, I'm aware," I said. "Why is that important?"

Laurel glanced at the paperwork. "Albert was the one who was bitten. It was your mother whose blood saved him."

"So, you think because it's the reverse, it doesn't work." The blood could protect me but not heal me from an ultimate death sentence like a vampire bite...or a poison-tipped arrow.

"Kind of." He twisted his hand back and forth. "I think your blood is preventing it from spreading as fast as it normally would."

"Yes, that's clear. I'd have turned by now if there wasn't something slowing it down."

The door opened and Marius entered in his unicorn form. Even in his natural state and without being in his head, I could tell something was bothering him.

"Laurel was recapping what we know about my situation," I said, ignoring the urge to scratch the wound to relieve the uncomfortable sensation. The irritation was mind-numbing.

He walked over to join us, where Laurel spread out papers and had some kind of graph and a jumble of numbers and letters up on a screen. "I'd like to try to heal you myself."

"I'm not sure it's wise to use random magic on it," Laurel said.

"So, we do nothing?" Rain asked, his tone laced with anger. "It's up to you, Ari."

"My magic is ancient. Random is an insult to it."

The inflammation had me on edge, and I wondered if

my physical discomfort rubbed off on the others. The tension needed to be broken, and that was on me.

I pulled up my sleeve and exposed the spiderweb of purple veins shooting out from the bite that had grown significantly in size. I pushed the material up just past my elbow, but the infection had advanced well beyond what was visible. *Goddess, it's so much worse.* Shocked it appeared to be moving faster as it spread, I realized how short my time was before I became something that wasn't me.

Rain made a low noise.

I hated he was worried about me. "We're going to try this."

Marius closed his eyes, and his entire body stilled. A single golden tear drifted over his lashes and down his cheek. I held my finger out and let the bead roll onto the end.

Overcome with the hope his tear symbolized, my throat tightened. I worked through a swallow to loosen the ache. "You're sure you want to waste a piece of you on me, Marius?"

He opened his eyes and nuzzled the side of my head, huffing hot air through my hair. "A tear would never be wasted on you."

Marius loved me. They all did, but Marius had been a father figure I didn't know I needed. He gave a part of himself because he wanted to save me. I pressed my lips together and ran my tongue over my front teeth until I could speak again. They were all staring at me, and my hand shook. Careful not to drop the precious liquid, I rubbed it over the original bite marks. Bubbles formed, but it didn't hurt. The tear soaked into the wound, and the incessant itching subsided. The wound didn't heal, but the pain had abated. The change was small, but it gave me a little hope. "It feels better. Maybe that's a good sign."

"May I?" Laurel held out his hand.

I placed my wrist in his palm.

He examined it without touching the skin. "It doesn't appear to be as inflamed. It's not healed, but maybe that will slow the spread down while we find the right answer."

"I appreciate all you've done, Laurel, and you, Marius, for giving up a tear for me...and Rain, for standing beside me." Bracing for their denial, I couldn't ignore what was happening in my body. As much as I didn't want to leave them or any of my loved ones, my time was finite. "I don't think this is meant to heal, for whatever reason. My second chance wasn't for a lifetime. Whatever task I returned for is either done or nearly complete."

"This doesn't sound like the fae I am in love with," Rain said, crossing his arms and staring out the window.

"I have to agree. The princess I trained from a young age is a fighter who wouldn't know how to quit."

"Maybe she matured. Acceptance is a sign of grace and humility." My mark from Nyx burned in my side. I reached for it. "Agh."

Rain grasped my arm, steadying me. "What is it?"

I lifted my shirt enough to expose the painful area. "Am I on fire?"

He shook his head. "No, but your mark is glowing. I think Nyx is sending a message that you have more to do here."

"It did that in the bathroom earlier too."

"Before you tried to destroy the training center?" Rain's mouth quirked up on one side.

"I didn't try to destroy it, but yes, it was right before I went there," I said, letting the hem of my tunic fall.

The door opened again. I expected to see Gemma, but Merrick entered instead. "Your sister said I could find you here. I brought my mother, and you're not going to say no because she has knowledge that can help."

"What's one more person?" I said, pulling my sleeve down.

She waved her mother inside. Zabrina came forward adorned in regal attire and perfectly coiffed. She looked much better than at the camp.

"Thank you again for healing me," Zabrina said, her hands tucked into her pockets.

"You're welcome."

"I'd like to look at your injury if you don't mind." She cleared her throat.

"What is it you think you can tell us?" Rain asked.

Zabrina leveled a gaze on Rain. "Whether or not Arianna is going to turn into a vampire."

I bunched the material up around my elbow in a rush, tired of showing people the wound.

Her lip curled in disgust. "I've never seen a bite look

like this, but I've never seen anyone with goddess blood who's been bitten."

I started to pull the sleeve down.

"I'm not done yet," Zabrina said in a scolding tone. She took hold of my arm, and her eyes clouded. "It's uncertain. Your decisions...I can't see them, but they will determine whether you are saved or turned."

She could read the future, but she couldn't see what mine held. In the prison kingdom, my freedom to make choices had been a façade. In the seat of the fae kingdom, every decision I made mattered, and the consequences were mine. The significance drained my strength.

"You're a seer," Marius said.

"Not a practicing one," she said, her voice low. "I gave it up many years ago."

"Thank you for trying, Mother," Merrick said.

"Of course. I'll see you at home." Zabrina touched Merrick's arm and turned her powerful gaze on me. The ferocity urged me to step back, but I maintained my position. "Trust Nyx's plan."

Her word choice, so similar to what Nyx herself had said to me, made me cock my head.

Merrick nodded and watched her mother leave.

No one spoke until the door was shut behind her.

"Why did she stop practicing?" Marius asked.

"The war. She couldn't take the death she foresaw. Fae would come from all across the kingdom for her. She wanted to help people, but foretelling death helped no one. Some would try to avoid it and beg her to tell them how, but she can only see what will be based on the decision."

"And she couldn't see mine," I said, and I didn't know if that was a good or bad sign. "That's why she couldn't tell me my future. Is that normal? To not be able to see someone's decisions?"

"I've never heard her say that before, and I don't remember much around that time in the war. My interests were elsewhere."

"Thank you for asking her to try." I squeezed her hand, knowing it must have been hard to ask her mother to help.

She looked at Marius. "I have read about healing properties—"

"We already tried my tear," Marius said. "And that is not for a fae to ask."

The mark ached and twinged again. I lifted the hem of my shirt and turned the spot toward Rain. "Am I glowing again?"

He nodded. "That has to mean something."

"Maybe the vampire venom is burning the goddess blood out of me." *Nyx, I don't know what you're trying to tell me.* The mark flared. "Fuck."

"Ari, has Whit seen that mark?" Merrick asked.

"No," I said. "I don't go around pulling my shirt up for everyone."

She smirked. "That's not just a symbol for Nyx."

"What do you mean? Isn't it the triple moon?"

"It is, but see that little swirling design?" She pointed

but was careful not to touch the glowing skin. "That is not part of it."

"I can't see without a mirror," I said.

Rain cast an uncertain glance at Laurel. "I've never seen that before. Have you?"

"No," he said. "Was it there from the beginning?"

Rain shook his head. "No, that's new."

"Is there a bathroom in here?" I asked. "I need to see what you're seeing."

Merrick handed me a small compact and held my shirt while I twisted to get a good look. "It stopped glowing, so I guess that's a good sign." My gaze travelled over the tattoo-like mark. "I don't recognize that symbol. Marius?"

He looked stoic, which meant he knew what the mark meant. "It's been many lifetimes. I cannot be sure, and it might not mean the same now. You should consult your historian."

I narrowed my eyes at him. *Really?*

"I don't want to give false hope," he said, speaking out loud versus replying down the bond. He wanted the others to hear. "The last time I know of reference to that symbol was passed down through unicorn leaders, so I am bound by an oath not to reveal the details. However, I can say, the last time I know of it being seen was when Nyx walked this realm."

Goddess...literally. What had she marked me with? And for what?

Rain cut his gaze to Marius. "Does that mean the goddess is returning?"

"I cannot say," Marius said, and his tone suggested he was honest.

"When I was with her, I got the impression she couldn't return. She could heal me and send me back, but she couldn't walk in the realm."

"She was barred from entering the realm in her full form," Marius said. "As punishment for her gift to my kind."

Fucking gods and their punishments. Everything was so shrouded in mystery with them.

"I'm sorry," Merrick said, blinking rapidly.

"Who has the power to punish Nyx?" Laurel asked.

"A being who is no longer, but whose magic still sews the realms together," Marius said.

I wanted to throw something at him. He wouldn't intentionally hold back information unless he was bound by an oath to not reveal. But would he let me die for the same oath? "You know I hate it when you answer questions in such a manner."

"Then I'm thankful we're not in the training center," he said, inclining his head toward me.

"We need to talk to Whit and maybe Orla too. She's a symbol expert," Merrick said, letting go of the hem of my shirt. She took slow steps toward the door.

"I'll call Orla and have her meet us there," Rain said, looping his arm around my waist. His support was the strength I needed. He looked at Laurel. "You coming?"

"No, I'm going to stay here and keep running tests. I have this feeling I've missed something."

I was relieved that my state of annoyance hadn't deterred him. He was trying so hard to save me. "Thank you, Laurel. I'm sorry the discomfort made me hateful earlier."

"I'm a healer. I've seen worse." His kindness and easy-going demeanor were a blessing. He was the exact support Gemma needed.

Marius walked toward the door. "I need to see how Cyrus is doing with the vampire younglings. I'll meet up with you afterward."

CHAPTER 36

BLOOD OF OLD

RAIN

Orla beat us to the museum, and Whit greeted all of us with a warm smile, even Merrick. Quinn sat at the desk, having been found at some point. Given no one was talking about it, I assumed it was in the bed of someone his family considered undesirable. In the same manner, they would have likely called Laurel and me had my father not been handed the throne by his sister.

"Rain," Orla said, embracing me. Her golden eyes were warm. "Always good to get a call from you."

She'd often brought fresh-baked goods to the house after my mother passed and before Father was thrust into the seat of the realm. She'd never married, and I often wondered why. They'd certainly seemed to care for each other. "Thank you for coming."

"Arianna," Orla said, bowing her head in reference. "Though I wasn't free to speak when we first met, I will tell you now. I'm impressed by what you have accomplished at such a young age."

"Ari, please." She held out her hand.

Orla pulled her into a hug. "I couldn't do this in front of the others. I have a reputation. But I loved your mother like a sister." She released Ari, and tears pooled in the corner of my mate's eyes. Orla pointed at Merrick. "You better not tell Zabrina, or I'll make your life hell."

Merrick remained silent and gave Orla a small smile. I was curious what Orla had over Merrick.

"You knew my mother too?" Ari asked, her voice sad. "It seems like everyone knew her but me."

"Everyone did know her, because she was the best of us," Orla said, nodding. "But only a few of us really knew her from our university days."

"I'd like to hear those stories sometime." Ari smiled at Orla, but it wasn't her usual smile. There was a bit of sadness in it, and her eyes didn't light up. "If I'm around to hear them," she said under her breath, but I caught it.

She was discouraged. Not that she didn't have reason to be, but I wanted to erase it for her...go back in time and be there to stop the vampire who bit her. Time traveling wasn't a fae skill, but if it was, I'd master it and rip the head from the vampire's shoulders before it ever got near my love.

"All the books we've been reviewing are still in the room. We can move there," Whit said, holding a hand out for the group to go first.

"Where is the symbol you need me to read?" Orla asked, thumbing through one of the books.

"It's not in a book," I said.

Orla's mouth formed an 'O.'

Ari lifted her shirt. "Me showing parts of my body is becoming a weird thing."

Orla laughed and knelt. The sounds died in her throat. "How long have you had this mark?"

Ari's gaze found mine, and anxiety wrinkled her beautiful face. "I trust Orla."

My mate swallowed hard. "The triple moon symbol appeared after Nyx cured me from being shot with a poison arrow."

"Interesting," Orla said, running her fingers over the marked skin. "And the other was part of it?"

Ari flinched from the touch. Her eyes went distant like she was trapped in the memory, but she recovered in seconds. "No, it just appeared today."

"The skin is so cold where the mark is," Orla said, touching the mark again. It glowed in response, though not as bright as in the Laurel's lab. "I've never seen a gifted symbol do that, but I do know what this mark means."

Finally, something wasn't like walking through fire to get an answer.

"And that is?" Merrick asked, moving closer.

"Blood of old."

I bit down on the inside of my jaw. The old blood running through her veins wasn't exactly news. "Why would a mark appear on Ari for that?"

"The saying has many versions of its meaning," Whit said, "depending on what part of our history you look to."

Orla straightened. "The way it's drawn here is the oldest. This is from the time Nyx walked our realm."

"Marius, my bonded, said that too." Ari's curiosity meant she had hope.

Thank the goddesses and gods. I thought the fight had died, but the warrior I loved was still in there.

Orla smiled again. "I know your bonded. We fought beside each other in the war. It's no accident he chose you or that these marks have appeared. You are our next leader. You will sit on the throne of old and usher in a new time, much like the blood that runs through your veins did. Nyx is urging you to change the world. The question is if you are ready to accept that."

Ari's posture was rigid. She didn't say a word, but her focus remained with Orla..

I'd known Ari was destined for greatness before I met her, but she didn't like change that wasn't of her own doing. "What kind of change?"

"That remains to unfold from what path Ari chooses." Orla rested a hand on Ari's cheek. My mate's attention was on Orla's every word. "Do not be afraid. You have the warrior spirit and strategic mind of your mother and the blood of a goddess in your veins. You are exactly what our realm needs to continue."

CHAPTER 37

JUST ASK HER
ARI

Nyx had given me so many gifts, and I still didn't know if I would live to see them through. What if I ushered in the change only to leave everyone I love behind? My heart cracked and shattered on that thought. Orla renewed my hope, though, and I refused to believe that my life was meant to end like that. My story wasn't at the mercy of anyone else but me.

Rain talked me into taking a nap before the sun came up, but I couldn't sleep. I tossed and turned until I found myself in the kitchen looking for some of the chamomile tea.

I threw up a wall of wind around the bedroom door to let him sleep while I fumbled around for the kettle. Filling it, I set it on the stove and turned the burner on to what I hoped was high enough to make the water boil.

I glanced down the hall and didn't see a light, so I

assumed Rain was still sleeping soundly. We'd come so far in a short time, and I wanted a future with him. *Nyx, what am I doing? What is it you want from me?*

Starlight glittered in the steam rising from the kettle. *You have all you need in front of you. The answer is already there. Look for it, not in the obvious places, but in those you wouldn't normally seek.*

The kettle whistled, and the starlight disappeared from view.

Apparently, being blessed by Nyx didn't make her any less cryptic than any of the other goddesses and gods. Look in a place I wouldn't normally seek—so, not elders, not books, not unicorn, not my own fucking brain. Where did that leave? Talking to trees or horses or children. Children...Phina had said something when she was groggy and half asleep. Asking a child gave me an awkward pit in my stomach. I was an adult, her aunt, and should protect her from the world, especially vampire.

"What are you doing up?" Rain asked, rubbing his eyes. Half-asleep looked sexy on him, but there wasn't a time he didn't look hot. "We haven't slept but maybe an hour."

"You slept. I messed up the sheets, twisting around before I gave in and got up."

He hugged me to him. "We're going to get through this. We will have our life together."

I looked up at him, my throat aching with unshed tears. "Will we? I keep asking Nyx for guidance, and either she doesn't answer or gives me something cryptic."

"She's talking to you?" He tipped his head to the side.

Marius had told me not to tell anyone, but this was Rain…my mate. "Kind of. If you call telling me to look for answers in places that weren't obvious, which I thought we were already doing, then yes, she's talking to me."

His expression turned contemplative. "Did you think of a place to try?"

"The only thing I came up with is kids because of the dream Phina had, but I can't ask a child that little if she knows the cure for her aunt's nasty vampire bite."

"Phina is wise well beyond her years. Have you seen her room? She solves problems that fae four times her age can't. If your gut is telling you to ask our niece, then I think you should."

"I don't know if I can take another dead end," I said, leaning my head against his chest. His heart thudded in a steady beat, and it calmed me better than any tea could. No other options had presented themselves, and I didn't know the right thing to do. Phina was a child…my niece.

"But what if it is the answer?" he whispered into my ear. "You were talking about living earlier. Don't you want to try?"

I smiled against his chest. "Since when are you the optimist?"

He chuckled, and the sound rumbled against me.

Even if I didn't think we'd cure the bite, I still wanted to live every minute I had left. "How long until sunrise?"

"Mmm…probably an hour or so."

"How about you take me to bed and remind me what

I'm living for?" Marius's tear had slowed the progression, and every moment felt borrowed. I wanted to be in the one place that made me feel cocooned in safety.

Rain scooped me up into his arms. "That is a request I will fulfill on command every time."

LEANA STAYED with Drew and Phina while Gemma met us in Laurel's lab. I wanted their permission to ask my niece if she knew the answer. If they disagreed with me and Rain, I wouldn't push, and we'd continue to look for other options.

"You look like shit, Brother." Rain clapped Laurel on the back. His brother had dark circles under his eyes as if he hadn't slept at all. In fact, he looked as if he hadn't left the lab all night.

"You're not looking particularly well rested to be so hap—" Laurel said, glancing between us. "Never mind."

"How's your arm looking?" Gemma asked.

Marius's tear had slowed the progress, but it expanded and itched more with every second that ticked by. I studied what I could see, fighting the urge to dig my nails in and scratch. It looked mostly unchanged, but the infection still spread. "About the same as the last time we saw each other."

"I wish I could say I discovered some miracle here, but I haven't," Laurel said, hanging his head in his hands.

Gemma rubbed his shoulders. "What did you need both of us here for? And you better not say you're running away to turn vampire or I'll throw every ounce of magic I have at you."

I smiled. "No, I'm not running away, at least not yet." I took a deep, calming breath. "Phina had mentioned a dream about knowing how to heal everything, and I know she's quite gifted. I wanted to ask your permission to see if she might know the answer here."

Gemma's face skewed in confusion. "Why would you think Phina would know that?"

"Nyx answered me, albeit cryptically, and told me to look where I hadn't for the answer. Children came to mind, and I remembered Phina's dream."

Laurel looked up, and Gemma draped her arms around his neck. "I don't have any concerns about you speaking to her. Maybe don't show her the bite."

I reached for Rain, and he laced his fingers with mine.

One side of Gemma's mouth quirked up. "Unless she asks to see it. She does like to look at some grotesque things."

I frowned at her. "Thanks a lot."

Gemma gave me the soft look she had done many times after Mother passed. "Seriously, Ari. You're her aunt, and she loved you before she actually met you. She'd want to help, and honestly, she's probably wondering why you haven't asked her already."

I pondered if my sister was still in denial that I might die or turn eventually. "You're not worried about protecting her from the trauma and knowing I might not be around?"

"Maybe we don't tell her that part," Gemma said. "Just ask her the straightforward question, like 'I'm sick from a vampire. Do you know how to cure it?"

"She's seen a vampire. She knows what they do. We've talked to her about it. It's not going to scare her if you phrase it the way Gemma suggested," Laurel said.

"Thank you." I walked around the desk and wrapped my arms around them both. I'd been so worried about how they would react, and they showed nothing but love, which is what I should have expected. "Thank you."

A weight pressed against my back. "I can't see the three of you hugging and not join."

"And it just got awkward," Gemma said, laughing.

Rain straightened. "Thank you both," he said, his tone serious. "I feel it in my gut that this is the right path."

"Yeah," my sister said. "It does feel right."

Their confidence gave me hope. Relief carried over me like a gentle breeze.

CHAPTER 38

THE CURE

RAIN

Leana had taken Drew to her home to play. Laurel, Ari, and I sat on the monster of a couch Gemma had chosen for their living room. I gave Ari space, so Phina could sit next to her if she wanted. I'd noticed how my niece liked to be in the personal space of the person she spoke to.

Gemma held Phina's hand as they walked into the room. My niece's eyes were wider than usual, but she carried herself with a confidence beyond one of her young age. "Are you okay with all of us here while Ari asks you some questions, or do you want to be alone with her?"

"We're family," she said, holding the doll I'd had crafted for her birthday last year. The dollmaker had used a picture to match the hair and face, and it looked so much like her. Phina wore the dress Gemma had made for her that matched the doll's. I found the doll and matching dress unnerving, but Phina loved it.

"That doesn't mean we have to all be here," Gemma said, giving Phina another chance.

"No, I like it. There's more love in the room when we're all together," she said. "I do miss Cyrus."

"So do I," Gemma said, her voice losing its power. "But he'll be back in a few days."

With their mate bond, I was surprised he'd been able to stay away this long. Marius had been rather tight-lipped with Ari over where Cyrus was and when he'd be back, only offering that he was with the vampire children. Her bonded had been firm in his stance that the two vampire were Cyrus's responsibility, despite their role in rescuing Gemma and Laurel.

"Can I sit with you, Aunt Ari?" Phina asked, swinging the doll in one hand.

"Of course." Ari smiled at her.

Phina crawled onto the couch next to her. Ari hugged our niece, and Phina took that opportunity to climb into her lap.

"That's better," she said.

Ari kissed the top of her head. "You give the best hugs."

"I know," Phina said. I had to stifle a laugh.

Ari touched the face of the doll. "She's so pretty. Just like you."

"Uncle Rain gave her to me. He doesn't like dolls."

I laughed. "No, they don't appeal to me. That is true."

Phina giggled.

"Is it okay if I ask you about vampire?" Ari asked, tentatively.

Phina's little brows furrowed in an expression that was identical to one I'd seen Gemma make many times. "Okay. But don't you want to ask me what the cure is?"

Of course, our brilliant niece knew.

Ari's eyes widened, and Laurel sat straighter. Gemma covered her mouth.

"Yes, I do. I was bitten by a vampire. She's no longer in this realm, but I'm sick from it. Do you know how to fix me?"

Phina flopped the arms of the doll back and forth. She pointed to one arm. "Your bite is here."

As far as I knew, Phina hadn't seen it, but she pinpointed the spot with accuracy.

"Yes, that's correct."

Gemma knelt in front of them and put her hand on Phina's arm in the gentle way a mother does to console a child. "Daphina, do you know the answer to Ari's question? Do you know how to cure her?"

"Yes, the sprite told me how when I was the healer in our game." Phina looked up into Ari's face. "Our blood is the same."

All this time...since that power outage, the answer had been in front of us.

Understanding registered on Ari's face. "You have goddess blood too."

CHAPTER 39
SMITED
ARI

The sterile scent of the disinfectant Laurel had wiped on my bite and Phina's arm permeated the lab. Laurel prepped everything to make it as easy for his daughter as he could. Phina sat next to me on the exam table, looking unfazed by the conversation. She was gifted beyond what any of us knew. I might not be privy to the future, but she could teach us all about how to approach our fears.

"I've had a shot before, Aunt Ari," Phina said, looking at me like I was being unreasonable. "I'm not afraid of needles."

"You are braver than me," I said, wrinkling my nose. "I don't like them."

"Nobody likes them. You just do it because you have to." She shrugged.

I held my hand out for her. "That's true, but I'll hold your hand if you want."

Phina nodded her head with extra enthusiasm. "Yes, I like holding hands." She studied me as if she were working out a problem. "You're wrong."

"About what?" I asked.

"You are brave, Aunt Ari. You are the bravest of us all."

I blinked back tears, breathing through my urge to sob. "Thank you. I think you are much braver than me, though."

"No, it's you."

I laughed. "Okay then."

Marius arrived with a grimace on his face. My anxiety spiked, disquieted Albert had shown up, and I wasn't going to be ready to fight.

What's wrong?

I was worried I wouldn't make it here in time.

We haven't started yet.

"How are you going to use Phina's blood on Ari?" Rain asked, concern flickering over his fine features and stretching the scar at his chin.

"Not on," Laurel said, pointing to the syringe. "In."

"You'll inject it in her arm?" Gemma asked, her lips curled, the corners pulling downward.

Phina put her hands over my ears. "You might not want to listen to this part."

I pulled her hands down and held them between mine. "I'm not afraid of doing what it takes."

"That's why you are the bravest." She sat taller.

"Once I withdraw Phina's blood, I'll inject it the same way Albert did with General Daphina's." He looked at me as if telling me to brace for it. "In every puncture wound."

"I told you not to listen," Phina said, shaking her head.

"It's better for me to hear. I don't like surprises." I smiled at my niece in an attempt to ease her concern.

Her brows furrowed together. "Not even on your birthday?"

"No, not even then, but I don't really like celebrating it either." Every birthday had been a reminder my mother was no longer here, and I didn't need those prompts.

Her forehead bunched harder. "We need to change that."

"We certainly do." Rain put his hand on my back.

His touch was like a surge of strength, even when discussing a topic I preferred to avoid.

Phina stuck her bottom lip out. "When are you going to marry Aunt Ari, Uncle Rain?"

I schooled my features to neutral as practiced. Since the prison kingdom, we hadn't talked about marriage. He might not even want to marry. If this didn't work, it was likely we wouldn't get the chance anyway. Marriage wasn't what we needed to focus on for the time being.

Rain chuckled. "As soon as she'll have me."

"Aunt Ari, can I be in the wedding?" Phina's expressive eyes widened with her enthusiasm.

I opened my mouth, but I didn't know what to say. No words would come.

Laurel came closer with a syringe in hand. "Phina, it's time. Do you have your doll?"

"No, but I have Ari's hand. She makes me brave because she's the bravest."

"You make me brave," I said, squeezing her tiny hand. "If it hurts, just squeeze as hard as you can."

"Okay." She squinted her eyes shut.

Laurel poked her arm. Phina didn't flinch, and her hold on my hand didn't tighten. Her fearless spirit was contagious, but my throat dried thinking about how many times that needle would pierce my skin.

My sister's mate filled the syringe about halfway up. "That should be enough."

Gemma was at the ready and put some gauze on the puncture wound. "You did so well, my little princess."

My niece smiled and swung her legs.

"You didn't even need my hand," I said, showing her she'd left no marks on my skin.

"It's because you were here," Phina said, holding her hand out to me. "You can hold mine now."

"I might hold Rain's this time." I put my hand up next to my mouth. "So, he doesn't get his feelings hurt."

Phina mimicked my actions. "Boys get their feelings hurt a lot."

I mashed my lips together. "You're so smart."

"Mommy and Daddy tell me that all the time."

Gemma barked out a laugh. "You repeat too much."

"Are you ready, Ari?" Laurel asked, trepidation in his voice.

I worried that if this didn't work, his daughter would

be upset she wasn't able to save me. "Do it before I lose my nerve."

"I'll start at the one closest to your wrist. That's the most sensitive skin, so we'll get it out of the way."

I eyed him. "Some details can be kept to yourself."

Rain chuckled.

I sent a lick of fire against his palm. He jerked, but I didn't let go.

"I love you," he whispered.

"Jab the needle in already," I said.

Laurel slid the needle into the first tooth mark.

"Aagh." Sweat beaded my face. The burn was excruciating as Phina's blood mixed into the vampire bite. I gritted my teeth.

My niece's eyes were wide as she watched her father stick me.

"Get Phina out of here. I need to say profanities." I wouldn't scar her with my language, or the guilt if this went wrong. She didn't deserve either of those kinds of memories. If this ended badly, I wanted as few people here as possible.

Gemma held her hand out to her daughter. "Come on, Phina. Let's go see if Drew's back yet."

"What are profanities?" Phina asked my sister.

"Bad words. Those words we told you not to say." Gemma ushered Phina to the door.

"Mommy and Daddy say those words all the time," Phina called before Gemma could get her through the door. "They even say them when they are napping."

Even in agony, I laughed so hard I snorted.

Laurel's face was bright red. "I don't know what she's talking about."

"Sure you don't, Brother," Rain said, chuckling.

Marius paced back and forth, and I noted a line of sweat on his upper lip.

"Why are you so nervous? I'm the one getting jabbed by Doctor Make It Hurt."

Laurel shook his head.

Marius studied me with concern. "I feel your pain, Ari. You can't block me out when I want to be in your head."

"Well, choose to get out of it," I said, matter-of-factly. The pain made me lash out, but it touched me that he was willing to experience my discomfort with me.

Sorry. I sent the apology down the bond.

Are you getting soft?

Maybe.

"Ready for the next one?"

"Yes, and keep going until we're done. No matter how many times I tell you I hate you," I said with a smile.

"Stop flirting with my brother," Rain said, smirking. His distraction was welcome.

Laurel rolled his eyes. "I don't pretend to understand you two."

He stuck the needle in again.

"Ugh...Fuck all the gods. Every last one can fuck off."

Laurel bit back a smile. "We're all going to get smited."

"Smiting would be over quicker." I ground my teeth together. "Just keep going."

The needle pierced the next one, and I turned my head into Rain's chest. I inhaled his minty scent mixed with a storm on a summer afternoon. Nothing could be a better distraction than him.

"You can bite me if it helps."

"Stop flirting," I said, through gritted teeth, throwing his words back at him.

"I can flirt with you. You are my mate." He kissed my temple.

Laurel sank the sharp point into another spot.

My vision blurred. "Godsdammit. Fuck that shot."

"I can stop."

"If you do, I'll stab you in the arm with my knife."

"Easy," Rain said. "Save that for me."

A breeze blew into my mind. *Let me talk you through it.*

Get out of my head, Marius. I can't control my thoughts.

Pain is a state of mind you can command.

I tried to close my mind to him, but he held it open. Goddess, I was going to say something awful. It was going to come out, and I'd have to deal with the aftermath.

Breathe. Remember when you broke your arm when the tree fell on you?

You mean when my magic went crazy and knocked the tree down?

Yes. How did we deal with the pain then?

I'd wandered off from the castle into a pasture and hadn't known he followed me. Determined to see what my magic could do, I threw it at the tree, but I didn't know what elements to reach for or how to be precise.

The trunk broke in half, and the top half fell on top of me. He'd lifted the tree off. *You took it away with your magic.*

No, I didn't.

What do you mean? I remember the glow of it. You healed me.

No, that was you, and it was the first time I saw the goddess's magic in you.

I don't remember it that way.

Try now. Think of a buffer to the pain.

The part that came later was what I didn't want to remember—a memory I'd pushed so far down it'd been forgotten for years. Father had been so angry with me for running off he'd told me I was the reason Mother had died. Looking back, that was probably his true self coming through. I just didn't know it yet. *You know what. I'm good. I want to feel the pain. It reminds me I'm alive.*

Liar.

"All done," Laurel said.

"Really? I didn't feel..." I gazed at Marius with his far too smug expression. Underneath, there was something else, a concern like he hadn't known what Father had said until I remembered it. "You distracted me."

"With the truth." He nodded.

I nodded back, having a hard time concentrating on anything other than the pricking sting in my flesh. The burning radiated up my arm as if it were tracing every last one of the purple veins.

"There is medicine that can help you sleep through the

next part, but I don't know if it will affect how your body metabolizes Phina's blood."

"No, I can handle this."

"The other phase is..." Laurel paused, looking at Rain.

My mate shook his head.

"What we're not going to do is keep things from Ari," I said, referring to myself by name.

"The next part is the part that hurts," Laurel said.

"The burning is mild, like an itch. It's fine," I said.

Fire raged up my arm and through my body. I gasped for air, but even my lungs burned. "Nyx, help me. Am I being smited for telling the gods to fuck off?"

My skin ached like I needed to peel it off, but my hands wouldn't respond. I fought against the restraint, and the room seemed to fall away. I was in the pits of hell to burn for eternity. My mind was going dark, and I fell through flames until there was absolutely nothingness.

CHAPTER 40

WAKE UP
RAIN

I patted the damp cloth around Ari's face. She'd been out for nearly two days, and I was worried. Laurel told me not to be concerned and that her heart rate and respiration were good. He said her body needed the peace to heal. Was this what it was like for her when I had been out for days? When she'd been near death with Nyx, the tempo of life had seemed to slow down, but she wasn't gone long. With the treatment for the bite, there was no time limit on when she would wake up. The purple veins had receded to a small radius around the bite, and the teeth marks were looking better. Laurel showed me the results where the vampire marker was still in her blood, but the rest of her results had returned to normal. She was cured. If she would wake up.

Gemma dozed in the other chair. She wanted to bring Phina by, but I wasn't sure Ari would want her niece to see her like this. I'd asked Marius when he came by, and he shrugged saying he told me he couldn't get into her head. She was unreachable to him too. So, we waited.

Laurel stepped around the corner. "How's the bite looking now? By Albert's journal, she should see it gone within a week. Although I don't know how long he'd been bitten before he administered the cure on himself."

I turned Ari's arm so he could get a better look. "It's improving hour by hour. So, why hasn't she woken up?"

"For the little we saw on the outside of her body, the venom was doing things internally that she needs to heal too. There's no time frame, because we're all different." Laurel clapped my shoulder.

I slumped under the weight. Everything seemed heavier. "Maybe we should let Phina come see her. It might be what she needs to wake up. She would do anything for your daughter."

"She would do anything for any of us. Including sacrificing herself because that is who she is." Gemma stretched her arms over her head and leaned side to side. "I'll go get Phina. She'll be eager to see Ari for herself."

"Can you bring me a sandwich when you come back?" Laurel asked.

"Of course," she said, squeezing his shoulders. "Anything for my mate. Do you need something, Rain? Have you eaten today?"

My appetite had disappeared. It was like I couldn't eat without Ari. I forced a smile for Gemma. "I'm fine."

"You sure? Because Ari will be angry with you and me

both when she wakes up and sees those dark circles under your eyes."

"I can handle mad Ari." I wanted any anger Ari could throw at me over her being out and unmoving like she was. "I don't need anything, but I appreciate you asking."

Ari was so still it broke me watching her, but I couldn't look away either. I took her hand in mine. "Wake up, my love. The world stops when you sleep."

"She's going to wake up, Rain." Laurel walked to his desk. "I'm wondering if there's anything else we can use in this journal."

"Hmm." I didn't want to think about Albert. Ari deserved all my thoughts. I pressed my cheek to the back of her hand. *Can you hear me, my love?* The other end of our mate connection was silent and cold. *I need you to come back. It's boring without someone threatening to stab me, and your sister keeps trying to feed me. All I want is for you to open those blue eyes that are like the clearest sky, because I don't think I can do another day in the realm without you. If you'd wake up, there is a question I want to ask you. I want to ask you if you'll marry me.*

"Yes," Ari said, her voice raspy and barely audible.

Thank the goddesses and gods, she spoke. I leaned in closer. "What did you say?"

"Nothing," Laurel said.

"Not you," I said over my shoulder.

"She's awake?" His chair scraped against the floor. I heard his footsteps, but I refused to take my eyes off my mate. Her eyes were still closed, but there was a little movement under her lids.

"Ari, what did you say, my love?"

Yes. Her tired voice drifted into my head. She was there.

I love you. My heart hammered against my chest beating out a rhythm of relief and happiness. "Open your eyes."

"She's not quite awake, Rain," Laurel said, pushing buttons on the monitors. "She's still in a sleep stage, but this is the closest she's been to waking. It won't be long now."

"Thank fuck," I said, relieved she was that far along.

"Language," Gemma said from behind me. I hadn't even heard her enter.

I glanced back, and she had Phina on her hip.

"Why are you crying, Uncle Rain?" Phina said, concern in her voice. "Aunt Ari is cured."

I nodded. "I know, sweet girl. We just need her to wake up."

Gemma sat with Phina on the bed next to Ari. My niece studied my mate in the way she did when she played a game and was planning her strategy. "She wants to wake up."

"How do you know?" Gemma asked.

"I just do." Phina placed her hand against Ari's cheek. A glow like the moon peeked out from her hand and enveloped Ari's body.

I'd never witnessed Phina with this type of magic.

Gemma's mouth fell open, but she closed it. Laurel blinked a few times.

"She'll wake up now." Phina sat back against Gemma and watched.

Ari's eyes shifted under her lids in rapid movements. It was working. I leaned forward and kissed her cheek. "That's it. Open those eyes."

"You can do it, Aunt Ari," Phina said, getting close to Ari's ear.

Ari opened her eyes. The power shut off, leaving us in the dark.

CHAPTER 41
ADVANTAGE
ARI

Was I back in deep sleep? No, I'd woken up. I pushed myself to a sitting position, and hands helped me. A pillow was shoved behind my back. My eyes adjusted, and I saw Phina smiling. The next face I found was Rain. Love filled our bond. *My mate.* I sent the endearment down our connection. Tears pooled in his eyes. I tried to raise my arm, but there was a needle in it connected to a tube, like when I'd given my blood for Gemma. Was I that bad that I needed a transfusion? No, the liquid was clear. Gemma and Laurel stood behind Phina. Everyone stared at me like I was art in the museum.

"The power." My voice didn't cooperate. I cleared my throat to try again. "The power is out again?"

"Yes, it just went out," Gemma said.

"Why aren't you all trying to figure out why?"

"Because you just woke up."

"That can't be a coincidence," I said, knowing the answer without much thought. Drew had told us all before. It was the 'not our father anymore' man. *Albert.*

"Probably not," Gemma said.

I rubbed my throat. "Can I get some water?"

Laurel poured a glass and handed it to me.

I raised it to my lips. "Can you all stop staring at me while I take a drink?"

Rain winked at me.

"Maybe we should give Ari and Rain a few minutes." Gemma squeezed my shoulder.

Phina frowned. "But we just got here."

"We'll wait in the hall," Gemma said.

"I'll call and check in for sightings of Albert." Laurel stepped away.

"Thank you." I gulped the water. I should be thinking about my father, but my body was so tired—tired of being in bed, tired of fighting the vampire bite, and plain fucking tired.

"What can I do for you, my love?" Rain asked in the gentlest tone.

"Help me up to get dressed." I set the glass on the bedside table.

"There's no rush." Rain perched on the edge of the mattress. He had the covers pinned down with his weight, and I wondered if that was on purpose.

"The power is out again. It's the third one unless another happened while I was out. We know of at least one sighting of my father. I need to get out of this bed and do what I was meant to do." Albert didn't care who he hurt, and I couldn't take any more deaths at my expense.

"You're not battle-ready." Rain didn't move.

"It's my responsibility. I'm the chosen leader for our lifetime, and he's the man responsible for one half of my life." The only person who could stop him before was my mother, and it would take someone with her strength to do it again. A realm didn't exist where I'd leave that duty to my niece.

"When you have your strength back," he said firmly.

"We both know the Fates don't work like that." I worked my feet free from under the covers and slung my legs over the side. "So, you can stay here, or you can help. Your choice."

"You know me well enough to know I'm not sitting on the side."

"I do. So, are you helping me get dressed or not, and who put me in this weird, white nightgown?"

Rain stood and faced me. "It's a dressing gown from the infirmary, and Gemma did."

"Where are my clothes?"

"Gemma brought some fresh ones this morning and put them in the drawer." He pointed to the table beside the bed.

I blinked the last of the grogginess away. "This morning? How long was I asleep?"

"A couple of days," Rain said.

"It didn't seem that long." I opened the drawer, my vision adjusting to the darkness with the help of the last of the day's sunlight peeking in from a window on the far side of the room. Thankful to see pants, I slipped them on underneath the thin, gauzy gown. Rain held my elbow. I didn't pull away, but I felt better than I had in days.

"You seem pretty steady."

"I feel better from the water, but I'm starving." I yanked the gown up over my shoulders. Rain held the tunic for me, and I pushed my arms into it. My muscles protested a little but were surprisingly good. He pulled the top down over my head.

"We can see what's in the kitchen. They won't be able to cook anything until the power is back on, but there's probably something we can get."

"No, the power being off is the top priority. I'm really curious to hear what's going on right now." I dropped into a chair and grabbed the boots.

Rain knelt in front of me and helped me into them.

"After we know everyone is safe, I'd like to reenact this kneeling you're doing right now, my mate."

Rain chuckled. "There's very little that would give me more pleasure."

"Are you decent yet?" Gemma called from the door.

"Yes," I yelled back.

"Good," she said, entering the room with one of the orb lights. Laurel and Phina weren't with her. "We've got a problem."

"I assumed so with the power out," I said, getting to my feet. Rain straightened beside me.

"There's a breach at the unicorn housing," Gemma said.

"Where are Phina and Drew?" I asked. Albert had tried with me, Gemma, and Laurel, and I worried the children would be his next target.

"Laurel has Phina. The nanny was with Drew, so Laurel is going to take them to the safe room. They can manually bolt the door from the inside."

"We're blind without the cameras."

"I'm not," I said. "The people here have become far too dependent on that technology. We're fae. We have powers greater than this"—I gestured up, but I wasn't sure at what—"electricity and computer junk that hums in our ears all day."

"The hum drives me insane," Gemma said. "What's the plan, Ari?"

I glanced at Rain. Seeing the eagerness on his face that I felt, I winked. My mate and I were born for challenges, and we'd face all of them together. "We go to the highest point for an advantage, right?"

A smile spread across his face. "We sure do."

CHAPTER 42
THE STAIRS
ARI

Laurel met us in the tower. The cool night air was welcome against my flushed skin. I tried to act like I was the picture of health, but exhaustion peeked through. The memory of the last time Rain and I were in the same location was hard to ignore, but I focused on the present. The city wasn't under attack...yet. Gemma and Laurel weren't captives of Albert.

"I don't see anything happening in the unicorn area. What do you see?" I asked no one in particular, but we were all monitoring different directions.

"Nothing unusual this way," Laurel said. "People are milling about, but they are definitely fae and not vampire."

"Same for me," Gemma said.

"All good over here," Rain said.

"What is his end goal?" I wondered out loud. Our magic hadn't worked one time, but it did this time. Was that what he was trying to do? Get all the magic? "Why keep turning the power off? If it is, indeed, him."

"He's testing us," Gemma said. "While not identical since we didn't have electricity, he ran scenarios with me while preparing me to take the throne in our kingdom."

"Agreed. I watched him go through similar motions with his advisors," I said. "He took away all the key elements for survival to see who was the weakest."

"But testing for what?" Laurel asked. "To see if we dive into chaos?"

"Maybe," Gemma said. "But it's more likely he's testing for vulnerabilities."

Where we were vulnerable...I believed that, but my gut said there was something more. He was about power. *So how does this get him more power?*

"I've got something over here," Rain said. "Move slowly and ease your way to this side, so we don't draw any unwanted attention."

My stomach bottomed out. It might have been partially from hunger, but the majority was dread. I was closest, so I went first.

Rain didn't point and barely moved. "Look between the two spires to our left. Use them as a guide to the target."

Figures moved through the shadows in unnatural ways. Hidden in the darkness, they clearly were not fae.

Gemma made it. "Isn't that near the museum?"

Laurel grabbed the beam over us for balance. "If Whit's there alone..."

"It's Wednesday. He's usually volunteering with the children in the evening," Gemma said.

Albert might not be here, but he had eyes and hands in the city. If he was trying to build his forces, it was a good time to take his army out.

Laurel let out a breath.

"It doesn't look like they are up to any good," Rain said.

"If we go investigate it, we'll know for sure." I smiled at my mate.

"You two could stay here," Rain suggested to Gemma and Laurel. "Ari and I can go see."

"Not a chance," Gemma said.

Unsaid was what happened last time we'd all been separated in a moment like this.

Rain wrapped his arm around me. "Meet you there."

Nothing happened. "Did you forget how to vanyshen?"

"You try," he said.

I took a step up on the ledge, and he pulled me back. "It's not working."

The heaviness of our magic being stripped wasn't present like last time.

"For me either," Gemma said.

"What protects the palace from anyone vanyshening inside it?"

"It was carefully and meticulously woven into every wall, roof, and floor. Every time something new is added, it receives the same treatment," Laurel said.

"Would we know if someone had done that out here?" I asked, concerned we had a traitor inside.

"The city is a large area to cover. I'm not sure it would work. It'd likely take decades if not centuries," Laurel said.

"What else could do it?" If it wasn't woven, then there was a source, and a source could be destroyed if we found it.

Rain let out a long breath. "Short of a god or goddess, I'm not aware of anyone capable of weaving protections this size."

"A sprite, maybe...now that we know they still exist," Gemma said.

"What about Albert's syphon thing?" I asked, hating I had to bring that up in front of my sister and her mate. The question needed to be asked, but I knew what remembering my time under Albert's torture did to me.

"I don't know its reach," Gemma said, her unfocused gaze trained ahead. "But it was definitely powerful."

"If he has the tech to do this, then I think it's safe to assume it's him," Rain said.

The answers weren't at the top of this tower. I started down the stairs. "Then, we'd better start walking." It seemed unnecessary to say into danger, but it repeated in my head.

"Ari, we don't know what we're walking into," Gemma said, leaning over the rail to look at me.

"We know it's Albert and that he has forces inside the city and where. We can gather help along the way." Because she had a child, she needed a choice to walk away.

"If you need to go check on your daughter and our brother, that makes sense."

Laurel kissed her cheek. "I've fought Albert once, and I'm not afraid to do it again."

"I'm sorry," Gemma said, her hands shaking. "I...I can't do it."

"You never have to apologize to me," I said. "Go be with the children and keep them safe. That is more important."

She nodded and hugged her arms around her middle.

"I can carry you down," Rain said. "It's a lot of steps."

I side-eyed him.

"He's not joking," Laurel said. "We used to race to the top when we were young."

They had normal moments growing up. I forgot that sometimes, thinking about how young they were when the war started. My mate and his brother had grown up together, matured together, fought together, and lived whole lives before my sister and I met them. "What did you do when you made it? See who could push each other off?"

The stairwell went silent except for our footfalls. I glanced up where they'd both frozen. "What? Did you do that to each other?"

"It's how we learned to vanyshen mid step."

"Fucking goddess, you two are morons."

"May I remind you that you vanyshened yourself for the first time by stepping off that ledge," Rain said.

"You did what?" Laurel asked, his voice cracking with surprise.

I shrugged, looking forward. "At least I didn't know better. You two did."

"We'd been using our ability to vanyshen for years at that point. You didn't even know if you could," Rain said. He clearly was harboring some kind of feelings over it, but this wasn't the time nor the place for that discussion.

"I did know," I said. "Maybe it was the goddess or just my body understanding its ability, but I knew I could."

We walked in silence, and my strength grew with each movement. Instead of feeling tired, the exercise invigorated me. The only noise in the tower was the ringing sound of our feet on the metal steps, until we reached the bottom. I peered up, looking for Gemma, and though I couldn't see her face, her shadow made a slow descent behind us. She was taking her time, and I hated how triggered she was by the mention of Albert's machine. *Nyx, it's not mine to ask, but can you soothe my sister and heal her? I didn't realize how broken she was from the events. It's only been a few days, but I've never seen her like this before.*

If Nyx was listening or even heard me, she didn't respond. I'd hoped she would find my request worthy of honor, but she owed me nothing.

Rain cracked the door open and waved us closer. "I don't see anything suspicious here, but be careful when we step out," he whispered.

Anything or anyone could be on the other side. I shook my hands in an attempt to release some of the tension.

Marius trained me well for this since my magic was useless most of my life. Rain and Laurel had trained before this dependence on electricity. I didn't fear what waited for us, but I feared for those I loved and the people of the city.

He pushed the door back just enough to squeeze through. Laurel kissed Gemma's cheek and went next. I squeezed my sister's hand and closed the door behind me. Gemma could stay as long as she needed. Part of me wanted to remain with her to help her back to the castle, but the part of me that wanted to take down Albert, kill him, was stronger.

We crossed the street, moonlight showing the way. I expected to see vampire, but there was no one—no fae, no vampire, no Albert. Standing between Rain and Laurel, I pinned my back to the wall.

I hadn't tried to connect to my bonded since magic didn't seem to work, but our bonds were different. If it didn't work, I'd probably regret trying. *Marius, Albert is in the city.*

I'm aware. Relief that I could communicate with him strengthened my resolve.

And you didn't think to...never mind. We can't use our magic. Can you?

Yes. He replied in a one-word response, and I knew what that meant.

You're already there, aren't you?

Yes.

We're on our way.

I scanned the street, but there wasn't anyone else here but us. *Thank the goddess.* "Marius is at the museum."

"You can speak to him?" Rain asked.

"Apparently, that bond is still working with whatever this is."

"Interesting," Laurel said. "Albert's machine must only target fae somehow."

"Or unicorn are beyond his reach," Rain said, his voice dropping low.

"As Marius likes to say, unicorn don't answer to fae." A soft chuckle answered in my head. "And apparently I can't block him out, because he agrees."

"Can you ask him if he sees Whit?" Laurel asked. "If the unicorn told him or he noticed there were vampire in the city, he'd return to the museum."

Is the museum curator, Whit, visible from where you are?

He's at my side.

"Yes, he's with Marius," I said. "Why?"

"Because there is a weapon store in the museum that might help us," Laurel said, his voice barely a whisper.

Rain halted so fast I nearly ran into him. "We can't use that inside the city."

"I don't know that we have a choice, Brother."

Could any weapon be worse than the destruction Albert had inflicted a couple of weeks ago? "What kind of weapon is this?"

CHAPTER 43

BURNING
ARI

We traversed through the shadows at a clipped pace toward where we believed Albert to be.

We're two streets away from the museum. Where should we meet you?'

Follow the fight sounds.

Very funny.

That wasn't an attempt at humor.

Some of Rain's soldiers crossed the street ahead of us, running toward the museum. It was the first we'd seen sight of anyone since leaving the tower.

"Who's giving them orders?" Laurel sounded bewildered.

"They are trained to respond in events like this," Rain said. "While you've been in your lab the last few years, we've been planning for the prison kingdom to fall."

There was no bitterness in his voice, only a pragmatic

tone. I glanced back at Laurel, but Rain's words hit him like a blow. His shoulders slumped. I knew what it was like to not feel good enough and like you disappointed those important to you. Laurel's work was important, and moreover, he loved my sister like she deserved to be loved.

"You were building a family, and your contributions in the lab matter," I said.

"I didn't mean..." Rain shook his head. "Can we talk about our feelings later?"

"Always a doer and not a talker." The toe of my boot tapped the back of his.

"I talk enough," Rain said, staring ahead. He inched forward.

I patted his back as we scooted down the wall. "You sure do."

He grunted something I couldn't understand and stopped. More soldiers ran down the cross street. Faint sounds of metal clinking and a noise akin to fire crackling echoed off the buildings around us. I studied the glow.

My heart sank into the recesses of my chest. The only records of who my mother was were in the building ahead. *Please tell me the museum is not on fire.*

It is not. The buildings adjacent are.

Not good. "We need to get water over there. The museum is close to multiple fires."

Rain jerked his head toward me. "Which buildings?"

"I don't know."

Rain took off in a hard run.

All the strength from before was gone. It must have

been a rush of adrenaline. My legs were weak, not just from the stairs but from what my body had been through. I waved Laurel around. Normally, I'd hide any weakness. That was how I was trained, but today was the exception. I needed a minute to catch my breath, and Rain needed someone else by his side. "Go with him. I can't keep up."

"I'm not leaving you behind, Ari. He wouldn't either if it were another building."

"What does he think it is?"

"He stored many of our father's journals and stories and different things in there. He hasn't been ready to turn most of it over to the museum yet, but he had it all cataloged for when he was. Whit talks him into moving a few pieces over each year."

"But that means there are hundreds..." I said, understanding the loss he feared. "You should go. They're your father's writings too."

"Rain still harbors a lot of guilt over our father's death." Laurel inched forward at a pace I could manage.

"He told me about the events," I said, my heart aching for them both. I reached for the strength deep inside me and forced myself to move faster.

"It's this way," Laurel showed me the path by pointing and making an L-shaped gesture.

"Could Albert have known this existed?"

"We haven't made it public record, but it's always possible," Laurel said.

"I think my father targeted it," I said, recalling how the writings in the museum had said he'd been ahead of every strategy they planned during the war. I caught sight of Rain a few steps ahead. He advanced toward two vampire who seemed unaware of his presence.

"If that's the case, then this is a trap." Laurel sped up.

"Fuck," I said, pushing my legs to run as hard as I could. *Rain.* I yelled down the mate bond, but it didn't seem to work like the one with Marius. I tackled Rain to the ground.

He started to fight, trying to push up and throw me off. Rain realized it was me and stilled. Brushing the hair out of my face, he studied me. "What are you doing?"

"Saving your ass," I said. "We need to get out of here."

"The vampire ran off." Laurel offered a hand to us. Then the building exploded.

CHAPTER 44
EVACUATION
RAIN

My ears rang, and my head throbbed. Dust and smoke filled the air. I coughed and tried to push up, but a piece of stone was on my leg. I lifted it off, and my leg was fine. My chest ached, and my lungs burned. Ari? Where was she? She knocked me to the ground right before.

The thick particles in the air obscured my vision, so I crawled along over the remnants. "Ari? Ari? Answer me."

My hand connected with a boot too large to be Ari's. Laurel. No movement. I scooted along his body, not finding any injuries. He was breathing. A heavy slab propped up on another one seemed to make a cocoon around him, but war had shown me that appearances could be deceiving. I slid my hands under his arms and tugged. He came out easily. His face was covered in dust, and he was out cold. I assessed him for injuries and found a piece of metal in his shoulder. Not risking pulling it out, I ripped his shirt at the wound for a better look. There wasn't much blood seeping from it. The metal didn't look to be too deep, but I couldn't be sure. "Laurel?"

His eyes opened. My brother wheezed and coughed. He winced and reached for his shoulder. "What the fuck?"

"The building blew up. I can't find Ari." Torn between helping my brother or finding the reason my heart beat, I scanned around me. Goddesses and gods, was there anyone else who could help? All I saw was the dust in the air.

"It's not hitting anything major. Get it the fuck out of me." Laurel had been a triage expert in the war, and I trusted no one more when it came to assessing injuries.

"Here I go," I said, yanking the metal free and pressing my hand on the wound. "I probably should have torn some fabric first."

"I can press my other hand to it if you can find something to dress it."

"On the count of three," I said. "One...two...three." Our hands moved in sync as they had many times during the Great War.

I reached for the hem of my tunic and tore a long length of fabric. I wrapped it around his shoulder and over the wound as many times as I could before tying it off. "Stay here. I have to find Ari."

"She was in front of me," Laurel said.

"I know." I pushed to my feet, wobbly but good enough. She'd knocked me to the ground. Why hadn't I flipped her over?

"She has to be nearby." Laurel worked his way to a standing position.

I took in the sight. Panic sliced through my thoughts. Everything was gray, and I saw no signs of life. Rubble from the blast was scattered several streets away. It was powerful and obviously planned to hurt as many as possible. I didn't see any indication of her—not her clothes, her hair, not a sign of life. My heart pounded with terror I'd lost her. *No. I will find her.*

"There," Laurel pointed ahead.

The dust had settled enough to see the street was visible further down. Standing so far from us was my love. She was alive. Thank all the goddesses and gods. Tears streamed down her face. She limped toward me. Dust coated every inch of her and streaked her beautiful face from the dampness. I ran to her, wrapping my arms around her. "Thank your goddess, Nyx."

"I thought you were…" She buried her face against my shoulder. The way her voice shook with fear was an experience she shouldn't have to remember.

"Me too," I whispered, my throat tight, against her ear.

Laurel patted my back. "I need to find Gemma, and we need to get out of here."

"But what about the people?" Ari said, gazing toward the remains of the building.

"We have to secure the space first. Then we can start rescue and recovery. We are no good to them if we die."

"They might not be able to wait. What if someone dies

because we sought safety first?" She pulled out of my arms.

"This is war, Ari. We assess and triage. Not everyone can be saved, but we will honor them either way."

She stumbled toward the blast site.

I grabbed her hand. "I know you want to help, but you can't like this. You are injured yourself."

"The hell I can't," she said with that fierceness I loved so much. She cleared her throat. "What I meant to say is people are hurt. I'm not leaving them and I'm going to do what I can."

I sighed and turned to Laurel. "Go find Gemma. We'll be here."

"That's not wise," Laurel said.

"Tell my mate that," I said, clapping him on the shoulder.

He gave me a nod, and I turned back to Ari.

She stood a few feet ahead, staring at the destruction.

"You don't have to save everyone."

"No, but I at least have to try." She opened up her arms. "Nyx, hear my call. Evil has marred this land, and I ask, as your granddaughter, to heal the people here. Restore this site."

Light sprang from her hands and what seemed to be every pore in her body. Pieces of stone flew past us toward the building.

The power she used wasn't fae, and I was concerned what the price for this kind of sacrifice would be. She couldn't be punished like Nyx. That was an option. "Ari, I think you should stop."

She didn't respond, and the building began to take shape, looking as it had before the explosion. My ears stopped ringing, and I could hear others moaning in the distance over the whoosh of wind as debris flew past. As the pieces went back together in a puzzle-like fashion, I stood in astonishment. My incredible goddess of a mate undid a horror that should have been impossible to reverse. No mere fae had power to reconstruct on this level. She wanted to live up to her mother's legacy, but she'd created a legend with her single action. The stories told from today would immortalize her in myth.

People emerged from the area Ari had restored. Dusty faces wearing bewildered and awed expressions surveyed for the source of the never-before-seen power. I couldn't shield her from this, and gods knew I wanted to. People would stare, and they would talk. Fae filtered in closer—some injured or covered in gray residue and others not. All took a knee in front of her.

The building was completely whole, looking as if it had never been ripped apart. The light ceased from Ari, and her knees buckled. I caught her before she hit the ground and felt my magic return. I vanyshened her to the grounds of the castle.

Laurel ran across the courtyard ....toward us, his mouth wide open. His shirt was still torn, but the bandage had been removed. No sign of his injury remained. "Ari did that?"

"She did, and now she's spent from the exhaustion."

"Something you know a thing or two about."

"Did you see anything on your way over?"

"No," he said. "No sign of Albert."

"Do you think he started it in motion and left?" I asked, trying to figure out his goal tonight. Was it to lure us out? If so, why didn't he confront us?

"He's more the kind to take credit for his actions."

"True," I said, as we entered the back door. "If fae are acting on his behalf, then we have bigger problems."

"Don't we always?" Laurel said. "I'll check on Gemma again and then meet you both in the infirmary."

I carried Ari into the room and gently arranged her on the bed. She was out cold, and I'd been there enough times that I knew the way everything shut down. I found a pan and ran some water in it, then located a rag and soaked it. I wiped away the soot from her face and her arms. I wanted to change her clothes, but I was afraid that would be too much movement for her. She needed to stay asleep while her body restored itself. I pulled a chair up beside her bed and contemplated what to say so she would know I was with her.

"Once when I was little and coming into my power, I called the lightning to hit the ass of another fae I didn't like. It wasn't very powerful then, but it struck true to its mark."

The power flicked back on, and all the dirt and debris were more visible. I used my fingers to try to brush the ash from her hair, but my touch only seemed to make it worse.

Her dark hair looked a dull gray with the soot clinging to it.

"There was another time, not too long after my father passed away, I vanyshened to a remote mountain and threw bolts and tornadoes until I passed out. Casimir and Laurel found me there, face down in the earth. I'd started a forest fire with the lightning, so it'd made me easier to find. By the time I woke up several days later, hungry and still tired, they'd had an earth elemental repair the damage as if it'd never happened. I was happy the realm didn't have to suffer from my destruction, but it saddened me too. It was like a part of me had been expunged—like my grief had been erased."

I'd never told anyone the story, and Laurel and I'd never talked about it. Admitting it now to Ari opened up the grief I kept buried deep, and my chest ached. The grief that made me the ruthless fae capable of destroying my enemies. Not sure I was that person with Ari. She'd healed parts of me.

A hand squeezed my shoulder. "I never knew you felt that way about it, Brother."

Before it might have bothered me he heard my confession, but that time had passed. I patted the back of his hand with mine. "It was a long time ago."

"Still, I didn't think about what you were feeling in the moment. I should have asked."

"You were grieving too." I looked up at my brother and found his expression sorrowful and full of remorse. "I was never mad at you over it. Those dark days were difficult for both of us."

"Indeed," he said, hooking up fluids for Ari. She didn't flinch or react at all when he inserted the needle. "How did she do it?"

"Goddess only knows, and I mean that quite literally," I said, stroking my fingers over hers. "She's amazing. I want to marry her, Laurel. Properly in a ceremony befitting her noble blood."

I could see it so clearly—marrying her at the waterfall by moonlight with the moonflowers around us.

"You're already mates. You don't need that."

"No, but I want it."

"What does she want?" Laurel asked.

I pressed my lips to her fingers. "I hope the same, but I guess she'll have to tell me when she wakes up."

Laurel adjusted the drip and the instruments. "That should keep her hydrated, so it will be easier when she wakes up. I can start the healing process."

Her body had been through so much with the bite and then overexertion with her incredible feat. Anytime we rushed the healing process, there was some discomfort. She deserved to have some normal recovery time with no pain. "No, let her rest for now. We can start later. How was Gemma?"

"Nervous, but they were all fine. She'd just made it to the room when the explosion happened. She said everything shook like an earthquake over here."

"It felt like the world was ending where we were."

He nodded. "I think I'm going to send her, the kids, and Leana to the coast for a while. Gemma's nerves can't take any more of her father's actions. She's been struggling."

Given how distraught Gemma had been and that they had Phina, I thought it was a good idea, but only if they had unicorn protection. Ari would want a say in whether Drew went, but I believe she'd ultimately think he should go with Phina. She didn't like separating them. "Do you think Gemma will allow that? Ari certainly wouldn't."

"They are so much alike, but they handle experiences differently. When we were locked in that cell, Gemma fought hard. Her perseverance never wavered. Since we've been home, she's been herself most of the time, but then there are these moments where she looks distant. I know where she is in those brief periods because of the mate connection, but there's nothing I can do, even as a healer, to keep them from coming back."

"You understand how it is. We both had our own issues coming out of the Great War. She'll find her way in time."

"I hope so," he said. "I'm really worried about her."

"Why don't you go spend some time with her?" I said. "I'm not leaving Ari's side. You can check on her later."

Laurel scrutinized the monitors one more time. "I'll be back in a few hours, and we can get started."

The door slid open. One of my personal guards ran inside. "We're under attack."

Alarms blared to life. I rose from my seat. *Albert.* "Where?"

"The unicorn village side."

"Fuck." I looked at Ari and back at my brother, torn on what to do. If I left Ari, she'd be vulnerable. No one else stood a chance against Albert alone other than me and her. She was in no condition to fight and might not be for days.

"Stay with her. The rest of us can handle it."

"How many?" I asked the guard.

"About a hundred or so."

When I met Laurel's gaze, my decision was made. I wasn't leaving my mate. "Take all my guards. Every last one of them. They are the best. A hundred can't stand against them."

"What about you?"

"We'll be fine. Who is going to look in the infirmary? Besides, I trust you'll stop them before they get here."

He clasped my forearm and I his as in the old ways.

"Kill every one of those fuckers."

Laurel smirked. "With my honor."

I studied Ari, her power almost undetectable as her body recovered. She'd been left in such a vulnerable state. The events had immobilized her. I twisted toward the door. Laurel was almost through it.

"Wait," I called to him.

He turned.

"I don't think it's a coincidence that the building blew up or that they are attacking now. Albert wanted his daughter incapacitated and us distracted, but why? What is he after here besides her?"

"Power," Laurel said. "It's always been about being the most powerful to him."

"We're missing something important," I said, frustrated I couldn't reason it out. "I just don't know what."

"Maybe he's so blinded by the need for power he doesn't even know," Laurel said, his tone pragmatic.

"No, that's not it."

"We need to go help the unicorn fight," Laurel said, inching toward the door. "We can't let the vampire have even one of them."

I nodded. "Keep your eyes open. He might have another bomb. Tell the unicorn too."

The alarms shut off. Laurel gazed up at the ceiling. "That's not normal."

I pulled my phone out of my pocket and dialed Armstrong. We kept him hidden in plain sight so no one would ever guess what a powerful fae he was. "Tell them to issue the evacuation order. Get all the citizens out of the city."

CHAPTER 45
THE CAVE
CYRUS

Every bone, muscle, and sinew ached as my body shifted between unicorn and fae over and over again. My punishment for my broken oaths was just and far less than I deserved, but days on end of the constant glamour and release left me begging for death. Guilt for considering it followed. I imagined Gemma and Laurel greeting me once this was over. Would they be happy to see me? Did they think I abandoned them again? Marius had said he told them I'd be away on a mission, but that I would return. Would my mates still love me and want me in their lives?

My mind raced on what I would do if they did and then switched to what I would do if they didn't. I'd spent my entire life thinking I couldn't be loved, but I'd really been waiting for Gemma and Laurel. All my devotion belonged to them, Fae mates in their own right, and I was mated to them. I smiled through the pain, thinking of the look on Laurel's face when we were eating sandwiches in the kitchen and Gemma's face when I told her I loved her.

The heavy metal door creaked and four hoof beats turned to two footsteps. I couldn't see who entered, but it had only been Marius or Casimir the entire time I'd been in the cave. Dampness clung to the air, but my unicorn senses were held at bay while I was stuck in purgatory.

"Cyrus, we need to go. The city is under attack," Marius said.

My stomach pitted. *Gemma? Laurel? Phina? Erebus, get me out of here.* I tried to move, but my body's constant conversion from unicorn to fae blocked my attempts.

Casimir murmured the incantation of the rite to release me. Slicing her palm with her horn, she placed a hand on the panel in the wall. The liberation assuaged the perpetual torture, but it mutated to terror for my mates, who'd only been saved from Albert days ago.

The shifting between forms slowly came to a stop, and I fell to the ground, hitting the rough cave floor in a painful thud. My body, in my natural form, refused me when I tried to stand. My legs splayed out in four different directions, and I grappled to get my footing with weak muscles.

"You have to get up," Casimir said, her tone dire. "We don't have time for you to rest."

I thought of my mates and all they'd endured. The fear of Albert ensnaring them again drove my determination. Fury for the heinous acts he'd subjected Gemma and Laurel to furrowed into my heart. Albert would never touch them again as long as I walked, whether as a unicorn or fae, in this realm. Rocks digging into my skin, I forced myself up from the ground.

"We have to hurry." Marius, still in his natural form, led me out of the cave. The passage's width accommodated unicorn in single file order, so Casimir took up the space behind me. I stumbled into the wall. A sharp rock protruding gouged my shoulder, but I ignored the throbbing of the wound. Casimir, back in her unicorn state, slowed but remained silent.

The darkness outside felt like a continuation of the cave. I'd lost all track of time and only knew the number of days because Casimir had told me at some point. My magic flickered in my veins, and I willed it to my extremities. I would not leave those I loved to die at the hands of Albert. His head would be mine.

PART THREE

A PROMISE

From the personal writings of General Daphina, as kept in private by the curator of the War Museum.

I swore a promise to Nyx today. I offered my time in the realm among the fae as an exchange so that my daughters and their children could live long lives. The sprite warned me years ago that I wouldn't see them grow into their power, and I accept that. Albert has matched every strategy I develop, defying Zabrina's foresight every time. It's like he anticipates her gift and changes his decision at the last minute to bypass it.

I led skilled weavers to build the ultimate prison for him at Veran's request. The king refused to entertain death as the sentence for Albert's crimes. Whit showed me the journal recovered from Albert's offices. No one has seen it except Whit and the king, and Veran ordered him to burn it. Whit, ever the historian, defied the orders and showed it to me. I wove the perfect concealing net for the journal, and only Whit will be able to reach it. He'll hold it until such time as the information is needed.

The trouble with the prison I built for Albert is that the magic wanes if I am too far away. Even with a dozen other weavers inside, they couldn't keep it going on their own. My magic, the power granted me by Nyx, was the extra boost to keep it functioning. What I didn't tell anyone, including Whit, was how tired the prison made me. I had to find a way to protect my own energy while fortifying the net of the kingdom. The hardest part would be sending my children to the other side after they arrive, whenever that day may be. They are our future, and I will gladly trade my life for theirs.

MATCHING MARKS

RAIN

At my bidding, Laurel sent the guards on to the unicorn houses, and he went to get Gemma and the kids and would meet us back here. I hadn't told him yet, but I was going to send Ari with them to the coast. Leaving her here would be optimal, but I would risk Albert finding her unconscious. Once they were all safe on the coast, I was going to end this once and for all. My mate would be angry with me, but I'd accept that outcome.

Ari stirred in the bed, and I wished I could tell her all the things I'd wanted to say and held back.

If I died ending her father, I wanted her to know.

"When I saw you the first time and you turned those sharp eyes the color of the lightest blue sky on me, I knew something was different. Part of me knew it was the mate bond, but I didn't know who you were. I knew you were Gemma's sister, but I didn't know what kind of person you were. The way you hated me because I dared to come court you showed me you weren't someone who gave fuck-all about status. You stood up to everyone, and I hadn't known anyone like that in a very long time. I'd told myself I'd never love anyone again, but there you were, capturing my heart even while you hated me." I smiled, letting the memory replay through my head. I wanted to make a million more memories with her, but if that didn't come to be, I'd known what it meant to love with my entire soul and not just a piece of me. That was all because of Ari.

"You asked me if I'd been in love before, and I told you I had. It was many years ago, and I was young. She was a couple of decades older than me, and it was before my aunt married King Veran. I was just a nobly born young man, and she was a warrior. We'd been together for a couple of years, and she was sent to the vampire border on a routine patrol. She never came home. They found her and her horse both drained. I fucked my way across the kingdom for the next decade and decided that was all I needed. I didn't want love, and I'd walk away if feelings stirred. Every time I walked away, it got easier and easier... until you."

"I don't like hearing about you fucking anyone else," Ari said, her voice hoarse but amused.

Goddesses and gods, she shouldn't be awake this soon, but her voice was the melody musicians tried to imitate with their songs. "You should be sleeping."

"My body says otherwise," she said, her eyes still

closed. "Did everyone…" She took a slow, shaky breath. "Did they all survive?"

I sat in the chair that allowed me to see the door and took her hand in mine. Her skin warmed under my touch, and I relished the contact. "Yes, you saved them all and rebuilt a building."

"Good," she said.

"I can tell you another story."

"Mmm. Hmm. No fucking anybody else." Her breathing evened out. She'd fallen back to sleep.

It wasn't unheard of to wake up during the recovery, and I was relieved her body pulled her back to the restful state.

"My father insisted that Laurel and I do chores. Even though most of the noble families didn't, he wanted us to understand what work was like and what we would one day ask others to do. He had Laurel and me alternate mucking horse stalls. It was my turn, and I was working out a strategy to get it done as quickly as possible. When I got to the end where the pitchforks and wheelbarrows were stored, there was a unicorn. Casimir came to claim me as her charge. I'd felt someone in my head off and on for years, and I guess she figured I was mature enough then. She'd been wrong. I told her I didn't want to be 'tied to a fucking horned horse.' She said she didn't 'want to babysit a sniveling, powerless fae.' I reached for my lightning and threw a powerful bolt directly at her. If it had struck true, she wouldn't be here with us today. Instead, she absorbed my power straight into her horn. Then she stepped on the end of a pitchfork and flung horse shit right in my face. I ran screaming like a baby out of the barn." I laughed at the memory. As disgusting as it had been, I realized how much training I needed.

A smile ghosted over Ari's lips. She heard me, and I wondered if she'd heard all the stories I'd shared. She blinked her eyes a few times. Her lids finally opened. "Hi."

I smoothed my thumb in circles over her knuckles, so thankful to see her awake. "Hi, my goddess."

"Where is everyone?"

"Laurel went to check on Gemma and the kids," I said, waiting for her to work through where she was. "If you were expecting days to have passed, it's only been a couple of hours at most."

"Noted." Remarkably, she pushed up to a seated position.

I rearranged the pillows behind her.

"What's going on outside?" She looked toward the window I'd largely ignored.

"The unicorn houses are under attack, but we're taking care of it," I said. "My best soldiers are defending them."

Panic filled her features. "We should be there. What if Albert catches Leana or one of the others?"

"He won't. The guards are my personal guard. No one will get past them."

"Marius might need me," she said, running a hand through her hair. Her fingers snagged on the gray soot.

"Should he need you, he can get in your head anytime."

She nodded, looking less than convinced. "Am I covered in grime? Even my mouth feels gritty."

"It's in your hair and all over your clothes."

She peered down at her garments. "This is pretty gross, but maybe the vampire won't want to eat me looking like this."

"You don't have to worry about that. In Albert's journal, he talks of the vampire being uninterested in him after he was cured."

"He takes an elixir…" She thought for a moment. "Unless he doesn't because he has this same marker."

I tilted my head toward her. Albert was a master of deceitful acts, so I didn't put anything past him. "He might have an elixir made to throw others off, but the journal said otherwise."

"Did it say anything about how to stop someone with a cure?"

"No, but you knew that." *Where was Laurel? He should have been back by now.* "I have something to say to you, and I want you to hear me out."

"I'm listening." Her eyebrow arched, and I knew this wasn't going to be an easy conversation.

She preferred all the details, so I was going to give it to her—straight and concise. "Laurel is going to talk to Gemma about going to the coast. I'd like you to go with them if not for yourself, then for me."

"I can't believe…" She paused, staring off in the

distance. "No, I can believe Gemma would leave. I saw firsthand how anxious she was, and she has Phina to think about. Our mother's legacy must live on, and if my sister and her family are safe, then that would ensure Mother's memory would too. I have no children, and I was literally born to face my father. Drew could go with Gemma. He feels secure with her and Phina." Her gaze came back to mine, and the resolution of her expression was easy to read. "Gemma should go with Phina and take Drew with her."

"But you won't go? Not even if it means it keeps me from getting distracted?" I attempted to hide my disappointment, but I could tell by the arch of her eyebrow that I failed.

"You can't ask me that or use guilt on me for this choice, Rain," she said, softening her voice. "Nyx chose me herself for this moment. As much as I love you, I would give my life for you. It's not fair to ask me to ignore what Nyx empowered me to do."

I let out a heavy sigh, trying to get control of the rugged emotions I sensed in our connection. Freedom to choose was hers. I wouldn't fight her. "You're right, and I wouldn't do it if you asked me either."

"Then, it's decided. We live or die together today." She'd been raised in a world where few truths were told, and all of our words held some kind of power.

"That sounds a lot like a fae promise. Be careful." My caution was offered not from children's stories but from my own experiences.

She sat tall, her posture strong. "I know what I want, whether that's here or in the next realm. We do whatever it takes to defeat my father permanently. The rest is up to the Fates."

My heart ached with dread. "I can't swear that to you. I want you to live, Ari. You have so many years ahead of you."

"I make my promise to you, Rain." Magic charged the air and sealed her oath.

No defeat ripped my chest open more than her pledge for life or death, because there was only one way those ever ended. I lowered my head. "Then, I make another commitment to you. I bind myself to you for however long our existence may be. Whether that is tonight or ten thousand years, my body is yours, my mind is yours, my heart is yours, and my soul is yours." Magic zinged through my hand and into hers.

"I accept your pledge and give you all of me—my power, my life, and my love for however long our existence may be." Our hands glowed together with the promise, and there on our ring fingers were matching marks, similar to the one that covered Ari's scar from the arrow. Nyx had blessed our union.

A jolt of happiness shot through my body. I leaned in, kissing the symbol on Ari's finger. Perhaps everything would be all right.

"That sounded a lot like a marriage vow," Gemma said softly, leaning against the door. "I guess that means you're not coming with us."

"No," Ari said, getting out of bed. She made her way to her sister. Although her steps were slower than usual, she was stronger than I expected. "I can't go. Nyx gave me this second chance to stop Albert. I have to do it."

"Make him hurt for all the pain he inflicted on you and me," Gemma said, tears in her eyes.

"I will," Ari said, embracing her sister. "Sorry for the ash." She dusted it off of Gemma. "Give Phina and Drew my love."

"Laurel is staying too." Gemma sighed, taking a pack off her back. "He told me I should come see you on my own first before he brought the kids down."

"I look like something out of a nightmare right now. They probably shouldn't see me like this."

Gemma handed her the pack. "That's why I brought you a change of clothes."

Ari gave her a small smile. "Thank you for taking care of me after Mother passed and for continuing to take care of me even when I didn't know it." She paused, looking down at her hands, then back to Gemma. "When mother told us we'd always be close, I don't know that I believed her. How wrong I was."

Gemma took Ari's hand in hers and patted it. "Get changed, and we can say our goodbyes."

Ari disappeared around the curtain with the pack.

CHAPTER 47
GOODBYES
ARI

Gemma thought of everything to put in the pack, even a hairbrush. Unfortunately, my hair was coated in the ash from the building. I pulled it back and twisted it up in a knot on top of my head. That was the best I could do without a shower.

"Any news?" I asked, emerging around the curtain. Rain and Gemma both stared at the dreadful pocket phones.

"The guards are holding the line with the unicorn. No sign of Albert yet." Rain put the device in his pocket.

"He's here somewhere." Mother's writings said he'd been on step ahead of them the entire war until they trapped him in the prison. It was my turn to end him, and what scared the hell out of me was not knowing if we'd all survive. "He wanted me incapacitated. I don't think he realized how quickly I would recover."

"Agreed. He set this trap, but the question is for what reason. What is his goal this time?"

"I think he's after you," Gemma said, looking straight at me. "He wanted you weak, so you were easy to get to. I think he thought he'd catch us all separated and didn't plan on us being together."

I considered it. Though I want to disagree, my sister's reasoning made sense. "He's had both of us in his hands and let us slip through."

"He fought to keep you, Ari. You got away with help he hadn't planned on," Gemma said.

"Griselda got me out of there, but I wouldn't have made it if you hadn't been there to get me." A sour taste formed in my mouth remembering Griselda's final moments. She'd dissolved into nothing in my arms, and I called the wind to carry her away, unwilling to leave her there. Then, my family was there fighting for me and getting me to safety.

Gemma glanced at Rain with a look of trepidation.

Zabrina and Merrick burst into the room. Merrick's face was lined with worry, but Zabrina appeared composed.

"Thank the goddesses and gods," Merrick said, coming straight for me. "You look awful."

"Well, I did just put a building back together," I said, embracing her. "You shouldn't be here. Take your mother and get out of the city."

Zabrina raised an eyebrow. "You have the two most gifted fire wielders in front of you. We're not running."

"Merrick?" Gemma's posture was stiff. Merrick turned to her.

Gemma clasped her hands in front of her. "Look, we don't have time to tiptoe around each other. My sister is important to both of us. If you promise to have my sister's back against my father today, I'll let the past go. I'm taking my daughter and my brother to safety, and I cannot be here."

"I always have your sister's back, but I promise this to you." Merrick's promise charged the air. I was uncomfortable with their promise having me at the center, but I was thankful there would be peace between them.

Laurel entered carrying Phina and holding Drew's hand. Dressed in travelling clothes, my brother and niece were far too little to be running for their lives. Neither seemed agitated or nervous, and I wished I had their demeanor. My throat closed up, and I rubbed my aching jaw. How was I going to tell them goodbye?

"Where's Leana?" I asked.

"She's gone ahead with the nanny," Laurel answered. "She wasn't happy about going without Drew, but she agreed to get things ready so it was a seamless experience for the children."

I knelt to hug my little brother. "You are so brave, Drew. Be yourself above all else. I love you."

He embraced me. "You smell like dirt, but I love you too."

I laughed and stood. Patting Laurel's cheek, I mouthed "thank you" to him. He gave me a grim smile of assurance.

Phina reached for me, and I hugged her, but didn't take her from Laurel's arms. "I love you so much."

"You'll see us soon. Don't worry, Aunt Ari."

I blinked back tears. "Someday soon," I said, knowing the likelihood was not very soon at all. Albert was powerful, and we'd have several battles where the best I could say we had was a draw. I was leading us into a war, and I didn't know when it would end.

My sister pulled me into an embrace like she had when Mother passed, and that was the reality of another goodbye between us.

I held onto her like I couldn't let go. "I'm so glad our destinies brought us back together, even if it was for a short time," I whispered against her ear.

She pulled back. "Don't say that. We will see each other again."

"Go. We don't know how much time we have," I said.

Rain was saying his goodbyes to Laurel and the kids and hugged Gemma. I didn't hear what my sister said to him.

My mate pulled back and met my sister's gaze. "I'll take care of her." His words rang true, and I realized they were close. My sister trusted him enough to ask him to protect me.

"Go." I waved. "I love you," I said before it was too late.

Laurel took Gemma's hand, and they were gone. I sagged against Rain in part exhaustion and part relief.

Zabrina took my hands. Hers were warm, but she

carried tension in her shoulders. "You will succeed tonight, because I can tell you what Albert has planned."

"Tell me what his intention is."

"He's been completely unpredictable, Zabrina," Rain said. "Are you sure you can trust this vision?"

"She wouldn't be here if she didn't," Merrick said.

Rain nodded.

"As I was saying"—Zabrina gave him a look of annoyance—"don't go to the current skirmish. His full force lies in wait to proceed here for you. They are currently traversing through the Forgotten Forest."

"At night?" I asked, my stomach turning, thinking of the way the spirits played games. They'd messed with me, and I didn't want to repeat the experience.

"Yes," she said. "The vampire are already dead, so what would the remnants of what was once a life do?"

I swallowed hard. "True."

"You have minutes and must go to the edge of the forest to stop them before they make it to the palace grounds."

"Albert expects you to make a stand and not go on the offensive there, but you must go now in order to intercept him."

Rain shook his head. "I can't redirect all our forces there on such short notice. It would take at least a day to move them all."

"You don't need them," Zabrina said, glancing at me and back to Rain. "Between the two of you, and Merrick and me, you'll have all the power you need. Arianna will know what to do when she gets there."

She had that wrong. I didn't have a clue what to do to stop Albert, and I was praying Nyx would hop into my mind to help me.

"I see the skepticism on your face, both of your faces," Zabrina said. "But did you know what to do before you put that building together and saved all those fae lives?"

"No," I said. "It just came to me like a piece of knowledge I'd once known but forgotten."

Zabrina smiled. "Because it is the goddess giving you what you need at the precise right moment."

"Or it's Ari's nature to want to save the innocent."

Both arguments had merit, but I knew it was Nyx's power. There was only one fear I had in the moment. "What if I can't save everyone?"

"That was never going to be an option," Zabrina said. "We are all here for a time and pass to the next realm. It's a gift, and one I believe you know personally."

I glanced down at the floor, lamenting what waited for us. Knots formed in my stomach, and I breathed through the anxiousness. Starlight twinkled in my periphery as if Nyx was urging me forward.

"We need to go now," Zabrina said. "Orla, Dariel, and Haisley are waiting in the courtyard for us. Whit will meet us at the edge of the forest."

It wasn't fair. They'd all fought in the Great War and the many battles that occurred during that time, and here they were again being asked to face the same foe—my father. As much as I wanted to deny him, he was my blood, and I'd have to reconcile later the cost to my soul after I killed him.

CHAPTER 48
DUTY & HONOR
CYRUS

Leana vanyshened with a fae, so she and her unborn youngling would be safe. Cleave stood on one side of me and Marius on the other. Two of the homes once occupied by unicorn burned. One unicorn had been bitten—a male I didn't know well. A fae vanyshened him to the coast so he could be treated. As for the remaining vampire, we'd exploded or beheaded most of them. They were possessed by their bloodlust, and eyed us as their next meal.

Cleave looked passed me to Marius. "We could stop this with one—"

"That is not our way," my brother said. "We fight fair."

"Of course." Cleave bowed his head. "I didn't mean to offend."

"You didn't, my friend."

I drew my sword and readied myself for the attack. Drool ran from the mouth of the vampire directly in front of me. The spit ran down the front of his black and red armor. He salivated over our blood, and it turned my stomach. His head would be the first one I would take.

"Where is Albert?" Marius called out over the couple of dozen vampire.

The one drooling laughed, and the others snickered behind him.

"This is a distraction," I said. Anger seethed from me and in the collective bond.

"Yes, but that doesn't mean we let them live."

I smirked, shifting side to side, keeping my tired legs warmed for the signal.

The vampire parted, and a grunting noise in the dark got louder and louder. One of the giant vampire like had been at Albert's palace came into view, occasionally knocking a normal-sized vampire out of the way. Anyone in their right mind would be terrified. I hoped the fucker came for me.

He ran straight for us with red eyes and mottled skin, a scrap of material hanging around his waist. Albert had created this monster, and it only wanted death.

"Steady," Marius said to our small group of seasoned fighters.

Letting my glamour go to my unicorn form, I looked down the line, recalling the many battles we had fought side-by-side, knowing this could be the last time I would do so as a unicorn. *Thank you, Erebus. My duty and honor belong to you.*

CHAPTER 49

TARGETED

RAIN

A line of guardsmen waited with Orla, Dariel, and Haisley. Relief crossed Orla's face as she laid eyes on Ari. Her face went back to neutral, and she took a knee in the pebbles in front of Ari. Merrick did the same, followed by her mother. Then, the soldiers showed their respect. I stared at Dariel and Haisley, waiting to see what they would do.

Neither had been particularly fond of me on the throne and had opined to the council at various times to replace me. Haisley had seemed to connect with Ari, and I knew it was fear of Dariel and his cruel ways that kept her f I snarled in their direction, letting a taste of my anger out. If they challenged Ari, I'd take their heads and serve them to their queen. Dariel and Haisley both dropped in reverence. I turned to my love, my mate, my everything, and bent my knee to her.

"I pledge my life to the queen of fae chosen by Nyx to

lead us into battle and return triumphant for the good of all fae kind." I'd made a similar vow to King Veran, but it never meant what it did to make the same commitment to Ari.

Her mouth opened, but she quickly closed it. A translucent sheen of starlight enveloped her.

The others behind me repeated the same words I'd spoken to her.

"Shall I fall, my death will be to the glory of the kingdom, the realm, and my queen."

The air around us electrified with a promise to our queen. There was no taking it back.

Ari shook her head and motioned with her hand. "Rise. All of you." Then, she did something no other queen or king had done to my knowledge. She took a knee in front of us.

Pride swelled in my chest. She changed all of us with her courage. General Daphina had once bowed before the entirety of the forces. Ari had no way to know that, but her mother would have been so impressed by the humble gesture.

"I'm not worthy of the honor you bestow upon me, but I pledge my power, my soul, and my life to the protection of our people and our realm." Her voice carried on the wind in a powerful song that could only come from a goddess.

Zabrina stifled a sob. I scanned the others and saw eyes brimming with tears matching mine.

Ari stayed on her knee. "Dry your tears. We will not go

into battle in sadness. We go into it with power and strength and on the right side of history."

Zabrina looked up into the night sky and gasped. "Blessed Nyx."

Heads turned up in the same direction. I held my hand out to Ari. She rose from her position and leaned against me as she gazed up. I took in the wonder above us. There in the moonlight sky, a mix of starlight and smoke formed the triple goddess symbol.

"Nyx, Mother, and me," Ari whispered, her tone one of acceptance.

My queen, bathed in the light of stars, emanated beauty and exhibited the strength of a warrior. For two hundred years, I believed there was no match for me, and I wouldn't know love. Thanks to The Fates, I'd been wrong and though, I was wholly unworthy of her, Nyx saw fit to make me Ari's mate. She had all of me, and that was something I'd never given another fae.

"We will be victorious today," Orla said.

The group cheered, and Ari led us out of the gate toward the Forgotten Forest. I hated the place and mourned for those tied forever to the poisoned grounds. Laurel had no fear of it, and mine wasn't fear of the spirits —it was fear of the memories and if history would repeat itself.

Whit met us at the edge as Zabrina had said, and he had something in his hand that made me smile.

Thank the goddesses and gods. "You were able to retrieve it."

"What is that?" Ari asked, studying the machine.

"This can temporarily remove an individual's power when directed at them."

"So just the one person? Not everyone?" Ari's eyebrow raised with her skepticism.

Whit nodded. "Yes, it has to be targeted on them to adjust to their magic vibration. Once it is locked in, you press this button." He pointed to the side of the gun-like contraption. "Then, you have about fifteen or twenty seconds before their power comes back."

"That's not very long," Ari said.

"It was long enough for your mother," Zabrina challenged.

The desire to intercede and chastise Zabrina was hard to ignore, but she spoke the facts. Our window was small, and Ari would have to be quick.

Realization crossed Ari's face. "This is how my mother trapped Albert the first time."

"He didn't even know it existed, and he was so focused on her that he never saw it coming."

"You invented this, Whit?" Ari asked.

He shook his head. "No, your mother, the master weaver she was, did."

"Even in death, she gives hope," Orla said, looking up to the sky. "Forever our general, my friend Daphina."

I remembered Daphina's bravery on the field, and my heart ached for the loss of our friend. Her achievements could never be eclipsed, but her daughter's efforts fashioned a new branch on their incredible family tree.

""How much time before he is here?" Ari asked Zabrina.

"Not long now. He should be here in minutes."

"And you're sure he won't expect us?"

Zabrina straightened to her full height. "Not that I've seen. He is surprised to find us waiting in the vision. It still stands as I saw earlier."

"I hear rustling in the distance." The weight of my sword at my back increased as I drew it.

The crowd went quiet, crouching low. We'd be forced to pursue them through the woods if they retreated, and I decided I would pin myself to Ari if that happened. Merrick stood on her other side, her massive sword drawn. I hadn't seen her carry it since the war and hadn't thought I would ever see her use it again. Ari withdrew her daggers from their sheaths and lit them up with Nyx's power. She would be victorious. Her reign would not end at the hands of her father. I'd make sure of that.

"Whit, how's your angle?" I whispered.

"I should be good from here if he's in the center as we suspect."

I nodded. The anticipation drowned my patience. I wanted blood on the end of my sword and to make them all pay for what they did to my love.

A line of red eyes glowed at the edge of the forest. I gave one last glance up and down the line, and my gaze settled on Ari. I sent love and respect down the bond. "Neck, head, or heart."

She smiled at me. "I love you too, but I expected something different given how much you like it when I stab things."

I winked at her. "Save that for later."

A screech pierced the air. I snapped my head to the forest. Two of the giant fuckers like I'd fought at the palace appeared. I owed some blows to those undead creatures. "They are mine." I leapt over the line in front of me and landed right in their path. They eyed me, and my mouth curved up as I summoned a small taste of my power. I struck true with dual pinpointed lightning bolts. The two giants stumbled and banged against each other, falling in opposite directions. Both of their huge bodies erupted into mounds of ash.

"Godsdammit, that felt good." My voice into the forest. My message meant for Albert's ears, I wanted him to know I wasn't afraid of him. "Who's next?"

How about you come back here and stick to the plan? Ari's amused voice sang into my head.

Whatever you say, my goddess. I vanyshened back to her side. "Ready to kill some vampire?"

"I'm ready for the private party afterward." She lifted one shoulder and gave me a quirky smile. "But killing some vampire before then sounds like a good warm-up."

Anything you say, my queen. I'll be worshipping you tonight.

"Is that foreplay for you two?" Merrick's top lip scrunched, and her nose wrinkled.

Ari laughed. "Let's have that discussion another time."

"I'm not sure I want to," Merrick said.

Zabrina cleared her throat. "Must you young ones always talk about sex?"

Ari, Merrick, and I all laughed. Orla covered her mouth.

"It's time," Zabrina said, her voice deadly sharp.

Albert emerged from the woods, flanked by a dozen of those strange, giant vampire.

CHAPTER 50
SECOND CHANCES
ARI

I'd take pleasure in wiping Albert's smug expression from his face. Even with the knowledge of a win for the battle, I was careful not to underestimate him. A quick survey of his forces gave me more hope. It was a large group of vampire but not as many as we'd faced at his palace. How many of those enormous creatures were in his ranks? And he had to have made the hideous vampire-ish creatures because they weren't native to our realm.

"This can all end, Arianna," Albert said, his voice echoing around me. "You just have to come with me."

If he spoke the truth, his offer would have tempted me, but lies flowed like a river from his mouth. There would be no peaceful ending to the battle.

"That's never going to happen," Merrick murmured beside me.

"Not as long as I'm alive," Rain said from the other direction.

I mentally prepared myself for what I expected next. He'd berate me or all of us, and I'd have to keep my temper in check. I wasn't fully recovered, and I could only have enough strength for one shot.

Is Whit ready? I asked through the mate connection to Rain. *I'm afraid he'll follow my line of sight if I look.*

He's ready. Whit's been ready for this for two hundred years. Rain's voice sounded heavy in the bond. All the excitement over his kills was gone. *You're sure about this, Ari? We don't have a prison to put him in, so it has to be death, but it doesn't have to be from you.*

Yes, it does.

I inhaled through my nose and held it until the rushing sound in my ears stopped. "I already did that—went with you before. It didn't work out."

"Oh, but it did, darling daughter." He moved forward, but I didn't care if he made it clear of the vampire. I was perfectly fine taking them out.

I ignored his goading. "You also took my sister and her mate. What you did to them is not the act of a father." I paused like I was choosing my words carefully, but I knew exactly what I was going to say. He moved a few steps closer. "So, no, Albert. I'm not your darling daughter. I'm vengeance personified—for me, my sister, my mother, and all those who have paid the worst price at your hands."

"Now," Rain whispered beside me.

Whit shook his head. It wasn't firing. *No. Fuck.*

"Did you really think you could get me twice in a lifetime with that, Whit?" Albert flicked his wrist, and Whit went flying through the air. A thud was the only indication he landed. No other sounds followed.

"Someone go check on him," I said through gritted teeth.

"I'm the only healer here," Merrick said.

"Then go."

"I'm not leaving your side. I promised your sister."

"Then pick someone to go see to him." I ground out.

Albert laughed. "You can't win, little girl."

"I'm not a little girl. I'm a descendant of Nyx," I said, summoning the power of my ancestors. I held out my hands and hurled everything I could at him. Bright, hot luminescence shot from me like starlight and was stronger than any fire I'd met.

Albert side-stepped it, and my beam cut a line through his vampire army. Dozens of them, including some of the giants, turned to ash along with any trees in between. The vampire hissed in eerie unison.

"How?" Zabrina said, barely audible over the noise of the vampire hoard.

Whit approached, no obvious injuries on him, but several unicorn flanked him. Marius, Cyrus, Casimir, and others I didn't recognize but assumed they were from the unicorn area of the city. Marius met my gaze.

My plan didn't work. I sent to him.

You gave up on the first try. Did we ever give up the first time in training?

No. I felt stupid—like a child who hadn't learned the most important lesson in front of her.

So, we adjust and try again.

I nodded to him. Cyrus stood next to him. He'd come back for us—or at least for Gemma and Laurel.

"I'm going to give you one last chance to save your precious friends," Albert said. "Then I'll kill them all if that's what it takes to get you to leave with me."

How's Whit?

He's fine. The machine is broken though.

Any ideas?

Your plan is solid. Distract him. Then give your goddess power free rein on him.

"Rain, I'm going to need some lightning. Can you drop everything you've got on him and the horde? I need a distraction he can't ignore." While I meant my request, I was posturing for Albert, and I wanted those standing with me to know I was no longer afraid. Nyx chose me, and I intended to fuck shit up for Albert and his vampire army.

"How about a little fire with that lightning from the other side?" Merrick asked, her lips tipping up in a smile.

"This is why we are friends, Merrick."

"Come on, Mother. We're going to set some vampire on fire."

Zabrina met my gaze, and it said everything I needed to know. We weren't in the future of foresight, and she didn't know how this was going to end. We might all die, but at least we would be doing the right thing.

"My answer is still no," I said, letting the wind carry my voice.

Albert chuckled a sound full of menace. "Then it might be time to wish your friends safe passage to the next realm."

I cocked my head to the side. "Or maybe I'll just tell you I hope you don't make it there."

Thunder crackled overhead. "Have you met my mate's lightning?"

Some of the vampire scurried back, but the giants stuck close to him.

"Whenever you're ready, my love," I said, drawing out the last two words like he did with me so often.

"My pleasure." The eagerness in his voice energized me.

Lightning hit in blinding strikes in front of us. I shielded my eyes but could feel the heat of Merrick and Zabrina's flames. Second chances were kind of my thing, so I believed it might work.

Marius and Cyrus took up the position left open beside me when Merrick and Zabrina had moved. More unicorn stood beside Rain, including Casimir. Our guards. Our protectors. Our friends.

"Nyx, thank you for the gift of the power to stop my father in this realm." The magic spread out under my skin, building with each second. A silvery light shimmered over my skin as if it couldn't be contained in my body any longer. Controlling it required considerable effort, and I fought to maintain the appearance of strength.

I unleashed everything built up inside me, all the hate I held in my heart for him, all the pain he'd put me, my sister, and my mother through. I sent it all to him tenfold with the power of starlight.

The unicorn dipped their heads and pointed their horns at him. Light radiated from them and joined with mine. There wasn't time to focus on how they were doing it. My limbs shook. If I fucked up, someone I cared about could be hurt or worse. I forced my body to still.

You're in control, Ari. Guide our light to yours and aim as you wish.

I'm scared I'll lose control and hurt someone.

Don't be afraid. You're stronger than you think. If this isn't what you want, someone else can take up the task. Marius lowered his head and added his magic to the stream of light.

There's a line of sight. The choice is yours. Rain's voice mixed with ours. I wanted to ask how it was possible, but I gave all my attention to the beam of light.

Albert looked scared as I gained control and launched it at him. His eyes widened, and he disappeared. The beam hit the giants. They disintegrated—not even any ash remained to mark where they stood.

My breath was ragged as I gulped down air. "Where did he go?"

Everyone was frozen. Rain's face reddened, eyes darting to the side. Chills slithered over me.

Hands grabbed me from behind, arms locking me into a cage. Albert dragged me back.

Marius trained me well in close combat. I wrapped my foot around his ankle, sending us toppling backward. It bought enough time for me to shove an elbow into his sternum, breaking his hold. I rolled away and scrambled to my feet. Retrieving my daggers from their sheaths, I sent goddess power into them. The emblems glowed in response.

"You can't kill me. I am your father." He scoffed.

Anger infused my magic, amping up the brightness of my blades. I circled Albert, crouched in my fighting stance. "There was a time when that would have been true. I remember the man who raised me. That man loved me. He took care of me, consoled me after Mother died and Gemma disappeared. That man wasn't real, and any semblance of him died when the prison kingdom came down. You are not him. You are a power-hungry tyrant who doesn't care about the realm or the lives you've broken or the sacrifice my mother to stop you. So, Albert, I can say without any remorse that I will kill you, and I will sleep better for having done it."

His expression changed into something unreadable, but there was no time to decipher it. He vanyshened away. Movement caught the corner of my eye. The others unfroze in stiff movements like the magic was slow to release them from its hold. Albert must be close. I turned in a slow circle searching for signs of his power. A weight lifted, lightening the air, and the others rushed toward me. I knew Albert had gone somewhere out of reach.

CHAPTER 51

STAND
ARI

He left his army to die, and we gladly vanquished them from our lands. Separating the heads of vampires would only be a temporary euphoria that evaporated when the memory of the look on Albert's face flashed through my mind. I promised him death for the horrors he'd inflicted, and I meant every word I'd said to him.

Wiping my daggers on a clean spot of my pants, I returned them to their sheaths. "Merrick, go to the coast and make sure that's not where he went. He can't get his hands on my sister and her family."

"I'd like to go if that's okay," Cyrus said, looking at Marius, not me. Since when did he ask for permission?

"Of course," Marius said, his tone solemn.

"I'll come back as soon as I find them," Merrick said. She paused in front of Orla. The look they exchanged was hotter than the fire Merrick had used earlier. I hoped I wasn't misinterpreting what I saw, because I had questions for my friend later.

The vampire tried to run, but some of the most gifted fae in the lands stood together. None of the vampire who entered our kingdom would leave tonight.

I took a step toward them, and my legs gave out. Standing in place, I hadn't observed any weakness in my body. The amount of magic I dumped toward Albert was equal to that of Rain's the day of the Moirai game, so the possibility I'd drained my power existed.

Rain caught me and held me up. "Maybe we should go to the coast too."

"No, I want to be here when our people return," I said. "And I'm hoping Zabrina knows where Albert is and when I can go after him again."

Looking utterly defeated, she turned her head away from the vampire across the field. "Nothing about tonight happened as I saw. Why would you trust what I tell you now?"

"Because you want Albert dead as much as the rest of us."

"I cannot see where he is now. Either he has someone to mask his location..."

"Or he's in the human lands," Rain said.

I wasn't as familiar with the human lands as the others, but I knew their lifespans were far shorter and their bodies more vulnerable than ours. That meant an easier and faster army to raise, which he would need if he was going to keep throwing distractions at us.

"Or on the sacred mountain of the sprites," Orla added, disgust in her tone.

"He wouldn't dare hide there," Haisley said, joining us.

"He's already done some heinous things. I don't think that's above him." I'd seen his atrocity firsthand and read about so many more. It was clear he didn't have boundaries in his thirst for unrivaled power. One thing was certain, he had to be stopped soon.

The light shimmered around me, and the sprite that had visited in my dreams stood in front of us. "He has not invaded our lands."

"Neala," Marius said, his voice softened. "How are you with us?"

"It's not unheard of for us to pass from realm to realm when needed, and the necessity is here tonight," she said.

Marius shook his head. "But you haven't in centuries."

My bonded's statement wasn't entirely true. *You let her in my head.*

That was different. You are different.

Neala smiled coyly. "Have we not?" she asked. "Your lack of seeing us doesn't mean we haven't been here."

"Why now?" Rain asked.

She turned to me. Her ethereal presence cast a soft glow on the ground. "Because there is a goddess with us now, and she needs our guidance."

Denial charged through my body like the hum of electricity in the city. "I am not a goddess. While Nyx has blessed me, I am fae."

She walked around me, her chin tipped up, and that same smile on her face. "You do look very much fae."

My shoulders relaxed.

"But looks can be deceiving. Your father looks fae as well, does he not?"

What was she talking about? The vampire bite. The goddess blood in my veins was the only known cure, but it wasn't really a cure since it was still present. Was she about to tell everyone here I'd been bitten too? That the vampire marker would remain in my blood just as it had Albert's? I looked at Rain's face, memorizing it in case the others turned on me.

"Do not fear, Arianna. They have pledged their lives to you."

Marius's trepidation about Neala's arrival had me on edge, but the way she played with matters that should be kept private pissed me off.

I straightened to my full height. Sprite or not, I took that as a threat, and I wasn't going to cower. "If you're so omniscient, then you should know there is very little I'm afraid of."

Ari... Marius warned.

She turned her patronizing smile on him. "Why do you caution her for speaking her mind?"

Shock filtered through me. She'd read his mind. He hadn't spoken my name out loud.

Are you going to tell her unicorn don't answer to fae? I sent back angry he hadn't warned me she could insert herself into something as sacred as our bond.

She inclined her head toward me, and I might have thought it was respect from anyone else. From her, the action seemed meant to disarm me. "You catch on quicker than some, but to your question for your bonded guard, normally unicorn do not answer to fae. Now ask your next question."

"Why did you phrase it like that?"

"Because you, like your brother, are so much more than fae. Although you are as different as you are alike, your paths are destined to be similar. Be careful not to end up on different sides."

"He's my brother. I love him and will protect him. We will not end up in opposition."

"I truly hope that is the case, young goddess." Neala clasped her hands in front of her. "Nyx was right to bring you here at this time in the realm."

Her logic made no sense. I was born into the realm. The discussion seemed like a lot of nonsense. Meanwhile, Albert was out there planning his next move, and maybe I'd already set up his next steps for him. "Are you here to help us end Albert or not?"

"I like you," she said.

"I don't think you're here to make friends."

"Ari," Rain said, squeezing my hand.

"I told you—"

He inclined his head in the direction the sprite had been.

Her ethereal body floated toward me like an apparition. "Look into my eyes, young goddess."

I glanced at Marius. His face was unreadable save for a subtle blink of encouragement. I met the gaze of Neala, and smoke clouded my vision. I was standing on one side of the field, and on the other side stood a man. He looked familiar, but I didn't know him.

"What am I seeing?" I asked.

"Look closer," she said.

I focused on the face of the figure, and the features were so similar to someone I knew. Drew. But he was all grown up. He'd survive whatever came next, and that gave me some solace. "Is this the future?"

"One of the possible branches," she said.

Albert stepped out of the forest and patted grown-up Drew on the back. Vampire closed ranks behind them. No, that would not be his future.

"I will never allow this to happen."

"No, it won't as long as you choose your path wisely. You must rule this kingdom in the most tumultuous time faekind has faced. If this path comes to be, you will not win, and the realm will lose all magic. The unicorn will die. Fae will become not much more than humans. My kind will not be able to return here in any form. It is much that Nyx has rested on your shoulders, but it is within you if you follow the right path."

"I don't suppose you will tell me the signs I'm on that path."

"Unfortunately, I cannot."

I gazed at her and saw something under the exquisite

mask of beauty. There was a connection to this realm she didn't voice. "You're not solely a sprite."

"Like you, I walk two worlds. I was born sprite long ago and was reborn a sprite again around the time your mother came into this realm. I visited her on occasion."

Shock skipped through me like a rock over water, but also a sense of interconnection to know she'd met Mother. "What did she think about your visits?"

"She was far less skeptical than you are." Neala smiled, genuine and warm. "But she saw me for what I was."

"You're a Fate," I whispered, understanding why she'd visited both my mother, me, and the children.

"Some answers are not meant to be said aloud."

"I want to save the realm," I said. "He froze time. How?"

She placed a hand on my shoulder in a touch as light as a feather. Both cold and warmth spread with the contact, but her touch was peaceful. "I know you do. Some things I cannot tell you, but as your power depletes your energy so does his. For now, your father has retreated. You are safe to plan your future or pursue him. It will take him far longer to recover and regroup than you, and that is the limit of what I can share without influencing outcomes."

Light flashed in front of my eyes. I was back at the edge of the forest, and she was gone. "Where did she go?"

"She will come back if needed," Marius said.

Do you know?

About her?

That's what I'm asking.

There was a long pause, and I thought he was going to cite unicorn business or just not answer. *Yes.*

He'd known she was a Fate. Godsdammit. *It makes it hard to remember why I trust you when I know you've kept a secret like this.*

It was never mine to tell, Ari, no matter how much I wanted to.

Sadness and remorse deluged the bond. It hurt him not to tell me.

I forgive you.

Merrick vanyshened back without Cyrus. "Why are you paler than usual? Are you hurt?"

"I'm fine. The others took care of the vampires. I need rest, but I'll be okay. How's my sister?"

"Everyone is safe there. No sign of Albert," Merrick said, her tone calmer. "Laurel is doubling the patrols."

I relaxed and looked at Rain. "I don't know for how long, but we have some time to prepare before he tries again. Thank you all for standing by me tonight. The events of the evening could have turned out much differently had you not stood with me."

Orla, Haisley, Dariel, and Whit formed a line in front of me and knelt. Zabrina crooked her arm through Merrick's and joined them. The guards, Rain's guards, kneeled for me again.

Their loyalty signified our future for the realm. Despite the veneration, which I did appreciate, I still despised the tradition. The visible unity held importance for the realm, but we would show our cohesion in other ways.

"There are few places I like better than being on my knees in front of you," Rain whispered in my ear before turning and dropping to the ground.

The only time it is acceptable for a fae to be on their knees. I whispered seductively into his mind while schooling my features.

"Hail to our queen," Orla shouted.

"Hail to our queen," the others repeated with her.

"Rise," I said, knowing what I wanted to say. "No one in this kingdom should bow to anyone else. You are citizens of this kingdom, and as such, you will stand with your heads held high in not only my presence but each other's."

Rain was the first on his feet, taking his place beside me. Merrick was next and stood at my other side. Zabrina followed and then the rest, standing as I'd instructed.

"I know change is never easy, but we will experience many new things together. Our common goal remains the same—to find and end Albert."

CHAPTER 52
PUNISHMENT
CYRUS

I sat on the blanket next to Gemma. Her feet in the sand, she watched Laurel play in the surf with Phina and Drew.

"You've been glamoured in your fae form for a long time," Gemma said. "Do you need to go run and be free?"

She was serious, but a laugh escaped my mouth.

"I'm fine, Gemma." I stretched my arm behind her back and buried my fingers in the sand, wanting to touch her but resisting.

"Something is different. Did Marius punish you?"

I winced. I wanted to tell her and Laurel together. Verbalizing once what I'd experienced would be hard enough to get through. "Can we hold that conversation until we're alone with Laurel?"

She leaned her head on my shoulder. The connection everything I wanted in this realm. "Of course. I'm just worried about you. He is too."

"There is nothing to worry about, but I will tell you both where I was. I didn't run away."

"I know you didn't." Her voice wavered in a whisper as if she was afraid to speak.

I rested my head against hers. Her belief in me was something I valued. I missed our bond when my punishment prevented me from communicating with her. "How do you know?"

"Because I was in your head," she said. "At least the emotions. I could feel how much you wanted to get back to us."

I tensed. My stomach twisted into knots the size of the sacred mountain. I'd been restricted from her but she hadn't been blocked from me. "Gemma…"

She sat up and studied me with the kind of love I never thought I deserved. "Tell me in your own time. I'm not pressuring you. It's your story to tell. For now, I want you to know how loved you are."

A tear flowed over my lid and rolled down my cheek. Gemma caught it on her finger and held it out to me.

"You've shared enough. Our love doesn't require tears any longer. Take this one back."

I looked up into the sky and swallowed against the hardness in my throat. "I can't."

She gasped and clutched my knee with her other hand. "What do you mean?"

I took her fingers in mine and pressed my lips to her soft skin. Maybe this was always what was meant to be, but my insides had a hole where a part of me was missing.

I hadn't reconciled the loss of my identity. I didn't know who I was anymore. The words wouldn't come to tell her I was different. "Let's discuss it tonight."

Phina ran toward us and jumped in the middle. Sand went all over me, Gemma, Laurel, and the blanket. "I love it here."

I did too. My heart was full, surrounded by the people I loved.

Drew dropped onto the blanket in a position that resembled a frog. "When is Ari coming?" Leana would be back for him soon. She'd gone to prepare a place for herself. Gemma made it clear Leana was welcome in the summer palace, but Leana wanted a separate space for her and the youngling growing in her belly.

Gemma smoothed Drew's hair back. "Soon. In a few days, maybe."

Laurel leaned over, letting his hair drip on Gemma and me. He gave Gemma a quick peck on the cheek and surprised me by repeating the gesture on me. The perfect happiness of the moment settled over me like the warm sun above us. Open displays of affection were not a practiced skill for me, but I'd learn to be for my mates. I wouldn't live in the shadows because unicorn frowned on my broken oaths. No, my mates deserved so much more.

Phina grabbed a bucket and scooped sand with it. Drew had a toy car in his hand and drove it through the sand and into the hole Phina made.

I tried to brush some of the sand off the blanket and was unsuccessful.

Laurel stretched out at the bottom of it and rested his head on my leg. "Do you think we can talk Ari into moving the seat of the kingdom here? This is paradise, and I'd forgotten how perfect the coastal lands are."

"My sister isn't known for her ability to relax," Gemma said. "But she needs to learn. I think it's better to keep this part of the kingdom free of court business."

"Are we ever really free of court happenings?" Laurel asked in a wistful tone.

"Not for me since I was fifteen years old," Gemma said.

"Not in my centuries either," I said, thinking of all the changes I'd seen over the years like the rise of the vampires with Albert's help. Or how the matriarchal society of fae had become a patriarchy in one generation with King Veran's seat on the throne. Ari's rule would reset their expectations, but it would take decades to repair...possibly a century to undo all the damage. I was curious if she would leave the technology developed under Veran. Gemma wasn't fond of it either but adjusted more easily than her sister. Together, they could reduce the reliance on electricity in the city.

Laurel stretched his arm over his head and draped it lazily on my thigh. Gemma and Laurel made life feel easy, especially with the laid-back lifestyle of the coast. It had been hard for me for so long that I had forgotten what it was like not to struggle. I didn't want to go back to the fae court. Did that count as running away from my problems? Even if I was happier in this piece of the kingdom that was paradise...

The kids moved closer to the water, not too far but at enough of a distance that they wouldn't pick up on our conversations. My heart cracked wondering if they'd accept a mate who wasn't, might never be, whole. The denial I grappled with did the situation no good. Gemma and Laurel deserved to know my punishment and be aware of my situation. They could decide if they still wanted me around once they understood.

"I'd planned to wait until we were alone tonight, but I know you both have questions about where I went after I left."

Laurel twisted, propping his head up in his hand. Gemma faced me. Love and sympathetic expressions met me, and I turned my head. Being unworthy was a feeling I knew, but the gravity of it sunk into my gut.

I stared out into the ocean, not sure I could get through it if I looked at them. "Honor is the most sacred thread that binds unicorn society. There are certain rules that, when broken, require punishment to be administered. We are well aware of this when we pledge ourselves and take our different oaths. While I can't share most of them, you are familiar with one."

I glanced at Gemma. Recognition passed over her face. I recalled the day everything changed for me, and the day I knew I'd give up my honor for her.

"The guardian and charge bonding ceremony," she said with no regret in her tone.

"Yes," I said. "It's one of our more sacred ceremonies

and one of the few fae are privy to, obviously, due to the nature of it."

"You broke the oath by being with me," Gemma said, her voice barely audible. "Because I was your charge."

"That is one oath I broke. After a lifetime of perfection, it was my turn, and I broke several over the course of a year," I said, looking back at the ocean. My chest nearly caved in at my confession.

Laurel brushed his hand along my calf in gentle caresses. "Are you able to tell us how you were punished? If you want to, of course."

Taking Laurel's hand in mine, I had the acceptance I needed to continue. "I do, and I wish I could tell you all of it, but what I am allowed to tell you is that I cannot release the glamour and return to my natural form. I'm bound to my faelike form until my punishment is complete."

A kind or release lightened the burden of the truth, but it didn't repair the gaping hole in my soul left by my confinement to fae form.

Gemma scooted closer, placing a hand on my bicep. She squeezed. "And how long is that?"

"It could be a year, or it could be a century. We are never told in cases like mine." From what I'd heard of these matters, no unicorn received their form or their ability to speak to the collective consciousness back in a year. The diminutions lasted at least a century, but rules barred me from sharing those details.

"That's so unfair to deliver a punishment that has no end," she said.

"What can we do to make the time easier for you?" Laurel asked.

Suddenly too hot, sweat beaded on my forehead, and I swiped it away. My insides quivered. I hoped my conclusion wasn't a miscalculation of what they offered. "You still want to be with me when I'm half myself?" I asked, glancing between them both.

Gemma rested her hand over my heart. "Of course. It's not your physical form that I love. It's who you are."

Laurel placed his hand over Gemma's. "I agree. I don't care if you are on four legs or two as long as you're here with us."

I bowed my head. I'd expected this conversation to go much differently. I hadn't expected them to accept me without all my unicorn glory.

"There is something I'd like from you," Laurel said, kissing my cheek. He kissed Gemma's neck. "Both of you."

"What's that?" Gemma asked.

"Marry me here on this beach. I don't care if it's today, tomorrow, or a year from now, but I want to be married to both of my mates."

PERMISSION

CYRUS

"I can't get married without Ari here," Gemma said.

Being bound to both of them was what I desired most. I'd do it however they wanted as long as I could claim them as mine, and I theirs.

"Of course. I'd want Rain here too," Laurel said, looking at me. "And I'm assuming you'd want your brother here as well."

My twin's relationship with me was complicated by my broken oaths and my punishment. He walked a very tenuous line, freeing me, and even then, he couldn't be the one to release me early. Casimir had to perform the rite and use her blood. The panel was a recent addition in the last hundred years. The crystals in the cave had some sentient property that held a unicorn until they felt remorse for their actions, and that was never going to happen for me. I'd have been there until my body gave out. Even after the pain, I had no regrets for my choices.

"Cyrus?" Gemma tilted her head at me. "What do you think?"

Our species were symbiotic, but our cultures were very different. "While you have fae with multiple partners and the same for unicorn, your status in the kingdom is different than most. As your bonded, I caution you both against this choice."

Their positions in the fae line of succession as well as mine would be a problem for both our kind but more so for the fae. Both wanted heirs, and that wouldn't happen between unicorn and fae. Our relationship would be challenged repeatedly. I'd accept the trials with no contrition. Was it fair to ask that of them?

Gemma frowned, and she turned her gaze to Laurel, lacing her fingers with his. "We've known since you left that you were the piece missing in our lives."

"So as our mate what do you say?" Laurel smiled.

"As your mate, I'm already bound to you for here and after. I am yours and you are mine until the last star in the sky winks out." I said the word "mate" out loud that had played through my head so many times since we were together again. Love radiated in my chest and lightened my heart. A single word had never held so much power leaving my mouth.

"And?" Gemma asked, her lips turned up expectantly.

"And there is no greater honor for me than to profess my love for you in front of those closest to us."

Phina squealed. When I turned, she ran straight for me, tackling me. "We're going to be a family."

I hadn't known she was listening, but the joy in her voice as she included me as family made me the happiest I'd been in this lifetime. My family...worth every ounce of penance my broken oaths required.

Gemma smoothed Phina's hair. "We are."

"I told you he'd say yes, Mommy." Phina leaned her head back and talked to Gemma from an upside-down position. She straightened. "I told Mommy and Daddy that we were all going to live together and all they had to do was ask you."

When I thought my heart couldn't hold any more love, our daughter proved me wrong. "Is that what you want, Phina? For all of us to live together?"

"Yes, I'm the luckiest girl in the world because I have Mommy and Daddy." She looked at both of them. Then, she looked at me and patted my cheek. "And my baba, Cyrus."

"Baba? I haven't heard that word in two centuries."

"She wanted you to have your own name for 'daddy,'" Laurel said. "So that you and I know exactly who she is talking to at the dinner table."

Erebus, I am unworthy of this love, but I am so grateful you are giving me this life. If I never earn my unicorn form back, this is enough for a hundred lifetimes.

"Thank you, Phina," I said, my words strained through my tight throat. "And was there anything special you wanted me to call you?"

Her nose wrinkled just like Gemma's. "Phina, of course. What else would you call me?"

"My daughter," I said. "Phina."

She smiled and hugged me. "My baba."

"Phina, can you check on Drew? I think he might be lonely out there," Laurel said, giving a side nod.

"Oh..." She took off running, kicking up sand on the blanket.

"Will Drew live with us too?" I'd become attached to him, but he wasn't mine to claim. Leana declared for him, and any relationship for us would be complicated. Setting Drew up for a successful future was important, and I'd work with Leana however needed to make sure he didn't suffer because of our convoluted past.

Gemma shook her head, a little pain in her eyes. "He wants to live with Ari. I tried to explain that her life was going to get so much busier, but he was insistent."

"He knows his mind. If he wants to be with her, there is a reason." Like calls to like drifted in my head, but I didn't voice it. We had enough to deal with, and that could wait.

"Or Ari and Leana raised him, and he barely knows me." Gemma sighed. "My father certainly broke our family in ways that have lasting repercussions."

Laurel scooted closer to her, and I slid my hand over the back of her neck, massaging the tense muscles.

I watched the kids play. "He didn't break any of you. You all have survived, and he will not win."

"I am broken. All the training we did, Cyrus, and I couldn't face him. I left my sister...my younger sister to deal with him while I ran away and hid in this paradise."

She misplaced the blame on herself. Albert deserved all of it, and my heart ached that she carried around guilt because of him.

"You had children to think of, Gemma," I said. "Lest we forget, Ari has a unique set of gifts."

"She does, but I don't think I can forgive myself." She hugged her knees.

"Let me ask Leana to take the children tonight," I said. "The three of us need to do some healing, and there was a place I saw when I was getting Kyle and Jenna settled that I think would be perfect."

"You don't have to ask permission, Cyrus. You are part of this family." Gemma gestured between the three of us. "We are a unit."

My heart heard her, and so did my head. She spoke the truth, and the love was real.

Laurel leaned forward. "Since you brought it up, how are the two vampire doing?"

"They've adjusted remarkably well, considering they are the only two vampire here. They like being near the water." Marius conceded and allowed me to bring them here before my punishment was invoked. I think he did so out of fear I'd do it anyway and add another crime to my list.

The sun dropped lower in the sky. Gemma stood, dusting the sand off, and kissed the top of Laurel's head. "I'll get the kids. You took them in the water."

I brushed my fingertips through hers as she walked toward the little ones.

Laurel reached his hand out, and I slipped mine into his.

"We're very lucky, Cyrus," he said. "We have extra love in our family."

"We certainly are." I might not be a unicorn anymore, but I didn't need to be to know what I witnessed was love. And it was mine.

CHAPTER 54

PROMISE
CYRUS

Gemma clasped her hands together, taking in the table covered in fine dishes, candles, and food. "It's beautiful in here. You did all this?"

"I did have some help, but it was my vision." My cheeks heated, but I wasn't embarrassed. Rather, it was my nerves.

Laurel surveyed the blankets and pillows by the lagoon, glowing turquoise in the dim light. One of the fae staff told me there were rumors that an evil water beast lived in the lagoon. While I didn't believe him, there would be no swimming in the beautiful waters tonight.

I took each of their hands and led them to the table. My palms were damp, but I didn't think I would ever have a big life-changing moment with a mate, much less two.

"There once was a tradition among unicorn that disappeared centuries ago. My parents were among some of the last to observe it. These gold bracelets represent the evolution of love and the continuous circle of fulfilling the three roles to our mates." I picked them up and turned them so the symbols aligned and pointed to the first one.

"We start here with Phillia. The heart with the twin flame represents deep affection earned through our shared experience." I turned the bracelets to the second symbol. "Next, we move into Eros. The bow and arrow have many meanings, but here is where we fall in love."

I twisted the metal one last time. "Finally, we reach Agape. The highest form of love for a unicorn. Some unicorn live their entire lives without reaching this stage, but I was granted the grace twice with both of you. Agape is represented here with a rose entwined in a love knot, and is selfless, unconditional love. My promise to you is bound in these bracelets, and that is to love you until the end of my days."

A tear rolled down Gemma's cheek, and I wiped it away. "No tears tonight. This is a happy occasion."

"Cyrus..." Laurel whispered.

"Let me finish." I brushed my fingers over his, fighting my own tears from falling. Proud to be able to share this private unicorn tradition with them, I pushed forward. "This next part is important."

"This was my father's." I placed the bracelet on Laurel's wrist. "And this one was my mother's matching one." I slipped the smaller one on Gemma's arm. "If you accept my love and my promise, I'll infuse my magic into them. By doing so, you'll be able to find me wherever I am in this realm. Should any of us enter in without a heart of pure love, the bracelets will return to the lands where the ore was mined."

Gemma and Laurel exchanged a look, and my heart dropped. They were going to say no after everything we'd been through...even though we were mates. The bracelets were a bigger commitment than a fae marriage ceremony. I'd went too far.

"Before I accept, will you be punished further for this?" Gemma asked.

To my knowledge, the ceremony had never been performed outside of the unicorn culture. Humans had a ceremony where they exchanged rings, but there were stories that they adopted it from us from the time when we shared space...before they were made to forget. What else could Marius do? My identity had already been taken away. While it could be throttled, they couldn't take my magic without killing me, and I hadn't committed an offense worthy of death.

"There's nothing left to take as punishment," I said.

A smile, mixed with sadness and happiness, appeared on Gemma's face. "Then I accept."

"As do I," Laurel said.

Thank you, Erebus, they'd both said yes. I swallowed against the tightness in my throat. My pulse sped up with excitement, and my heart thrummed in my chest with their acceptance. The overwhelming urge to run and jump through the fields energized me. I'd have to wait for that, but one day, maybe centuries from now, I would celebrate in my natural form.

"Hold your arms out," I said, wrapping a hand around each of the bracelets on their wrists. "Erebus, I call on you to bless our union. Bind my promise to my mates as my gift to them."

Magic zinged around us and sealed itself to the gold. I wasn't sure how much of my magic I'd have access to without my true form or my horn, but I was grateful Erebus had seen fit to allow the union. A sense of completeness wrapped around me, and that was the love of my mates. They pulsed in my chest, and if I'd done the ceremony, I did in theirs as well. Forever bound to them I'd remain, and that exhilarated me. "It is done. All that I am is yours."

Leaning forward, I captured Gemma's lips with mine. Her mouth opened, granting me entrance to claim her. I broke the kiss and pulled Laurel to me. He crushed his mouth on mine, eagerly tasting, and I let him explore. I leaned back, giving space for them. Laurel buried his hands in Gemma's hair. They pulled me into the tangle of arms, and our foreheads rested together.

"I love you both and my life is yours," I said.

"I've loved you for so long that I wouldn't want to find out what it's like to not," Gemma said. Then, she turned to Laurel. "I love you as if I've known you all my life."

Laurel blinked back tears. "I can't imagine not loving you both. My life never felt complete until you both walked into the Forgotten Forest."

"That was a lot like a fae wedding ceremony, Cyrus." Gemma winked. Her voice, low and sultry, stirred my libido. "A very intimate and private one. Maybe we should have a honeymoon tonight to match."

My cock hardened. "I've thought about all the ways I could have you both if you want me. It's going to take a lifetime to get through my list."

"Then we should start ticking them off tonight." Laurel pulled his tunic over his head. His abs were like chiseled rock, and most healers didn't have a hard body from training like him. I palmed the front of my pants.

Gemma ran her hand over his bare chest. "The kids are with Leana all night."

He grasped her hand, so her index finger was the only one extended. Bringing her hand to his mouth, he slid his lips down over her finger, taking it all into his mouth. Gemma's breath quickened. Laurel pulled her finger out in a slow, torturous motion. Raking his teeth over Gemma's skin, he never broke eye contact with her. I might die from pleasure tonight, and I was fine with that.

Laurel reached for me. He curled his fingers around the waist of my pants and pulled me closer. His mouth was on mine, and I relinquished control to him, letting him taste and suck. I reached behind me for the table and grabbed one of the chocolate truffles I'd had made.

When he pulled back, I held it at his lips. He opened and took a bite. His eyes closed, and he hummed with delight. My dick twitched, and I had to adjust myself.

I turned to Gemma and offered her a bit from the same piece. "As was said before, you are always in control. If you become uncomfortable, you say so."

"I don't want control tonight. I want everything," she said, her voice smoky with desire. She opened for the truffle, but I waited.

"You can have whatever you want, but tell me you will speak up if something hurts or isn't what you need," I said.

"The only thing I don't want is what I said last time. Nothing in my ass, but yes, I'll tell you."

I brushed my lips over hers and brought the chocolate near her mouth. "Bite."

"Mmm," she purred.

I watched her swallow and ate the remaining piece, sucking the rest of the chocolate off my fingers.

Gemma slipped her hand into my hair, and her lips covered mine in a gentle caress. She tasted of chocolate. I undid the laces on the front of her dress. "It has a zipper in the back."

I blinked and met Laurel's gaze, and with my eyes, directed him to our mate's back.

He pushed her hair over one shoulder and kissed the exposed part of her back. The zipping sound was loud as he pulled the tab through the teeth. I worked the dress down her arms. Gemma wore no bra, and her breasts were exposed to me. Her nipples hardened in the night air of the cave. I licked my lips, desperately wanting to taste her.

"Is this okay?" I cupped her cheek.

"More than okay." She stepped out of the dress, and Laurel tossed it to the side.

"You look every bit the goddess." I ran a thumb over

her peak, taking in the black lace panties and black heels she wore.

Laurel kissed her neck. His hands slid over her stomach and up to her breasts. He fondled one and gripped my hand over the other. Gemma turned her head, giving him access to her mouth. His tongue slid in and met hers. I kissed along Gemma's jaw.

She wiggled between us, looking for friction. Laurel slid a hand over my bulge. An aching warmth spread through my groin area, and I rocked into his palm.

"Both of you have too many clothes on. Do I need to call the wind to knock them off of you?" Gemma's voice was raspy and demanding. A subtle breeze blew through the cave.

I chuckled, stepping back. Laurel jerked his boots off and tossed them near Gemma's forgotten dress. Gemma inched back toward the plush pallet near the water. She kicked one shoe off and then the other. I yanked my shirt over my head and undid my boots. Laurel had made it down to his underwear, and his muscles rippled as he watched me. I slid my pants off and held my hand out to him.

Gemma waited, standing on the blankets. Her gaze raked over both of us, and I'd never felt more desired. She placed a hand on each of our cheeks and guided mine and Laurel's faces together. I reached my hand around Gemma's neck and pulled her between us. Laurel slid one hand down the black lace she still wore. His hand began to move, and my cock hungered for release. I ran my fingers in light touches over her breasts and down her stomach. She lifted one of my hands to her mouth and sucked on my finger as Laurel had done with her earlier. I groaned, craving a taste of Gemma.

Hooking my thumbs in her panties, I slid them down her legs, trailing kisses as she stepped out of them. I sat in front of her, positioning my legs out in front of me. I grasped her calves and urged her down, reclining backward until she sat on my face. I licked from her slit to the bundle of nerves, swirling my tongue on her clit. Gemma braced her hands on either side of my head. Her breath came in little pants. I grabbed her hips and guided her back and forth.

Laurel's hands were on my dick through my underwear. The head of my cock popped out, and Laurel ran a finger through the precum beaded there. Yearning for more skin-to-skin contact, I pushed toward him. He started working the fabric down. I lifted my hips to make it easier for him. He ran his tongue along the underside of my dick. The euphoria of pleasure rocketed through me, and I hummed against Gemma's pussy. I worked my tongue, tasting her arousal. She fisted my hair, letting out a gasp and came on my face.

"Cyrus." My name was a breathless whisper on her lips.

Bucking my hips into Laurel's mouth, I tapped the back of his throat with my cock. He sucked harder. My erection painfully hard, I was about to erupt like a fountain, but I held off, needing to be joined with them both.

I scooted back, immediately missing Gemma on my face and Laurel's lips on my cock.

"Turn around, love," I said, urging Gemma to face Laurel. I grabbed a pillow to prop under my back and head.

She positioned the head of my dick at her entrance.

"Lean back if you want to give Laurel access to join." She did, and I eased into her as she did. She was so wet I had to control the movement to keep it slow, afraid I'd find release too early. I wanted to memorize this moment, because there was a time I thought I'd never unite with them again. I groaned against Gemma's back from the intensity and reached around to cup her breast, twisting the nipple between my thumb and forefinger. She arched her back and cried out. I slid my hand to her hip and held her still.

"Laurel," she reached for him. "Please."

He knelt between my legs and hers. His hand slipped in her hair, and he kissed her deeply. "You never have to beg, love. I'll give you whatever you want."

Laurel rubbed the head of his cock over the exposed part of my shaft and through Gemma's slickness. My release was so close I could have come. I bit my own lip to hold off for the reward I wanted most. After several passes, he paused. "Are you sure?"

"Yes," Gemma gasped.

He slid in, and the friction against my dick was paradise in physical form. I moved in time with him, and Gemma was so tight. The realm existed for only the three of us like this. I couldn't get close enough to either of them no matter how deep I drove. Gemma's back bowed, and I kissed the space behind her ear. I slid a hand over her breast and down her midsection until I found where the three of us were joined. Erebus, it was incredible.

"You both feel so good," I said, my hand finding her clit and applying pressure as I moved my fingers in circles.

"I..." Laurel's voice trailed off, and his strokes became erratic. He was close, and I was ready to tumble over the cliff together with them.

Gemma swirled her hips, and her pussy contracted around us. The base of my spine tightened. I drove up hard into her and moved my fingers faster.

Laurel grunted, and warmth filled the space. Stars filled my vision. My toes curled into the blankets.

"Fuck," I said, spilling my seed to mix with his. The ecstasy was perfection because it was with my mates.

Gemma cried out in incoherent syllables. She collapsed back on me, and Laurel rolled us on our sides, still connected. Gemma's aftershocks milked me and Laurel. I never wanted to move from the spot afraid I'd lose the closeness with them. When Albert took them and when I faced my punishment, I did so with no expectation or hope I'd make love with Gemma and Laurel ever again. Bound to my mates in every way possible, I felt like we were one.

I draped an arm over both of them, letting my hand rest on Laurel's back. Gemma reached one hand for

Laurel's neck, and the other around mine. "I love you two so much."

Kissing her temple, I eased out of her, feeling Laurel slip out with me. "I love you." I tightened my hand on Laurel. "And I love you."

"That was incredible," Laurel said, his voice thick. "My heart is yours forever—both of yours."

CHAPTER 55

SHATTERED THRONES

ARI

A week had passed since Albert disappeared, and I'd tried to be the leader the fae needed. A coronation date had been set for next month, and I was to declare the name of the city for the duration of my reign. My mate and my bonded were the only two who knew I planned to break from the tradition of using the seated ruler's name. I'd tell Gemma at lunch that the seat of the fae kingdom would be known as Daphinos after our mother, Daphina. Opposition might arise against me on other changes, but recognizing my mother with this honor was one I believed the majority would support.

While I constantly had to look over my shoulder for the next attack from Albert, I carried on with the duties as expected. Sitting on the throne was tiresome. I understood the importance it represented, but I didn't like it. Rain advised I start with smaller things rather than removing the monstrosity of a chair, so it remained in the room on the dais. Albert coveted the chair and the power of it, and I wanted it gone. The irony wasn't lost on me, but I found no humor in it. All the time I'd thought I was like him, I'd been wrong. I wasn't anything like him.

No one was in the room. I'd asked them to give me a few minutes to collect myself. Nyx and Neala had both confirmed I was to bring about change, so why not start with this hideous chair?

I opened the box with the Night Sky Crown given to me when I still considered Albert my father and held it up in front of me. When I came to this kingdom, I'd sworn to myself the crown would sit on my head again, but that would be no more. The black metal matched the darkness of the throne, and my mind let go of the last of my attachment to the object. As I set the crown on the seat of the chair, I imagined a light and vibrant throne that was still regal. The heaviness of the room shifted. Light shimmered from me to the ugly chair and shattered the throne. The metal transformed into wood with carvings and metal accents—a twin flame, a unicorn, and a triple moon. Moonflowers intertwined with butterflies connected all of them. A dark stone, like obsidian, had been hidden under the base of the old throne and maneuvered itself into the bottom of the new one, closing the gap between the legs. The stone itself was unremarkable except for the carving —a deer. Diamonds scattered along the top like stars in the night sky. Purple velvet cushions padded the bottom and the back. "Perfect."

I stepped forward, tracing my fingers over the etchings. Each groove hummed against my touch as if it knew my presence. The wooded scent was very familiar, like the scent of the Forgotten Forest from the periphery before the other fragrances from deep within melded with it. I sat on the step in front and ran my hand over the deer. Was it the same black deer we'd seen?

Some fae, those who didn't like change, wouldn't like the new throne, but they would have the option to get over it or deal with it. I didn't have a choice about taking this position, but I did have various alternatives for how I executed it. No longer would I exist in the space of how others thought I should. My life was going to be lived... even while we hunted for Albert.

CHAPTER 56
ACCOUTREMENTS
RAIN

I decided to try again. When I brought Ari to the park last time, she jumped in the water midway through dinner, and my plans shifted to accommodate what she needed in that moment. My mate needed to feel alive that night, and I gave her the safe space to do it.

The staff would have everything arranged in the park before we arrived, and I'd walk her to the waterfall. Dinner would be set up, and during dessert, I'd ask her to marry me. She'd already said yes, but that was under duress. Even more so was the time she agreed in the prison kingdom. She deserved a real proposal, and one where no extenuating circumstances impacted her decision. I wanted everything to be perfect for Ari.

I walked into my meeting. Laurel was already at the table reviewing something on his tablet. He came back this morning to help review the reports of possible hiding places for Albert. The calm around us was a false sense of safety, and none of us could afford to be complacent. No one else was in the room yet, and my brother gave me a rude gesture. I returned it in kind. Gemma hadn't reclaimed her seat at court opting to stay with Cyrus and the kids on the coast, and Ari wouldn't push her to come back. Gemma's focus wasn't here anymore. She had a little fae to raise and two mates.

I studied the bracelet on my brother's wrist and took the seat to the right of him. The symbols on the gold looked familiar, and I realized what they were—three symbols for love. "Brother? Did you perform a commitment ceremony without me?"

"Says the fae who has a matching mark to his mate on his hand."

I wiggled my finger, appraising the symbol that complemented Ari's. "True. Your mate isn't as prone to violence as mine is though."

Laurel's face twisted from confusion to surprise and then his eyes dropped to his bracelet. He swallowed, and my easy-going, light-hearted brother became so serious I thought he was going to choke.

"Do I need to pat your back like when we were kids?"

"No, it's just...I didn't think anyone would know what it meant before we told them."

I leaned back, resting my hands over my head. "I, of all people, am not judging, but if you married Gemma without Ari there, my mate may very well stab you."

He gulped. "It wasn't like that. They're my mates, and

I asked Gemma and Cyrus to marry me. Cyrus gifted us the bracelets that were his parents'."

I patted the back of his shoulder happy for him to have found not one but two who he loved. It didn't surprise me he had two mates with as much love as he was capable of giving. "Congratulations, Brother. I couldn't be happier for you."

His mouth turned down, and he gave me a thoughtful look. "Do you think the court will accept us? I know it's not unheard of outside of court, but we're more visible."

"I don't think you have anything to be concerned about. With King Veran on the throne, maybe, but not anymore. If anyone speaks out against the three of you, Ari will likely launch a dagger at their heads."

"Who am I throwing daggers at?" Ari entered the room with the power of a goddess, and I wanted to drop to my knees and show her the power she had over me like I had last night.

"No one," Laurel said, fidgeting in his chair. "Hopefully."

She eyed him carefully. Her eyes landed on his new accessory. "That's quite the accoutrement you are wearing, Laurel." A broad smile spread across her face. "Something to share?"

The scared look on his face almost made me laugh. I had to cover my mouth to hide my smile.

"Ari, Gemma said she wanted to tell you."

"She did," Ari said, closing the space and hugging him.

"She came to get some of Phina's things this morning and told me. I'm so thrilled for the three of you."

"Thank you," he said. "I love her so much. I love them both with my entire heart."

"I know you do," Ari said. "Gemma is the happiest I ever remember seeing her."

"I thought you were taking the day off to rest?" I wrapped an arm low on her hips and pulled her toward my side.

Ari leaned against me. "Gemma couldn't carry everything, so I'm taking some things to the coast for her. Val and Theo were relocated there, and it will be the first time I've seen them since the prison collapsed. I'll stay for lunch, and if Drew is ready, I'll bring him back with me. I'm assuming you can handle all of this without me since you have been doing it for years?"

I pressed my lips to her shoulder. Doing the work was different now. I felt a pressure I hadn't felt before, because it was Ari's name at stake. Before, I didn't care if people liked me or hated me, but I wanted them to love her as much as I did...well, maybe not quite as much as I did, but close. "In your name, I will do the best of my ability."

"Please don't act weird now," she said. "I need you to be Rain, the fae I fell in love with."

"If you could read my thoughts right now, my goddess." My gaze dipped to her breasts, conveniently eye-level, and back to her. "You would know I'm the same."

"That's better." She kissed the top of my head. "I'll see you this evening."

As she crossed behind my chair, I reached out. Grasping her hand, I tugged her back to me. She didn't resist and collided hard against my chest, putting her perfect breasts in my face. I licked my lips and turned my head up to hers. "We're not leaving each other like that ever."

Her eyes glittered in the light. "I love you."

"I know." I gripped the back of her neck the way that had her moaning last night and pulled her face to mine. "I love you too." Then, I brushed my lips over hers in a slow seduction. "I will show you how much tonight."

"Tonight," she said, walking backward out of the room.

Laurel cleared his throat.

"Sorry, I almost forgot you were there."

"I see," he said, shuffling some papers.

"I'm going to ask her to marry me." I imagined her standing in front of our family while I proclaimed my unending love for her. My chest warmed with the thrill of making it known for all that we were mates. Not that most didn't know, but I wanted to shout it to the entire kingdom.

"Haven't you already asked her twice, and she said yes?" Laurel looked at me.

"The first was in the prison kingdom and swimming in lies, so that doesn't count. The second time, she was in one of your infirmary beds. She deserves better than that," I said. "I'm doing it in the garden tonight."

"Congratulations, Rain. You and Ari are the kind of mates other fae dream about."

"Thank you, but she still has to say yes...this time." If she didn't want to marry now that she'd started settling into her role, I'd understand, but I wanted her to be mine in every possible way and the reverse for me to hers too.

"She will," Laurel said.

"I had this made for her," I pulled the velvet box out of my jacket pocket and passed it to my brother.

He opened the box and studied the necklace. The 'R' and 'A' were intertwined with the triple moon goddess symbol, a lightning bolt, and a star. Our diamond-encrusted initials sat in the center of the full moon part of the symbol. The crescent moons were carved from blue goldstone and sparkled like the night sky. I chose diamonds for the tiny lightning bolt and star as well. "Is it too much?"

"Not at all," Laurel said, handing it back to me. "I think she'll love it."

"Rings are usually a human marriage thing, but I'm hoping she'll be okay with it." I pulled the smaller box out of my pocket and opened it. The blue goldstone glittered in the center with a crescent moon hugging it. "They are separate bands by design. I wanted it to represent two halves coming together."

"I think she'll be proud to wear any symbol you give her." He smiled. "I don't hardly recognize you any longer."

"Love changes all of us," I said. "And we have an abundance of it."

DARKEST NIGHT

ARI

I couldn't shake the strange feeling I had in the coastal realm, despite how peaceful and beautiful it was. Leana's eagerness to return with Drew and me only stoked my concern. If she was willing to return to the fae seat of the kingdom, knowing Albert would most likely attack here, what was she afraid of on the coast? Maybe she was uncomfortable being there with Gemma, Laurel, and Cyrus.

Or maybe she just wants to be closer to her declared charge, Ari. Stop overthinking everything.

Laurel returned to the coast not long after I arrived back, and I hadn't missed the look he and Rain exchanged in some kind of brother code. Rain went to a last-minute meeting with Armstrong, leaving me alone to prepare for a special dinner by the fountain. I couldn't wait to be back in that water with him. So, why had I ended up in the throne room again instead of in our apartments getting ready?

I walked up and caressed the arm of the throne. My fingers glided over the smooth wood, tracing the intricate designs. A kaleidoscope of purple butterflies fluttered from behind the chair and encircled me. The sight so beautiful I thought I imagined it when they disappeared.

Dark mist swirled around me. My eyelids were heavy with sleep even though I wasn't tired.

Neala appeared in front of me.

Time is short. A voice whispered into my head, strong like my bond with Marius.

Why are you—?

Speaking in your mind? Amusement laced her melodic voice in my head. *Because I can.*

I don't like you.

You don't have to like me. Her tone turned serious but kind. *You only need to listen and act.*

If you haven't noticed, I don't like being told what to do. I'm capable of making my own decisions.

The corner of her mouth twitched up. *So defiant. All of what you said is true, but if you don't change course, all of what you have fought for will perish.*

The sleepy haze fogging my thoughts cleared. *What do you mean?*

You've seen some ancient texts, but there is one that is important. She paused. *When Nyx's blood returns to the realm, all the magic shall be replenished to the glory of old. Those who bear the burden must prove their worthiness not only to Nyx but to the realm. From darkest night and raging storms to the brightest stars and dancing moonlight, life will be reborn.*

Yes, I've heard a similar text.

Now is the time you must prove your worthiness.

Nyx has deemed me so.

But has the realm?

Dampness coated the cool night air. The mist disappeared along with Neala, and I was no longer in the throne room.

Ari and Rain's story continues in Book 3,
Crown of Storms and Starlight.

CRAVING MORE PASSION AND MAGIC?

The magic you've experienced in these pages is just the beginning of the Empire of Curses and Dreams world. Join my newsletter family for exclusive content—from deleted scenes to sneak peeks of upcoming releases. I share writing updates, behind-the-scenes views, and magical surprises with my most devoted readers first. Let's continue this journey together

ACKNOWLEDGMENTS

To my friend, Lizzie, thank you for going to events with me and making silly videos with me. When they say the best friends are a blonde and a brunette, they must be right!

To my sister and my nieces, thank you for celebrating the milestones with me and for reminding me to enjoy each moment. Sis, no one creates a better table to display my books at an event than you. Love you!

To my editors, Dawn and Lisa, I can't imagine this series without you both. Thank you for not only telling me what needs to be fixed but what is good and what you like about the book too. You keep me inspired.

To my cover designer, Laura, you continually impress me with how you think outside the box. Thanks for reminding me to trust the process and for hanging with me through a literal thunderstorm for this cover.

To my beta readers, ARC readers, and fans, you mean so much to me. The way you embraced the characters, especially my man, Cyrus, has brought me so much joy. I love how passionate you are about what happens to your favorites. You are the reason I keep writing.

About the Author

Susan Person is a best-selling and award-winning author of fantasy and dark paranormal romance. After years in the business world, she returned to college to pursue a degree in anthropology and graduated in 2021. Susan enjoys meeting writers and readers alike at conferences and events. She knew at an early age she wanted to write powerful heroines and fulfills that dream by writing badass empowered heroines who take charge in their paranormal worlds.

Susan grew up on a thoroughbred horse farm before moving to the big city of Dallas. She considers herself a Texan but is loyal to her home state of Arkansas. A lover of travel, she has visited several countries with many more to go on her list. She particularly loved dowsing at Stonehenge and seeing the Parthenon in Athens. The outdoors is a place where Susan finds inspiration and can often be found in a park, at the lake, or on a road trip. She especially loves the mountains. Furry animals hold a special place in her heart, and dogs tend to seek her out as a friend.

Connect with her at susanperson.com

WANT TO LEARN MORE ABOUT SUSAN PERSON?

Scan the QR code below to see where you can find more of Susan's book or see what reader events she is attending.

ALSO BY SUSAN PERSON

The Night and Rain Series

Crown of Night and Rain, Book 1

Crown of Shattered Thrones, Book 2

Crown of Storms and Starlight, Book 3 (Coming in 2026)

Crown of Broken Promises, Prequel

Crown of Ruined Oaths, Book 1.5

The Falling From Hell Series

Fallen, Book 1

Reverie, Book 2

Marred, Book 3

The Blood Moon Prophecy

Queen of Sacrifice, Book 1

Queen of Darkness Book 2

Queen of Moons Book 3

A Vampire Ice Age Series

In Blood & Ice, Book 1

Reclamation In Ice, Book 2

Book 3: TBA

Enchanted Rock Immortals World

Fae Undone, The Enchanted Rock Immortals Clan Fae

Fae Redone, The Enchanted Rock Immortals Clan Fae

— Quase espero que você se recuse a obedecer — ele murmurou. — Sua pele pálida ficaria vermelha de um jeito tão lindo. E eu gostaria muito de persuadir suas reações ao longo do caminho.

O vidro tocou minha pele mais uma vez, mas agora ele o inclinou para derramar o líquido cor de bronze no meu peito.

Minha pele arrepiou.

Então minha respiração ficou presa na garganta quando ele inclinou a cabeça para pegar as gotas com a língua.

O calor acariciou minha pele. Sua boca era um beijo inesperado aos meus sentidos.

Ahhh...

Senti um estremecimento violento no abdômen, lançando faíscas em cada terminação nervosa. Faíscas que se transformaram em chamas quando suas presas perfuraram a área sensível ao redor do mamilo.

Gritei de surpresa e uma leve dor, apenas para congelar quando ele ergueu a bebida para a ferida recente.

— Como eu disse — ele sussurrou, suas íris geladas capturando as minhas. — Posso tornar sua vida confortável. Ou posso torná-la absolutamente miserável.

Ele inclinou o copo, fazendo o álcool escorregar pela borda direto no meu seio mais uma vez.

A queimadura confortável se transformou em um inferno pungente que provocou um assobio agudo da minha garganta.

Sua língua perseguiu o tormento, lambendo meu sangue misturado com álcool e acalmando a queimadura.

Durou apenas um segundo.

Mas seu ponto estava claro.

Sou seu mestre agora. Trabalhe comigo e considerarei recompensá-la. Trabalhe contra mim e vou te destruir.